thizz

a love story

NICOLE LOUFAS

This is a work of fiction. Names, characters, places, and incidents are either the product of the author's imagination or are used fictitiously. Any resemblance to actual events, organizations, or persons, whether living or dead is entirely coincidental.

THIZZ, A LOVE STORY

ISBN: 978-0-9964946-0-1

www.nicoleloufas.com

Cover art by Indie Solutions.

Formatting by Elaine York/

Allusion Graphics, LLC/Publishing & Book Formatting

to the lost

1 Dani

March 2006 - Eureka, California

I really don't want to deal with life today. I don't want to fake smile or do that thing where I sit up really straight and pretend I'm paying attention when I really just want to go back to bed and sleep away the rest of my senior year. There was a time when I could lie in bed until noon without raising concern about my mental well-being. Now sleeping in is a sign. Slouching and scowling are signs. Any time a rainbow isn't shooting out of my ass—that's a sign that I'm not ok.

I'll never *be* ok.

Of course, I can't let anyone know that, because then they'd have to care, and it's easier for everyone, myself included, not to care.

I sit up and grab my mom's faded gray CAL Berkeley sweatshirt from the end of the bed. She left it here at my aunt Lucy's a few summers ago. I found it hanging in the hall closet and reclaimed it for myself. I get out of bed and pull it on as I tiptoe across the cold hardwood floor to a pile of clothes in the corner. Lucy converted her attic to a playroom for me when I was six. When I moved in last January, Johnson, Lucy's boyfriend, swapped the dollhouse and plastic sofa for a bed and desk he bought at IKEA. It took him two days to put it all together. He left the pink fabric Lucy draped from the ceiling; it's really girly, but it hides the spider webs. The attic looks like a bona fide bedroom now. It's just not my room. This room will never be *my* room any more than this house will be my home. Lucy wanted me to move into the room across from hers, but that was my parent's room whenever we came to visit. It didn't feel right. Nothing about Eureka feels right.

I look at the calendar on the wall above the desk. Three weeks until acceptance letters are mailed. That letter is the only reason I get out of bed in the morning. Every day is another day closer to knowing my future. I have only one goal—getting into CAL Berkeley. I have the grades and, thanks to my mom, I have tons of extra-curricular activities. She listed me as honorary chairperson on dozens of projects she ran through her charities. I rarely did anything at the events other than show up and eat, but they looked really good on my college application. My parents went to CAL. It was their dream for me to continue the legacy. I plan on making that dream come true, even if they aren't here to see it.

"Dani, are you up?" Lucy calls from the hall downstairs. That's my cue to put on a fake smile— one that slides off my face just as quickly as it appears. Nothing I do these days will make it stick. I give myself a few more minutes of real as I pull a pair of cargo pants from the pile on the floor and put them on. I finish getting dressed and avoid the mirror hanging on the back of the door as I open it and head downstairs.

Lucy comes out of her room in green scrubs with a towel wrapped around her head. She's a registered nurse at St. Joseph's Hospital. "Morning, Lucy." I stretch to make it look like I just woke up even though I've been awake since dawn. "I thought you had the day off?"

I follow her to the bathroom and lean in the doorway as she plucks a couple of wayward hairs from her eyebrows.

"Two nurses called out today. Looks like another round of stomach flu," she says and unravels her hair from the towel. "I get off at six, then I'm teaching my Friday night Pilates class, so I'll be home late. There's some leftover Chinese food in the fridge." She plugs in the hair dryer and looks at me before switching it on. "Do you have any plans tonight, besides work?" She knows I have no plans, but she asks anyway, hoping one day I'll have a different answer. She's consummately optimistic. I guess you have to be in her line of work.

"*The Real World* is on tonight." I pick at the chipped paint on the door frame. I hate the look of pity on Lucy's face. She thinks I miss having a social life, but even back home I preferred being alone. I've never been good at making lasting relationships. I had friends, but none that mattered. There isn't a single person from my old school I want to call or write, or friend on Myspace. Besides, I moved to Eureka to get off the grid. My old life doesn't exist anymore. I don't even exist.

I walk into my final class of the day—computer lab—and take my seat in back. I've made it through the entire day without speaking to anyone. It's a game I play with myself. Once I went three days without uttering a single word at school. I don't know if it's something to celebrate or if it's just really fucking pathetic. The bell rings and Mr. Davis closes the door. He walks to the board and writes free time in big chalk letters. He adds three exclamation marks at the end to really drive the message home. Like free time in this class is something special. Building a Myspace is part of the curriculum, which tells you a lot about the seriousness of our seventh period computer class. You have to respect his enthusiasm though.

I log on to my B-minus Myspace page and wait for it to load. I could have bumped my grade up if I added a photo to the background, but I was going for a minimalist approach. Solid black background with white Arial font lettering. Mr. Davis told me he was hoping to see something with more personality. I moved here from San Francisco three months ago. My parents are gone, Lucy is the only family I have left, I have no friends, and I haven't kissed a boy since sophomore year.

I think I nailed it.

My page loads, and the first thing I notice is the flashing envelope at the bottom of the screen. I click it, and sitting in my inbox are two words: MATT AUGUSTINE.

Matt Augustine—the blue-eyed, Axe-body-sprayed boy who sits at the terminal next to mine has sent me a message. Feelings. Lots of feelings that I can't categorize flood my body. I take a deep breath then exhale like I just took a drag of a cigarette. Lots of words run through my mind. None of them make sense. If I were a comic book, there would be a huge white bubble with gibberish floating over my head because I have no freaking clue what is going on or why Matt Augustine sent me a message. I saw him at lunch; he was sitting in the middle of the quad surrounded by friends or fans. I can't tell the difference. They never look at me. Nobody does, except for him. Well, that's the lie I tell myself whenever I see him scan the yard and then smile when his eyes land on me sitting under the redwood tree across the yard. Why would he send me a message, then ditch class? Maybe he ditched class because he sent the message? *Quit dreaming, Dani.* It's probably nothing, like one of those chain letters telling me I have to forward to ten people or I'll never find true love. I hold the mouse over his name, daring myself to click.

I'm scared it won't be a chain letter.

I'm scared it will be.

There is only one way to find out. I click the mouse and the message opens.

Hey Dani,

Can you meet me in the parking lot after school?

Matt

I read it again—and one more time, hoping the words will scramble into something more informative, like why he's requested this clandestine rendezvous to the student parking lot. Guys like Matt don't message girls like me, let alone ask them to meet after school. Matt and I share one class—computer lab. Since we have no homework and the assignments are available on the school intranet, he doesn't need me to take notes for him. So why does he want to meet me? I'm a filler kid, the ones you know by face, but never remember their names. Matt Augustine is, well, he's the reason they give out free birth control. Dark brown hair, blue eyes so crisp and clear they make the Caribbean ocean look like a dirty swimming pool. He's the kind of boy you dream about when you're ten. The one that rides in on a horse and sweeps you off your feet. The one you love forever. I don't think I'm capable of that kind of love. I love things—like coffee and the smell of fresh lavender. I've never used the L-word in reference to an actual human that wasn't blood related. Except maybe Johnny Depp. I'm getting ahead of myself. I'm not in love with Matt. I'm not even in like with him. I am intrigued by the possibilities though. *Wait, what am I saying?* Matt Augustine is the last thing I need in my life. I have three months left in Eureka; I don't need any distractions, anything to knock me off course. I have a plan. Boys are not part of the plan. Not really. Ok, maybe I will make an exception for the right boy.

I watch the clock above the door click along minute by excruciating minute, debating on how to respond. I could ignore the message altogether, pretend I never saw it. No, I can't. The words, his words, can't be unread, unseen. I have enough regret in my life. Wondering why Matt Augustine wants to meet me is not going to be added to the list.

I stare at the clock, read the message, stare at the clock some more. The bell rings and I stand up, lift my backpack from the floor, and point myself in the direction of the parking lot. I'm on auto pilot. I don't want to think about where I'm going or what I'll say. I don't even know what to say. I don't want to open my mouth at all. I wish I had a mint.

I turn the corner to the hall that leads to the parking lot and I freeze. Through the crowd I see Heather King swaying towards me. *Crap.* I dip my eyes to the floor and pretend not to notice her even though the smell of her Bath & Body lotion burns my nostrils. You can always smell her a mile away. I step in line with a rather large boy from the football team when suddenly her flip-flopped feet appear in my path. I stop so I don't bump into her. As small as she is, she takes up all the air and space around her.

"Hello, Danielle." She addresses me like I'm some commoner that should drop to my knees in her presence.

I look up with the most strained smile I can manage. "Hi, Heather."

She poses in front of me like someone with a camera is going to jump out of a locker and snap her picture for a magazine. "Got any plans for the weekend?" she asks as she twirls a strand of her new blonde hair around her finger. I have to say the blonde suits her much better than the fiery red she had last week. With her sun-kissed skin and gray eyes, she looks like a poster girl for Abercrombie & Fitch.

"I'm working all weekend." I grip the strap on my backpack and step around her. "I'm actually going to be late." I would say have a nice weekend, but Heather is incapable of nice.

"So, I guess you didn't hear about the big party?" Heather loves to ask me about parties she knows I wasn't invited to.

I take a few steps back to gain some distance. "No, parties really aren't my thing." I stop in front of the girls' bathroom. I've hid in this bathroom more times than I care to remember. Maybe I should wait in here until Heather clears out. I can't risk her following me outside. There's no way Heather would sanction someone like me meeting a boy like Matt. I'm sure there's a high school rule that forbids it, and Heather is just the person to enforce it.

"I guess a high school party would be boring to someone from *San Francisco*," she snickers. "I bet you're more the rave type." Heather is jealous of the fact that I'm from San Francisco. I don't understand why it bothers her. I'm stuck here now, just like her. We're even.

"The only clubs I've been to are book clubs," I tell her. "I really gotta go." I push open the door to the bathroom and hear her laugh echo down the hall.

The door closes and the lights flicker on. I do a quick check under the stalls—all empty. I lean on the sink and look into the warped mirror. A distorted version of my face stares back at me. My limp brown hair is months overdue for a haircut, but I wouldn't even know where to start. My mom always took care of stuff like that. Makeup, hair, nail polish, those were mom's specialty. My mother held a degree in liberal arts, but she never had a real job. I was her job. I was a good little mannequin. I sat still when my hair was being curled. I closed and opened my eyes when prompted during my mother's many make-up sessions. I never thought to watch or learn. I didn't think I would have to. Or maybe I just didn't care. I went along with it because it made her happy. The same way a boy would play catch with his dad in the backyard when he'd rather be inside playing *World of Warcraft*.

I miss her. I miss her hand on my head when she ran the brush through my hair after a shower. I miss the lingering smell of her perfume after she left the room. I'm lost without her. I don't even think I'm wearing deodorant today. So, why the hell am I meeting Matt Augustine? I'm not nearly as groomed as I should be. I'm not Heather, not even close, yet a voice in the back of my head is telling me I have to do this. I have three months left in this town. If my mother were here, she'd tell me to make the most of it. *Not a day wasted, Dani.* Those are the words I hear in my head as I stare at a carbon copy of her eyes in the mirror. I smile, her smile, and lift my backpack from the floor. I think she would approve of Matt. He's smart and charming and tall and oh-my-God good looking. His smile, holy hell, it lights up the room. Who knows, maybe Matt is the glue I need to make my smile stick.

I open the bathroom door and peek into the hall—it's clear. I hurry down the hall and shove open the green double doors to the parking lot like a burglar escaping the scene of a crime. I step into the afternoon sun and slide my backpack onto both of my shoulders. I'm two-strapping it and don't care. I'm totally out of control. I scan the parking lot and find Matt leaning against a shiny black car. He stands a bit straighter when he sees me and runs his hand through his hair. It's in its usual disheveled mess, but I can see where his hairline naturally parts to the side, giving him sort of a clean-cut look. He's got on baggy jeans and a black No Fear t-shirt. The sight of him makes me warm and tingly inside, a feeling I missed when he skipped class today.

A chilly, ocean-scented breeze flings discarded papers at my feet as I cross the parking lot. A flutter tickles the inside of my belly at the thought of having a conversation with Matt that doesn't involve HTML. Suddenly, a car pulls out in front of me. I stop right before a silver Volkswagen takes out my legs. The driver waves to Matt, then yells, "Later, Nick" as he speeds away.

I follow the driver's gesture to the boy standing beside Matt and find him staring back at me. It isn't like I've never seen him before. I pass him in the hall at least three or four times a day. He's even been in the café where I work. *Small latte—extra foam*. This is the first time I've seen him look at me. I mean really, consciously look at me.

"Hey Dani," Matt greets me. "This is Nick Marino."

I try to say hi, but my throat has seized, so I give a faint smile and wave my hand. Nick smiles and nods back. He's leaning against the car beside Matt with his hands shoved into the pockets of his blue jeans. His clothes aren't as baggy as Matt's, so I can see his body bulging from beneath his white t-shirt. He's a cross between Leonardo DiCaprio and the dude from *John Tucker Must Die*. And he's smiling. At me. And my first thought is—run.

I'm pretty sure I've lost the ability to speak as sweat starts to pool at the small of my back. I try to focus on Matt, but my eyes keep wandering to Nick, who is just as quiet as I am. Nick doesn't seem like the silent type; he always has a crowd of people around him, and his picture is often plastered on the front page of the school newspaper. One week it was about the basketball game he starred in, the following week he was named the most spirited student. I think the editor makes up any reason to print his face on the cover, just so people will read the worthless periodical.

"Earth to Dani?" Matt waves his hand in front of my face. "Do you need a ride home?"

A ride? Home? Eureka isn't my home. He doesn't know that. He doesn't know anything about me. I'm a clean slate. I can be whoever I want to be. I don't have to be the weird new girl or the stuck-up city bitch. I can be a new and improved version of me.

"Yeah, a ride would be great." I wipe my sweaty palms down the front of my khaki cargo pants.

Matt steps to the side and opens the door. I climb into the car and marvel at the size of the enormous leather backseat.

"Where do you live?" Matt asks as he closes the passenger door.

Before I have a chance to respond, the driver's side door opens and Nick slides into the seat in front of me. *Holy hell, this is Nick's car.* Nick Marino is the most popular boy at Eureka High School, and I am sitting in *his* car. He is driving *me* home. I bite my lower lip and look around to make sure this isn't a dream. I find that pain keeps things real. It's one emotion you can't fake. You can laugh when you're sad, and cry when you're happy, but when you hurt, you feel it. You can't fake the hurt. Matt is turned in his seat with a smile on his face. A smile so bright and friendly that I smile with him. How did I go from hiding in the bathroom from Heather King to sitting in Nick Marino's car with Matt Augustine smiling at me with his perfect teeth and soulful eyes? This is not my life, but I'll take it.

Matt clears his throat. "You do know where you live, don't you?"

I suck at addresses and phone numbers. I know where the house is, but the actual address escapes me. I picture myself writing out Aunt Lucy's address on the yearly Christmas and birthday cards we used to send her. "Uh, three-three-two-seven Pine."

"Are you sure about that?" Matt asks, sensing the hesitation in my voice.

I give Matt an exasperated look. "Yeah, I'm sure." Matt has one of those friendly smiles that make you feel welcome and less like a freak. I love Matt's smile. *Did I just use the L-word?*

"I'm not a human GPS. Where is that exactly?" Matt teases.

"Don't be a dick." Nick gives Matt a friendly nudge in the shoulder. "I was raised in this shitty town, I'm sure I can find it."

Matt's grin fades at Nick's remark. He turns away from me and looks out the window. I feel bad. Nick thinks Matt's being mean, but it's just our thing. Not that we have a thing. I mean, we talk in class about class stuff. Other than the occasional interrogation by Heather, Matt is the only other person I've ever had a conversation with. I wouldn't call him a friend. A few more discussions about music or books, and I might say we know each other. Unlike Nick. He definitely doesn't know me or anything about me. I sort of want to keep it that way.

"What's the cross street?" Nick's hazel eyes smile at mine in the rear view mirror—they are a kaleidoscope of yellow, brown, and green. I look at his reflection, which gives the impression that he's further away than he is. He's sitting in front of me. I could reach out and touch him—touch Nick Marino. Freaking insane.

My back breaks out in a full-blown sweat, the kind that leaves marks under your arms. Thankfully I'm wearing a thick hoodie, so any pit stains I may develop are well hidden. "West Harris," I tell him, then sink into the seat out of his view. I can't imagine what it's like to date a guy like Nick. The pressure to look good, speak intelligently, breathe. An hour ago I couldn't fathom the idea of Matt asking me out, now I'm fantasizing about dating Nick Marino. I need medication.

I look out the window and see Heather King, her mouth agape, as we drive by. My ego fist pumps the air, but my brain is telling me I will pay for this later. Nick joins the line waiting to leave the parking lot and I start to wonder if this is why Matt sent the message. Did he want to offer me a ride home, or was it a set-up so I could meet Nick? My heart sinks at the idea. Nick seems like a nice guy, but we have nothing in common. A rush of disappointment fills me. I really thought Matt might like me. I'm not great at reading people, but I thought we had a connection. I suck at boys, but I know guys don't set up girls they like with their friends.

Matt turns up the volume on the stereo and Nick swats his hand away. He presses play on the CD and "Lucky Go Leah," one of my favorite songs of all time, by one of my favorite bands of all time, blasts through the speakers.

"Dude, not this again," Matt complains.

"My car, my music," Nick tells him.

Nick likes Audiodub. We actually have something in common. Something that I think is really cool. Who knew a guy like Nick would like an indie band.

Suddenly, Nick's hazel eyes pop into the rear view mirror and I stop breathing. "Do you have to go home now? Cause we're going to the Rack Room. You want to come?" Nick looks to Matt for backup. Matt just shrugs and gives me a half-ass smile. I can't tell if he really wants me to go. I don't know if I want to go. I have an hour and a half to kill before my shift at the café. I can't think of a more terrifying way to spend it.

The Rack Room isn't as dingy as it looks from the outside. There are a dozen pool tables lined up on one side of the building. The other side has a small area with video games and an air hockey table. They're separated by a seating area in the center of the room next to the bar. It's only three forty-five and the place is packed. The synthetic melodies of the video games drown out the music playing from the jukebox as the arcade fills with the same kids I just saw at school.

I try not to watch Nick walk over from the bar, but I can't help sneaking a glance. Everyone in this place is staring in his direction. Some wave while others just gawk. He exudes more confidence than anyone I've ever met. When he finally turns towards our table, I pretend to watch a game of pool going on in front of me. Nick sits down with a beer in his hand and sets a soda on the table for me. Matt disappeared to use the bathroom and hasn't returned, leading me to believe he's giving Nick and me time alone. "Do you play pool?"

"No, but if you want to play, go ahead." I take a sip from my soda like I'm totally fine, when I'm totally not. Practically everyone in this place is staring at our table, including three girls in the corner that have been eyeballing me since we got here. I don't know what I've done to offend them, but it looks like I'm about to find out. The trio stand from the stools along the wall. One of them fusses with her boobs before they head to our table.

They walk up behind Nick, and one of them places her hands over his eyes. "Guess who?" She leans downs and kisses his cheek.

Nick pulls her hands away from his eyes with an exasperated look on his face. "What's up, Katie." He takes a drink from his beer and leans towards me. "Dani, Katie. Katie, Dani," he says in that bored way people do when someone they can't stand is in their presence.

Katie shoots me a dirty look through her overly mascaraed eyes and ignores Nick's introduction. "So, what's up tonight? You want to hang out?" She leans into Nick's side, if he turns his head, her boobs will poke him in the eye.

"We're busy." Nick scoots his chair away and smiles at me. His rejection doesn't faze Katie. She runs her hand over Nick's head and starts to pull out the chair beside him. Nick stops her. "Matt's sitting there," he says as he holds the chair in place, denying her access to join our table.

"So what, are you with *her* now?" Katie looks at me like I'm gum on the bottom of her shoe. I think I finally get that saying, *if looks could kill.*

Nick takes a pull on his beer and tilts his head to the side with a coy smile. "No, she's with Matt."

"I'm not with Matt," I say quickly, trying not to choke on my soda. *I like Matt, he's a nice guy, but we're not together. Not that I don't want to be with him. I don't know. Maybe I do. I don't think Katie really cares about Matt. She isn't standing here with her boob in Matt's face.*

My internal rambling isn't helping my case. I look at Nick, then to Katie. "I'm not with anyone," I tell them both. I don't know if I can be any clearer. Katie's death glare subsides slightly.

"That's good to know," Nick raises his right eyebrow and my heart does a backflip. Why is he giving her the impression he's interested in me? Is he trying to get me killed?

Katie shoves the chair against the table and soda splashes out of my glass. "Whatever," she hisses and stomps away with her friends in tow.

I take a napkin from the dispenser in the center of the table and place it over the puddle of soda. "She seems nice." I laugh nervously. "Is she an ex-girlfriend or something?"

"I barely know her." Nick smiles and takes another pull on his beer.

I barely know Nick, and I can tell he's full of shit. I roll my eyes and look around the room. Everyone looks away. Nick seems like a nice guy, and I bet most people wouldn't mind the attention, but I can't take much more of this. Just when I'm about to make an excuse to leave, Matt comes back to the table. He tells Nick that Pete—the bartender who serves minors—is asking for him. Nick leaves and Matt sits down. He looks as uncomfortable as I do. I wonder if he hates the attention too. Or maybe he's just uncomfortable around me. I don't think he wanted to bring me here, which sort of hurts. The longer I'm in his presence, the more I realize how wrong I was. Matt definitely doesn't like me.

I check my watch; I have an hour until my shift. Eureka Coffee is just up the road. If I leave now, I'll only be thirty minutes early. Any place is better than here.

"Do you have to go?" Matt asks. These are the first words he's spoken to me since we got here.

"Yeah, I should get to work." I stand up and see Katie nod to her girls. One of them starts to take off her earrings while the other pulls her hair into a ponytail. I look towards the door where Nick disappeared with Pete. Maybe I should wait for Nick to drive me; it's probably safer than walking alone.

Matt stands and picks up my backpack. "What do you have in here?"

"Books." I blush. I like to carry my favorites with me just in case I feel like reading. Maybe I can use my backpack as a weapon if Katie tries something. I hold out my hand to take my bag, but Matt slides it onto his shoulder.

"I'm going to get a workout carrying this thing." He smiles his sweet, genuine smile.

I get really happy at the idea of Matt walking me to work. Even happier when he touches my shoulder as we walk to the exit. I look back at Katie, who seems to be settling down now that she sees me leaving with Matt. Crisis averted.

Matt and I are halfway to the door when Nick emerges from the backroom. "Hey, where you going?" he calls out and hurries towards us.

Matt keeps walking, but I stop. I don't want to be rude. "I have to work. Thanks for the ride and the soda." I smile a fake smile.

"I'll drive you." Nick places his hand on the small of my back and guides me out the door. I don't want it to feel good, but it does. His hand on my back feels so damn good. I look back and see Katie seething. Maybe not that good. I've been in one fight in my life. It was in the seventh grade, and it isn't something I want to repeat.

Matt is standing next to Nick's car, glaring at us as we step outside. "Dude, you were drinking. You really want to drive?" I appreciate Matt's concern, but I don't mind taking the ride. I want to put as much distance between me and Katie as possible.

"I had half a beer," Nick scoffs. "I'm fine." He looks at me to make sure I'm ok with accepting a ride from a slightly intoxicated chauffer. I shrug like it's no big deal. With that body, those muscles, I'm sure he can handle driving after a shot of tequila.

Matt holds out my backpack with a sad smile. He looks disappointed that we won't get our walk. Part of me is sad too. I like Matt, at least I thought I did. I'm pretty sure Matt set me up with Nick, which is why he left us alone in the bar. If that were true, he wouldn't be trying to stop me from riding in Nick's car. I'm almost positive it has nothing to do with Nick's blood alcohol level. Boys are harder to figure out than the Pythagorean Theorem. I want to walk with Matt; he makes me feel safe, comfortable. I like comfortable. I take my backpack from Matt and turn to Nick, who looks like he just won a bet. Those eyes smiling at me feels like riding a bike with no hands. It's scary, but I don't want to grab the handlebars just yet. I want to see what happens next. Nick moves to open the door when his cell phone rings. He takes it out and flips it open.

"See you Monday, Dani." Matt waves and offers me a small smile.

I look at Nick as he walks away from the car on his call. I can't hear what he's saying, but he has a serious look on his face. The call doesn't look pleasant. I'm grabbing the handlebars now.

I close the car door and slide my backpack strap on my shoulder. Nick looks up and ends his call. He hurries back to me and gives Matt a perturbed glance. I don't want to make this awkward. "I can walk from here," I tell them as I start towards the intersection. Nick tries to protest but I stop him. "I don't want Katie hunting me down and killing me." I'm only partially kidding. "You should stay."

"Don't even worry about that girl, she's just putting on a show. We're not together or anything." Nick nudges Matt to back him up, but Matt just shrugs. His silence tells me he doesn't want me to take the ride from Nick. Maybe he knows something I don't.

"Thanks, but I'd rather walk." The light turns green and I start across the street. "I'll see you in class, Matt." Nick looks disappointed, but Matt is smiling at me. Once I'm safely across the street I look back to make sure I'm not being followed. Nick is walking back into the Rack Room, but Matt is still standing in the parking lot, watching me. For some reason I feel safer knowing he's there. I speed walk to the next light and exhale when I turn back to see the parking lot is empty. As much as I would've liked a walk with Matt or a ride from Nick, this is the safer decision. I'm all about being safe.

2
Matt

I pull a pillow over my head and try to ignore the incessant ringing coming from the desk. There is a girl in a bikini waiting for me in the dream I was just ripped from. My phone goes silent and my body relaxes back into sleep mode. Just as the world starts to fade, the ringing starts again. I jump out of bed and grab my cell. "What!" I scream, ignoring the caller ID.

"Dude, get up. I'll be there in five minutes."

I should've known it was Nick. No good morning, just get up I'm on my way. Only he can get away with this kind of shit. It isn't just me—everyone obeys him. I like to think I'm different though, that he somehow respects me more than the other guys. I did save him from being kissed by Molly Wells in kindergarten. Even at five, she had a mustache. He still owes me for that one.

"Matty!" Ashley yells as she opens my door.

"Ash, a little privacy, please." She pauses while I pull on a pair of jeans. "Ok, come in."

She bursts in my room and jumps on my bed. "Mom wants to know if you're coming with us today," she asks as I leave the room to take a piss.

Damn. St. Joseph's Hospital has a yearly ceremony for the volunteers, and this year Ashley is being honored. If it were me, I'd never step foot in that place, but she can't stay away. Ashley had leukemia and is in her second year of remission. She spent half her life in and out of the hospital, so I guess it's the only thing she knows. If she stays cancer free, she will return to school in the fall. I hope once she's around healthy kids, she overcomes her obsession with the sick ones.

I return from the bathroom and find Ashley curled up in my bed. She's fourteen, but seems so much younger. She's the strongest person I know, yet she still seems so fragile, like a cracked windshield ready to shatter into a million pieces.

"I can't. Nick's coming." I hate seeing the disappointment in her face. "I still don't get why you hang out there so much. Isn't it depressing?"

She throws aside my comforter and gets up. "Yeah, that's why I do it. I try to make it less depressing. I wish someone would have done the same for me." My little sister has the guilt trip thing down to a science. She snoops through a pile of CDs on my desk while I put on my shoes.

"Don't you have a better way to spend your time? Wouldn't you rather be outside?" I pluck a CD from her hand and put it back in the stack. She knows I hate when she touches my stuff.

"I go outside," she protests. "The hospital has a really nice courtyard. You'd know if you ever visited me."

Ouch. There is only so much guilt I can take. I'm about to call Nick and tell him I'm busy when I hear his car rumbling outside. Too late. I know it's wrong, but its way easier to flake on my forgiving sister than it is to tell Nick I can't hang out with him. Ashley's already forgiven me for so much worse.

"Hey, I'll make it up to you." I grab my Stanford sweatshirt from the back of the chair and kiss Ashley on top of her head.

"I know you will." She sits in my chair and spins around.

"Don't steal my CDs and we'll see," I warn as I run out the door.

Nick is all smiles when I get in the car. "What up!" He holds out his hand and we perform the handshake we made up in the fourth grade.

"Where we going?" I ask, feeling shitty about missing Ashley's day. This better be important.

"I need you to come to San Francisco with me." Nick backs out of the driveway before I have a chance to object. "I'm meeting my uncle. We're picking up some inventory." Nick's uncle Will is a mid-level gangster in San Francisco. He has a bar in North Beach that he uses to front his real business—weed.

"What the fuck. I don't wanna get involved in all that." The car rumbles to a stop at the light and I consider jumping out, but it seems like such a chick thing to do.

"How much weed are you holding for me right now?" Nick raises his eyebrow in that way he does when he knows he's right.

Ok, so I have an emergency stash hidden under a loose floorboard in my closet. I sure as hell don't want to know where it comes from or be an accessory in its transport from San Francisco to Eureka. "Dude, I can't get busted." I sound like such a punk.

"I got your back, Matty." The light turns green and he stabs the gas.

Nick has never involved me in his business. "Where's Arnie?" He's the one that usually goes with Nick on these runs. Selling weed has always been Nick and Arnie's thing. They've been doing it since the eighth grade.

"His old man is on his case about the army again. He's got a meeting with a recruiter. But I also thought it'd be cool if we hung out today. It's been a minute since just me and you kicked it."

I smile, feeling weird that Nick's comment makes me feel happier than it should.

As many times as I've been to San Francisco, I'm in awe as we drive through the city. I wonder if the people that live here appreciate this magnificent skyline. The symmetrical balance of the Embarcadero buildings offset the jagged tip of the Transamerica tower. I've always been intrigued by architecture. I seriously debated between architecture and law. Law won. I've wanted to be a lawyer since the first time I watched my father pick a jury. Plus, I suck at math.

Nick makes an illegal left from Columbus onto Broadway. I count at least three neon signs flashing LIVE NUDE GIRLS. Even though it's the middle of the day, a couple of them have half-naked women standing in the door, coaxing people to join them inside. I fucking love this city.

Will's place, the Lucky Charm, is one of the seediest-looking bars on the block. We find a spot right in front and park, but neither of us have the fortune in change it takes to feed the meter.

"Fuck it, we'll just come check on it every few minutes." Nick locks the doors and we head inside.

The Lucky Charm reeks of stale beer and cigarettes. Nick goes straight to the back room to find Will and I take a seat at the bar. I realize the twenty-one and over sign and the no smoking sign are just pieces of artwork on the wall when the Asian girl behind the bar offers me a beer, and the sweaty guy next to me lights up a Camel. I decline the drink, then step back towards the door to check on the car and get some much-needed fresh air.

Some chicks walk past and smile at me. They must think I'm twenty-one. I lean on the wall like I belong here and smile at the pretty brunette. I wish I was this confident yesterday after school. I wasn't sure Dani would show, and then bam, there she was. We had a good vibe in class. She laughed at all my lame HTML jokes and always smiled at me when we passed each other in the hall. I have been wanting to ask her out for so long. She never seemed ready. The last couple of weeks I noticed her open up a little. She smiled more and she even asked me how my weekend was. I finally decided to make a move then I pussed out and sent the message instead of going to class. I should've had at least had her meet me alone, because having Nick beside me was like growing an extra head. He can't help but suck all the attention his way. Then he opened his big mouth about the Rack Room and well, the timing didn't feel right. I thought maybe Nick Marino's charm had won her over. Then she shocked me and Nick when she decided to walk to work. I don't think I've seen anyone, male or female, pass up a ride from Nick. Guys love his car and chicks love Nick.

I think I still have a chance. Maybe I'll stop by the café tomorrow and see if she's working. Or maybe I'll just wait until Monday. It isn't like she's going anywhere, we don't graduate for a few months. I still have time.

The girls disappear around the corner just as Nick walks by holding a small bundle in his hand. He pauses in the doorway as I scan the street for black-and-whites; going to jail today would suck. I give Nick a nod, and he makes a beeline to the car. I have to admit, it's kind of exciting.

"Was'up Matty?" A thick city accent startles me. I turn around as Will Walker emerges from the darkness. He's wearing baggy black sweat pants, a white and gold Rocawear t-shirt. A cross dangles from a fat gold chain around his neck.

"S'up, Will." I try to sound a little more street. I hold out my hand for him to shake. Will takes it and pulls me in for a hug. The show of affection worries me.

"So, my nephew says you're a stand-up guy." I look back at Nick, who is carefully placing the new inventory in a hidden compartment under the dash. I wonder what the hell he's told his uncle about me. "Nick needs people he can trust. I'm not there to watch his back, so it's good he has a close friend like you." I nod to let him know I'm listening, but I'm unsure what to make of Will's sudden interest in my friendship with Nick. We've known each other since kindergarten. I've had his back for more than half my life.

"Nick said you could use some money. Who doesn't need a little green, right?" He chuckles and slaps my back. "Nick's business is growing; the boys that stayed with me from the beginning are all ballers now. You know what I'm sayin?" Will's grip tightens around my shoulders as he escorts me to the bar.

I think I know why Nick brought me on this run today. I clear my throat, hoping my voice doesn't crack. "I get you, but, um, I'm going to college in the fall."

"There's nothing wrong with an education. Shit, even Nick's gotta go to college, but he said you were down. He's vouching for you." His friendly demeanor fades slightly. "I thought you wanted in?" There's a tinge of annoyance in his voice. What the hell did Nick tell him?

Sweat runs down the side of my head as I contemplate my options. Because of Ashley's medical bills, my parents can't afford to send me to college. Since I plan on going to Stanford, by the time I graduate from law school, I'll have a quarter of a million in student loans. That alone is reason to say yes, but it isn't my deciding factor. None of that really matters when you're standing in the arms of a gangster, being offered a job, while your best friend hides drugs in his car. "Yeah, I'm in."

Nick conveniently reappears just as I agree to Will's offer.

"Sandy, three shots of Patron." Will knocks on the bar, prompting the young girl to put down her book and pour the drinks. We pick up our shot glasses, clink them together, and slam the shots. Will takes the bottle from Sandy and suggests we take our celebration to a quieter spot. We sit at a table in the back corner of the bar. Nick holds out his fist to me and I bump it with mine. He's sporting the goofiest grin I've ever seen. I want to be pissed, really I do, but he knows how badly I want to go to Stanford. He's just looking out for me. I can't get mad about that.

Will leans back in his chair and looks at Nick. "How's school?" I think it's kind of strange that he cares about his nephew's grades, considering he is grooming him for a life of crime.

"It's all good." Nick leans back in his chair, mimicking Will.

"Do you know where you're going to college yet?" Will leans towards the table and looks from me to Nick. "I don't know how this shit works. Do they send you a letter or something?"

Nick fiddles with his empty glass, unable to look Will in the eye. I don't know why he looks so nervous. He has legacy status at Stanford. His family has a fucking wing named after them. He's pretty much guaranteed admission. "I haven't applied yet."

I choke a little on my spit when Nick says he didn't apply. We've been planning on going to Stanford together since our freshman year in high school. Nick finally looks at me with an apologetic smile and I pour myself another shot.

"Hey, I'm just looking out for you. You know you gotta go to college." Will reaches across the small table and playfully grabs Nick's neck. "You hear me boy?" He laughs as his knuckles scrape Nick's scalp.

"Alright!" Nick shouts in defeat. "It'll get Mariann off my back too." He looks at me. "Don't worry, dude. We're gonna run shit down there." Nick holds out his fist and I bump it. I've never even considered going to Stanford without him. I assumed we would live together, which would save me money on housing. If Nick doesn't go to Stanford, I'm fucked. Maybe that's why he's bringing me into his crew; he knows I'll need the money. It isn't just about the housing, I've never gone to school without him. We've always been there for each other, no matter what.

"How is granny?" Will couldn't sound more sarcastic if he tried.

"She stays out of my way and I don't embarrass the family name." Nick hates talking about his grandmother. He moved into a cottage in the back of their estate and rarely sees her. It's kind of sad since he's her only grandchild. He's the only family she has left.

Will's sister, Maria, was Nick's mother. Nick met Will at his mother's funeral when Nick was thirteen. Will and Mariann have been fighting for Nick's loyalty ever since. "You're too serious, Nicky." Will pours another round of shots. "I got something that'll put a smile on your face." He pulls a plastic bag from inside his jacket pocket. "You knuckleheads ever heard of thizz?"

Nick looks at me as if I would know something he didn't. Will tosses the bag at Nick and smiles. The bag is full of small blue pills. "What is it, black market Viagra?" Nick laughs.

"It's ecstasy, and it's going to make us a lot of money." Will takes his shot and nods for us to do the same. The lukewarm alcohol is hard to swallow, but I force it down in one quick gulp. "The kids in the bay call it thizz. But it ain't just the kids taking it. Some of my biggest clients are in their forties. It's cheaper than coke and it lasts all night. And the chicks, oh man, the chicks will do anything you want!" Will grins. "Just wait until those little girlies up north to get a hit. They'll be all over you and each other." Nick and I high five at the possibilities, then I immediately think of Dani. She's the only girl I want all over me.

Will takes a pill out of the bag. He holds it between his thumb and forefinger and says, "One hundred percent pure MDMA is a rare commodity. Most of the small-timers are cutting it up, mixing it with caffeine or speed. But that's not what I'm about. My shit is the Mercedes of MDMA." He puts the pill back in the bag and tells us thizz is a top priority since the market is still open in most of Northern California.

"What about the cops?" I ask, then regret it immediately for sounding like a pussy.

"Are they giving you any heat?" Nick adds, making my question sound less pathetic.

"From what I've seen, it isn't on anyone's radar." Will takes another shot of tequila. He doesn't even wince. "Unless you count Devon's bust." He mumbles some curse words under his breath. "Remember that punk I used to run with, Devon Brown? Yeah, he had the right idea, dealing it to the yuppies. He was doing alright, until he got popped. Fucking idiot."

Nick and I agree that this Devon guy is a loser while we each take another shot. My head is fuzzy from the tequila, but the last shot goes down like water.

"If Devon didn't dodge that third strike, he would've been in San Quentin for life, and I'd own this half of the city." Will flips his glass onto the table. It echoes through the bar. "You gotta be smart and you gotta have smart people around you." Will points at me and then at Nick. "Devon is still selling dime bags on street corners. He'll never leave the hood now. He's too scared. That's why we parted ways. I wanted more. I branched out to other businesses, like this bar. I'm diversifying!" Will opens his arms and looks around the dirty bar like it's something to be proud of. "Shit, I'm about to be the next Tony Montana, fuckin Scarface." Will sits back and pops his collar. "You feel me?"

We bump fists with Will in a show of respect and I realize why Nick admires him. Will is a tough guy, and who doesn't love having a tough guy on their side? Knowing Will trusts me enough to bring me in his crew gives a huge boost to my ego. Sitting in his musty dive bar discussing the distribution of an illegal substance suddenly feels less criminal. More like three business partners brainstorming marketing ideas.

After a brief tutorial on disposable cell phones, Will walks us to the car and scans the street before hugging Nick. We get in, and Will leans into the driver's window to tell Nick to keep it under eighty.

"Yeah, yeah." Nick smiles, but we both know it isn't going to happen. Nick's engine roars to life. He gives it a little gas and watches the gauges. "How much are we selling the thizz for?"

"Give out some freebies to first-timers. When they come back, its twenty a hit."

Nick whistles at the price tag. "Isn't that kind of high?"

"Don't worry, they'll pay."

Twenty dollars might fly in the city, but it's pretty steep for Eureka.

"Thizz." Nick repeats the strange word. "What the fuck does it mean?"

"Look it up. There's a whole music scene dedicated to thizz." Will points at me as I fumble with the radio. I nod and search for the hip-hop station we were listening to earlier. I want to soak up as much of this music as I can before we lose the stations. I turn the volume up on a Kid Rock song and sit back.

"You need to ditch your hillbilly shit and get with the times, boys," Will says. "You have product to sell!"

The drive home always feels longer. Having a carload of illegal drugs doesn't make it any easier. It's taken four hours to drive back from San Francisco, because Nick actually stuck to the speed limit. I know it was hard for him. His muscle car wasn't built to go sixty-five, and he has a stack of speeding tickets to prove it. Nick never has to worry about things like speeding tickets or money in general. The Marino's own most of the land in Humboldt County, which is why people kiss Nick's ass. They think he's their future landlord. Little do they know Nick has other plans. It doesn't stop Nick from getting free movie tickets, complimentary haircuts, and sometimes a free oil change, just because his last name is Marino. He's really gracious about it all. Every time the manager opens a new line for him at the grocery store, or an attendant leaves their booth to pump his gas, he acts shocked at their sudden burst of hospitality. Nick's one of the most powerful people in town, but he wants to believe he's just like everyone else. There might be some fucked up psychological explanation for this, but I think it has something to do with losing his parents. His father died when he was two, and Mariann made sure he never knew his mother. Will told Nick that Mariann made his mother, Maria, sign her parental rights over after Nick's father died in rehab. Will said she saved the money, hoping to get Nick back one day, but that day never came.

Nick pulls in front of my house and I yawn. "Fuck, I'm tired."

"Yeah, it's hard work sitting in the passenger seat, Matty." Nick puts the car in park and comes inside to use the bathroom.

My parents let me have the little apartment that sits beneath our main house. It's a one-bedroom with its own living room, bathroom, and kitchenette. Nick goes straight to my bathroom and I head upstairs two at a time. I stop on the landing in the hall and listen to make sure nobody is here. When I pass Ashely's room, her door is ajar. I peek in and see the evening sun spotlighting the pillows on her bed. When she was sick the last time, the worst time, my parents offered to switch rooms with her. That way she'd have her own bathroom and more space for the hospital bed they were going to rent, but Ash refused. She wasn't about to move to an uncomfortable hospital bed in our parents' bedroom. It sort of negated the whole point of being sent home to die. She wanted to stay in her room, in her bed, with the afternoon sun shining on her face.

I close her door and head to the bathroom in the hall. Evidence of Ashley's condition is everywhere. From the industrial-size mouthwash for when she's puking her dinner, to the stacks of garbage bags and never-ending bottles of medications that cover every available counter space. She's in some kind of remission now, but I don't think this stuff will ever be put away. The first time Ashley got better, my mother dumped everything and threw this huge party. Seven months later she was back in the hospital. This time she isn't being that optimistic. Or maybe she's superstitious. Either way, we all have to live with the daily reminder that life can really suck.

When I get back to my room, I find Nick on my computer—he's on Dani's Myspace page. I swipe the mouse from his hand and click off her page before that Audiodub song has a chance to load. It's weird enough they like the same band. I don't want her earning any more points with him.

"What the fuck, Matty?" Nick reaches for the mouse and I pull back.

The shock on Nick's face finally registers and I snap back to reality. "Sorry, I'm just tired."

I've never challenged him when it comes to girls. I never had to; every girl we meet loves him. The rest of us are just background noise. Dani didn't seem interested in him yesterday, but what if I'm wrong?

Nick spins the chair around to face me. "Do you like her or something?"

I shove my hands in my pockets and shrug. I know how I feel about Dani, but how I feel doesn't matter if she likes Nick.

Nick kicks my foot. "If you like her just tell me, dude."

Nick isn't trying to stake some claim, like Arnie does whenever we see a group of chicks at a party. So, why can't I look my best friend in the eye and tell him to back the fuck off? I want to, but I know it's wrong. If Dani likes Nick, I don't want him to blow her off because of me. And if he likes her, I can't compete. All I can do is get to her first.

3
Dani

My job at the cafe was a sympathy offer to get me off of Lucy's couch. It was one sympathy perk I didn't mind taking advantage of. It offers a very important element in my life—coffee. I love coffee anything—candy, candles, ice cream, mints. If there was a coffee perfume, I'd wear it.

The bells above the door jingle as I walk into the cafe. The owner of Eureka Coffee, Patty, is at the corner table in deep conversation with Mrs. Montgomery. She doesn't even look up when I walk past her to the storeroom. The gossip must be good today. Patty is a short, gray-haired woman with two grown children about Lucy's age. She opened the café when her husband passed away six years ago. She told me she needed a reason to get out of bed in the morning. Lucy thinks it's a really sad way to look at life, but I get it. It's sort of how I feel about getting into CAL.

I really like Patty. She is the only person that knows about my parents that hasn't given me the look. You know that look people give when they feel sorry for you, like it is killing them to even speak to you. I hate that look.

"What the hell are you smiling at?" the heavily perfumed she-devil at the register squeaks when I walk past her.

I only have one gripe about working at Eureka Coffee. Her name is Mary. She's Patty's granddaughter, so there isn't much I can do about her. I think Lucy and Patty hoped we would be friends. A small part of me thought we would be too, but Mary didn't get the memo. She's been a bitch to me since the moment I walked through the door because I actually get paid to be here. She works for free as a favor to her grandmother, or so she says. I think she does it to get out of the house. Her parents are super strict. Mary isn't allowed to date until she turns eighteen. If I had a daughter who looked like Mary, I would keep her locked up too. Mary has a flawless smile and amazing blue eyes. Both compliments of her father, who is the town's dentist and George Clooney's long-lost twin. Her mother owns a fancy salon and day spa next door, Lady Luxe, so she always looks like she just stepped out of a magazine. She's a senior at St. Bernard's, an all-girl Catholic high school, and today she has decided to work in her uniform. The few boys that come in love it. These little acts of rebellion are what keeps me from totally hating her.

"Please tell me you heard from CAL so I don't have to listen to you whine about it to my grandmother anymore," she quips and applies a fresh coat of pink lipstick in the hand mirror she keeps next to the register. "I'm so glad I was accepted early to the University of San Francisco. All this waiting must really suck for you." Mary loves to throw her early admission in my face. I decide to take the high road and ignore her snide comment. It makes my shift a lot smoother when I don't try to defend myself.

I pull a cup from the order line and wonder how long it's been sitting up here. Customer service isn't a high priority at Eureka Coffee. Most of our customers are friends of Patty's. They don't mind waiting ten minutes for their order if the gossip is good. The café is small. There are only seven tables inside and four outside, and they're all full. It's very rare to find an empty table at this time of day.

I make a large vanilla latte, set the cup on the counter, and reach for a lid to find there are none. *God forbid Mary restocks the counter.* I tell the customer to hold on and head to the storeroom. I'm only gone a few seconds when a piercing squeal that resembles my name echoes through the café. Mary has only one physical flaw, her voice. She sounds like a three-year-old that sucked all the helium out of a balloon. I would take my time, but I don't want to torture the customers. I grab a stack of lids and hurry back.

"There's a line." Mary spins on the stool at the register, and her thick black hair floats behind her like a super hero cape.

"Thank you Captain Obvious." I toss the lids on the counter and go back to work.

I get three cappuccinos and a large Americano out in record time. I'm working on my fourth cup when I hear someone say, "Excuse me, can I have extra foam on that?"

"No problem," I reply without looking up as I pour the steamed milk into a cup and add a dollop of extra foam on top. "Small latte, with extra foam." I place the cup on the counter and start on the next order.

"Thanks," says the voice. This time I recognize it.

I whip my ahead around and see Nick Marino standing in front of me.

"Hi, I uh, I mean, you're welcome." I look behind him to make sure Katie isn't in the corner with a dart gun ready to take me out. I also kind of hoped to see Matt. But Nick's alone. Totally alone and talking to me.

"What time do you get off? Can I give you a ride home?"

Holy hell, Nick Marino is offering me a ride. First Matt and now Nick. I wonder if Matt knows he's here. I wonder why I even care what Matt thinks. He isn't the one standing here with a smile that could melt an iceberg. For all I know, Matt was setting me up with Nick yesterday. That doesn't change the fact that I sort of like Matt. Even if he doesn't like me. I don't have time to debate this. Nick is waiting for an answer. "A ride would be awesome," I say with way more enthusiasm than called for.

"Ok, let's get back to work." Patty steps between the counter and my view of Nick. "She gets off at eight, hot shot."

Nick nods politely at Patty, then looks around her and smiles at me. He takes two backwards steps, holding my gaze, then turns around and leaves. When the door closes, every female in the café exhales. Mary looks at me like I've just sprouted horns and a tail. I escape to the bathroom before she can launch into her interrogation.

The lighting in here is a lot better than the bathroom at school. It doesn't make me look like the undead, but I'm still me. Boring. Weird. Me. My nails are too short, my chest is too small, and I have on the same socks I wore yesterday. *Why the hell would Nick Marino ask me out?* I know I shouldn't care or even think about Matt, but I do. For an hour I agonized over the idea that Matt was interested in me, and I liked that feeling. I definitely felt something. Although, it could've been the egg salad sandwich I ate for lunch. None of that matters now, because I was totally wrong. Matt didn't invite me to the parking lot to ask me out, he was setting me up with Nick. I didn't see that yesterday because I obviously suck at boys. Ok, so Matt doesn't like me. That doesn't mean I don't feel something for him. His smile, those eyes. I sigh just thinking about him. Do I just ignore the tingles he gives me? Forget all the juvenile fantasies I have about Matt and horses and happily ever after just because Nick Marino asked me out?

Yes. Hell to the yes. I have an opportunity to spend six or seven minutes alone with Nick Marino and I'm taking it.

As soon as I step out of the bathroom, Mary slides off her stool and meets me at the train. Patty calls the espresso machine *the train* because of its steaming process. Her late husband was a train collector; they visited dozens of railroad museums, and he preferred the old steam trains over all the others.

"Why is Nick Marino talking to you?" Mary crosses her arms and leans her hip against the counter.

"How did you know that was Nick Marino?" Mary's overprotective parents barely let her out of the house to work here. I doubt she's ever crossed paths with him.

"Everyone knows who Nick is. He's the grandson of Mariann Marino, owner of JM Developers; they only own half the real estate in the county and the largest construction company in California." Mary rolls her eyes. "So what, are you tutoring him or something?"

Mary doesn't believe a guy like Nick would be interested in me. I don't believe it either, but I'm not going to let her ruin the moment. "I know him from school." *Sort of.* "We hung out at the Rack Room on Friday." I push her aside. "He was just offering me a ride home."

Mary's eyes widen. "You went to the Rack Room. With Nick Marino?" The bells above the door jingle, and three women from the neighboring health food store walk in. Unlike most of our clientele, they're always in a hurry to get back to work.

"We have customers."

"Fine," Mary scowls and returns to her perch. I catch her eyeing me the rest of my shift like she's trying to figure out how I managed to fool Nick Marino into thinking I'm someone he wants to hang out with. *You and me both, sister.*

Somewhere around seven o'clock, I stop trying to analyze why Nick has offered me a ride home and whether or not Matt had anything to do with it, and I start to freak out. Questions, doubts, and nightmares flood my brain. Did he come into the café knowing I would be here? Does that mean he was thinking about me? My heart does this thing where it stops beating for a minute then bounces against my chest like a mental patient trying to escape capture. I don't like Nick. I don't want to like him. Being with someone like Nick means being on everyone's radar. I like to fly low, real low. So far below the radar that nobody knows I exist. I'm overanalyzing this. He offered me a ride home, that's it. I'll take the ride, thank him, and say goodnight. This doesn't have to turn into something it's not.

At five minutes to eight, Nick's car pulls in front of the café. I say goodbye to Patty and ignore Mary's dirty look. I open the door and walk through it as if I'm walking through a portal to a land where someone like Nick Marino is waiting for someone like me to get off work. This is a fairy tale moment if I've ever seen one. Or not. Maybe it's just a really nice guy offering a really pathetic girl a ride home.

Nick's leaning against the passenger door in a pair of jeans and a plain white t-shirt. His arms are crossed over his chest like one of those old photos of James Dean. *Holy hell.*

"Hey Dani." He smiles and opens the door for me. I say hi without meeting his eyes.

Nick gets in and starts the car. A classic rock song blares from the speakers. "Sorry about that," he apologizes and turns the music down.

"It's ok, I like that song." It was "More than a Feeling" by Boston. Johnson has been schooling me on classic rock since I was eight. I know way more about seventies rock and eighties hair bands than anyone my age should.

Nick smiles like he doesn't believe me and switches to the radio. "What time do you have to be home?"

The question catches me off guard. Why does it matter, if we're going straight to Lucy's house? "Uh, I'm not sure." I don't want to tell him I've never been out before, so I have no idea if I have a curfew.

"Well, there's a bonfire at Gold Beach, do you think you can go?"

Something that feels like excitement brews in my belly. Do I want to go out with Nick, or do I want to go home and stuff my face with chips and salsa while watching old episodes of America's Next Top Model? This is exactly the kind of thing Lucy was hoping for. Me out on a Saturday night. This is her idea of normal. I'll do it for Lucy. "Yeah, I can go."

"Sweet." Nick pulls out of the parking lot and heads towards the highway. His car is loud and takes some effort to drive. He's constantly shifting gears and checking gauges. It takes the pressure off making small talk. Once we're on the highway, he turns the volume up on the stereo to drown out the silence that I wouldn't really call awkward. The stereo is on a local radio station. Through the static I can barely recognize the Killers' "Mr. Brightside."

"The reception sucks out here. You want to hear a CD?" Nick pulls a leather case from between the seats and hands it to me.

I take the case from him and set it in my lap. You can learn a lot about a person through their music collection. "Sure." I flip it open and look through the first few pages. He's got all the latest music—Weezer, Snoop Dogg, even Gwen Stefani's "Hollaback Girl." It's the other stuff that impresses me, like Otis Redding's *Greatest Hits* and an old Bon Jovi CD. "I didn't think guys like you were so eclectic."

"Oh really, what kind of guy do you think I am?" Nick raises his eyebrow in that sexy, curious way sexy guys like Nick do to make self-conscious girls like me feel like they're going to pee their pants.

I can't say what I'm thinking—the kind of guy that gets what he wants, who he wants, whenever he wants, the kind of guy that would never ask me out. Instead, I open a page that contains the Rolling Stones, Dr. Dre, Sublime, and Santana. I hold it up so he can see my point.

Nick smiles. "My uncle owns a bar in San Francisco. I know most of the music from his juke box, but I pretty much listen to everything. What about you?"

I'm about to tell him we have a lot in common musically when I flip the page. My eyes drift to the last slot on the right, to an Eagles CD. I run my hand over the picture of the sun setting behind the hotel and remember the long melodic guitar solo that filled our SUV the last time I saw my father. I never realized how much missing him hurt until this moment. I bite my lip until I taste blood.

"Do you want to hear that one?"

"No." I close the case. "This is fine." The static is so bad it sounds like aliens are trying to make contact.

"How about a little classic rock?" Nick hits a button on the CD player and Motley Crue's "Without You" fills the car.

Johnson's tutorials on classic rock versus eighties hair bands have finally paid off. "I love this song." I feel the smile form on my face. An honest-to-God smile. I look at Nick and feel the urge to thank him, but I have no idea why. All he did was push play.

I listen to the very romantic lyrics and wonder if this song will ever mean something to us. Do I even want there to be an Us? I have a plan, a mission—CAL. Nick is not in the plan. Nick is a plan killer. I look at the one thing that can deter me from my future, and his lips are moving. He's singing. His eyes flit in my direction. He's singing to me.

Without you, without you, a sailor lost at sea. Without you, woman, the world comes down on me.

This song is telling me one day my heart will wilt and die. It's a risk I'm willing to take, because right now I can't think of anything better than falling madly, deeply in love with Nick Marino.

4
Matt

I'm sitting on a log outside the glow of the fire when I see them. Dani looks like a frightened animal being lured to slaughter. Nick is oblivious to the anguish he's causing her, parading her around like she's a prize. *Congratulations, Nick. You win.* I slam the beer in my hand and reach for another. He could've had the balls to tell me he was going out with Dani tonight. I wonder if he had this planned when he asked me if I liked her. *Why even ask?* I slam another beer and crush the can before tossing it in the sand.

"Hey Matt," Haley calls from somewhere in the dark. "I thought you were coming with Nick? Where is he?"

Nick is never hard to find in a crowd. He shines like a fucking lucky coin. "He's over there."

Haley turns towards the fire then murmurs some obscenities under her breath. "What is he doing with her?" She plops down next to me.

I shrug and take the cup from her hand. I sniff it; it smells like fruit juice and alcohol—Sex on the Beach most likely. These chicks are so predictable. I down it and toss the cup.

"Hey!" Haley retrieves it from the sand. "What's wrong with you?" She dusts it off and I notice she's blinged out the red solo cup with her name in glittery girly writing.

I shrug. I don't know why I'm so irritated. It isn't like I have a right to be. I don't own Dani. Hell, I didn't even ask her out. I didn't have the balls and now it's too late.

Haley sits next to me and follows my line of sight to Nick and Dani. "I'm not the only one that got snaked, huh?" I don't answer her. I don't know the answer. "So, you like her?" Haley offers me a joint. She always has weed.

I take it from her and she hands me a lighter. I put it to my lips and inhale as I hold the flame to the other end. Smoke fills my lungs. I hold it in for a long time before exhaling. I hand the lit joint back to Haley. "She's cool," I say. It's all I am willing to admit.

Haley takes a puff and hands it back to me. "Don't worry, it won't last. She's not like us. She doesn't party."

"How do you know?" How does anyone know anything about Dani? I've never seen her talk to anyone at school. Believe me, I would've noticed.

"She told Heather she doesn't party. She goes to book clubs or something."

"Yeah right." Probably just another lie Heather made up about Dani. I can't keep track of all the rumors she spread about her. I take another hit and look at Haley. She's wearing her Eureka High hoodie with black jeans and furry boots. Her hair looks curlier than normal, and she has on a sweet-smelling perfume. I can smell it through the weed. Out of all the girls in her clique, she's the only one I bother to talk to. I've known her the longest. She's a regular fixture in all my class pictures. "So, what's up with you and Nick?"

Haley looks at Nick, who hasn't let go of Dani's hand since he got here, and takes a puff. "We hooked up a couple of weeks ago, after the game against McKinnleyville. I thought he liked me, but you know Nick. With guys like that, you just sort of wait it out until it's your turn."

"That's all you want? To be some douche bag's turn? You're too good for that, Haley." I look at Dani. "You're too good for him."

I fall onto my back and stare at the stars. "I bet Ashley is looking through her telescope right now."

"How is your sister? I heard she's...better." Haley falls next to me and passes back the joint.

I take it from her and check the end to make sure it's still lit. "She's good," I say in between hits. I don't want to think about Ashley right now. I close my eyes. I don't want to think about anything.

5
Dani

The laughter and bright glow of the fire fades as we walk in the brisk night air. Anxious butterflies have replaced the knot in my stomach. I focus on him, his hand, his smile, his eyes—and try to forget the horrible welcome I received when we got here. That was exactly the thing I was trying to avoid. Luckily, Heather wasn't among the gaggle of blondes that looked like they wanted to push me in the fire. I have a feeling dating Nick Marino is going to be bad for my health. Mentally and physically. It's obvious to me and everyone else that I don't belong with Nick. But I can't leave. I don't even want to. He's like a drug and I can't say no.

I'm not even sure any of this is real. I would say I'm dreaming, but I never dream this big. Nick grips my hand and pulls me closer. He leans towards me and I feel the warmth of his breath on my face. That's real. *He is real.*

"You make great lattes," he says with a little laugh.

"That wasn't the first latte I made for you."

"I know," he says with a smile.

He knows, which means he has noticed me before today. "So, is that why you asked me out, you like my lattes?" He must've asked

Matt to send the message so we could meet properly. Knowing this makes me feel better about Nick and me becoming us.

He sort of laughs then bumps me with his shoulder. "Nah. You seem like an interesting person and I thought it would be cool to hang out."

"Yeah right, I'm the least interesting person you'll ever meet." The only interesting thing about me is the one thing I can't tell him.

Nick stops walking and turns to face me. We're standing so close, no wind passes between us. He slides a loose strand of hair behind my ear. "You really want to know why I asked you out?"

I could care less. The *why* doesn't matter, all that matters is now. This moment. Staring into those perfect hazel eyes. Nick runs his finger across my jaw and stops under my chin. *Is he going to kiss me?* The last time I kissed a boy was over two years ago. It was in a closet during a Christmas party at my father's firm. His name was Charles, the son of the CEO. His breath tasted like peaches from the cheap brandy he had hidden in his coat pocket. The kiss was sloppy and wet. I am so ready for a new first kiss. I don't care if we just met. Kissing a boy like Nick isn't something that happens every day. Screw the rules.

A sly smile forms on his lips. I feel his breath on my mouth, my lips part, waiting, wanting. *He's going to kiss me. Nick Marino is going to kiss me.*

He leans in closer, his lips brushing my ear. "It's your lattes," he whispers. "It could also have something to do with the fact that you're beautiful." He kisses my cheek and backs away with a playful grin.

Did Nick Marino just call me beautiful? I know I'm not horrible looking, but the positioning of my nose and the curve of my lips have nothing to do with why I find his compliment shocking. I find it unbelievable because I know I'm not up to his standard. I've seen his standard: Katie. She could do a Victoria's Secret catalog shoot tomorrow without having to puke her dinner. She was perfect. *And he didn't want her.*

I don't douse myself with make-up every morning or give two shits about my hair. I never wear perfume and I can't even remember the last time I plucked my eyebrows. Nick and I don't match on so many levels, yet being here feels right.

Nick swoops down and picks up something from the sand. He examines it for a second then puts it in the pocket of his jacket. I think it was a shell. Oh lord, he collects shells too. My heart bursts into song. You can't look like Nick *and* collect shells. It's just not fair. I'm going to fall in love with this boy, whether I want to or not.

"How old are you?" Nick spins around and walks backwards, facing me.

"I just turned eighteen." My birthday was last Saturday. I had to work and I didn't want to make a big deal out of it. Lucy brought me a cupcake from the hospital cafeteria during her lunch break and I let her and Patty sing "Happy Birthday" to me in the back room. Celebrating didn't feel right without my parents.

Nick stumbles back and puts his hand over his heart. "Oh man. You're older than me." He's blushing like this really bothers him. "I won't be eighteen until next month."

"Good thing you told me this now, because I have a rule about dating guys younger than me." Nick raises an eyebrow, and I realize he's reacting to the fact that I just said the word dating. "I mean, I'm not saying I want to date you." Nick clutches his chest again. "I mean, of course I want to date you, if dating you was an option." I feel my face turn red hot. "I just need to shut up." *Just run now, Dani, before you make a bigger fool of yourself.*

Nick reaches out for me. I let him take my hand and pull me to him. "To be honest, knowing you're older kind of makes me want you even more." He runs his hand down the side of my face then turns around and continues walking down the beach.

Being wanted by Nick is the best feeling in the world.

Being wanted by Nick is the scariest feeling in the world.

I don't like needing things, because when you don't have them anymore, it hurts. The idea of Nick not wanting me someday is almost worth walking away right now. Almost.

We are pretty far from the bonfire. Pale moonlight and the fuzzy orange glow from the parking lot is the only thing lighting our path. I stumble a few times and bump into him, not totally by accident.

"Whoa." Nick catches me. He takes my hand and pulls me into his arms, holding me as we walk. My hormones are raging in a way that I never knew was possible. All of Lucy's lectures on birth control and safe sex make a little more sense now. Even when I was making out in the closet with Charles, I never felt like this. Nick and I are just walking, and thoughts of him ravishing me won't stop running through my mind.

"So, you've lived in Eureka your whole life?" I ask, desperate to say something.

"Yep. Depressing isn't it? But I'm out of here after graduation. I have some things lined up in San Francisco." He lets go of me to pick up a rock, then he throws it into the darkness ahead of us. The gesture looks so juvenile. So unlike something the man walking beside me would do. His face looks like it belongs on the cover of a romance novel. There is nothing about Nick Marino that says boy, even if he is only seventeen.

"I applied to CAL, but I'll probably live in San Francisco." I don't want him to think I'm stalking him if we end up living in the same city. Even though I would totally stalk him; he's so stalkable. "Did you apply to San Francisco State or USF?"

"Oh yeah, school." Nick stares at the sand as we walk. He runs his hand through his hair and clears his throat. "I do have to go to college, it's a family thing. I just don't know where I'm going yet." Nick pauses. "My family owns a bunch of property around town. I don't know what you've heard."

I remember what Mary said about Nick's family being the largest developers in California, but it's Mary. How credible can she be? "Not much. I hate gossip."

"Me too." Nick smiles and takes my hand. He corroborates Mary's story about his family, only he tells the story like he's embarrassed. "It's no big deal. Besides, it's my family's money, not mine. I don't want any part of their business." Nick's tone turns hard. "I'm going to make my own money. I'm going to take the Marino name to places it's never been before."

The fact that he separates himself from his family's wealth is commendable. He isn't a typical spoiled rich kid. Not that I thought of him as one, but hearing the conviction in his voice when he talks about making his own money tells me he's passionate about his future. It only makes me admire him more.

We walk a few feet in silence. I get the feeling he's finished talking about his family, so don't I ask any questions. The last thing I want to do is talk about my family.

"What was it like growing up in the city?" he finally asks.

"Foggy mostly." *Please don't ask me anything else.*

Nick laughs. "Yeah, the weather kind of sucks, but it beats the shit out of Eureka. Why the hell would you move here? Did your parents want to torture you or something?"

I could tell him the lie Lucy made up for her coworkers and friends. She tells people my parents are on some bullshit philanthropic mission helping indigenous people in the South Pacific. I don't want to lie to

Nick. It will just make it that much harder to tell him the truth later. If there is a later. I shrug and force a smile. "Yeah, something like that."

Nick is waiting for me to elaborate, but I can't. I won't. We keep walking hand in hand, both of us holding on to family secrets we don't want to share.

"So, you like Audiodub?" It's the only safe topic I can think of. It's also something I've been curious about since I heard "Lucky Go Leah" in his car.

"Are you kidding? I *love* Audiodub. My uncle Will knows one of the guys in the band. Maybe we can go see them sometime. I'll introduce you." Nick's face lights up at the thought. "Have you ever seen them live?"

I tell Nick I haven't seen them, but it's a lie. I saw Audiodub play at Slim's last year. My mom freaked out when I asked her if I could go. She said Slim's wasn't an appropriate venue for a girl my age, even though the place has no age limit. The night of the concert, my father told my mom he was taking me to dinner and a movie. Instead he took me to see Audiodub. I couldn't count on my father for much, but when he came through, he came through big. We never told my mom, it was just our secret. It still is.

"Then I'm definitely taking you." I love that he is already thinking about future dates, because I can't imagine my future without him in it. I'm so screwed.

We stop at the end of the cove and stare in the direction of the ocean. I try to maintain some dignity as my hair whips around my face from the unrelenting wind. I look up and catch Nick watching me like a puppy in a pet store window. "Are you cold?" He lets go of my hand and holds open his jacket. I don't even hesitate. I wrap my arms around him and bury my face in his shirt. He smells like jasmine and car exhaust. Normally, that would seem like an odd pairing, but on Nick it's divine. I'm surprised at how easily I succumb to him. He offers to hold me and I jump in his arms. It's so unlike me—the old me. This is a new Dani. Who knows what I'm capable of?

My smile is frozen in place, partly by the freezing wind, but mostly because I feel good. I don't think I've ever felt this kind of good. I place my ear against Nick's chest and listen to the quick rhythm of his heart—it's beating as fast as mine. I want to remember this moment forever—the cold wind on my back, the uneven sand under my feet, the warm sensation in my chest, and the safe feeling of his arms around me. Nothing exists in the world but us. I look into Nick's smiling eyes, they are a plethora of earth tones—light brown and yellow with hints of green. Looking at him makes my body tingle in all the right ways. He pulls me closer and kisses my forehead. The gesture is sweet, but I want more. I need more. I focus on his lips, willing them to want me.

Kiss me, I scream with my eyes. I bite my lower lip; it draws Nick's eyes to my mouth. He brushes his hand across my cheek and I inhale as if I'm about to dive underwater. My eyelids flutter as he draws closer, my lips part, waiting to feel his mouth on mine. Then I hear the faint call of his name. The salty night air replaces Nick's warm breath as the yelling grows louder. *How was this moment suddenly ruined?* I look past Nick and see Matt running up the beach towards us.

Oh no, Matt.

6 Matt

My heart folds in on itself when I see her in his arms. Nick looks like he is about to make his move, so I yell his name. His eyes shoot in my direction and I wave. I put on my best fake smile and walk up to them like I didn't just cock-block my best friend. I tell Nick its ten thirty, but I don't say anything about the party at K's house. Neither does he. I don't think I can stand to watch them thizz together, not after what I read online about how it effects inhibitions, sex drive. Will was right. There is an entire culture built around this drug. Music, hairstyles, clothes. I can't wait to release thizz culture on Eureka. Just not on Dani.

"I have to be home at eleven," Dani says.

Nick looks at her curiously. "Ok," he says. "I'll drop her off then come back for you." I know from the look on his face he doesn't want me to say anything about the party. I nod my head once to let him know I get it. Nick and I have known each other forever. We can read each other like nobody else can. We always know what the other is thinking.

He takes Dani's hand and starts back towards the bonfire. I follow two steps behind. I wonder if she'd be here with me if I wasn't such a punk, if I would have just asked her out in class or at least talked to her in the parking lot. I knew better than to have her meet me with Nick around. He's like a black hole, sucking up the attention of everyone around him. He can't help it. Hell, I don't even think he likes it, but he can't escape it. None of us can. Dani being here is my fault. I put her in his path and she couldn't fight the pull. I know she liked me, at least a little. I saw the way her cheeks turned red when I sat down next to her in class and the huge smile she gave me when I passed her in the hall. We had a good vibe, I know it. I felt it. I fucked it up.

When we get back to Nick's car, I remember what Haley said about Dani. I wonder if Nick knows she doesn't party and that's why he isn't bringing her to K's house. Dani is standing on the passenger side of the car while Nick and I say goodbye. "Later," Nick says, and we clap our hands together. He whispers that he wants me to wait for him to get back before giving out any freebies. As if I would do it without him.

Dani is watching us. More like she's watching Nick. She doesn't even see me. I'm just background noise. As Nick's partner, it's my duty to let him know about Dani before things get serious. "I heard Dani doesn't party," I whisper.

Nick looks at me like I'm speaking another language. "Who told you that?" I know Nick, and his defenses just went up.

"Haley." The mention of Haley's name makes Nick grimace. He runs his hand through his hair and looks back at Dani. "Alright, I'll drop her off and meet you at K's."

I feel a huge weight lift from my chest knowing she won't be at the party. I won't have to watch her smile at him the way she used to smile at me. Nick unlocks the door and opens it for Dani. Before she ducks down to get inside, she looks up at me and smiles. "See you on Monday, Matt."

My entire body erupts in pleasure with that one small look. I don't want her to go, I want to stare at that smile a little longer. "Wait," I yell as her head disappears below the car. "Don't I get a hug goodbye?" I have no idea where that came from. It must be the six-pack of beer I slammed. Liquid courage.

Dani looks up with a strange expression. She looks shocked or disgusted by the words coming out of my mouth, which makes what I'm about to do even more pathetic—but I really don't care. I walk to her side of the car and wrap my arms around her frigid body. She smells like coffee and car exhaust. Weird—but fucking awesome. She doesn't say a word. I'm practically assaulting her. I'm such a loser.

"Ok, ok, hands off my girl," Nick says as I let her go.

His girl. She's Nick's girl.

7 Dani

The house is dark when Nick pulls into the driveway. Lucy isn't home yet, which means she won't know I went out tonight. I'm not sure what is happening with Nick, but I'm definitely not ready to talk about it with Lucy. She has this way of blowing things out of proportion. I also don't need another lecture on birth control. I try to say goodnight in the car, but Nick insists on walking me to the door.

"Do you work tomorrow?" he asks as we reach the porch.

I tell him I have the morning shift.

"Can I come see you? Maybe we can do something after you get off." He takes my hands and smiles, as if he has to convince me to say yes. He doesn't realize how badly I want to see him again. How I hate letting him go right now.

This is crazy. I can't be attached already. "Yes, of course." *I'll be counting the minutes.*

Nick smiles like I just told him he won the lottery. I think that's what makes being with him feel so nice. The way he looks at me like a coveted piece of art. He sees something that nobody else can, not even me. "Good night," he says, then leans in and kisses my cheek. I exhale slowly, and the next thing I know, his lips brush my mouth. We kiss softly two or three times then break away. My heart sputters in my chest when I open my eyes and see him staring back at me. This wasn't my first kiss, but it is the one I will commit to memory and pull up whenever I need to smile.

"Good night," I whisper into the air between us.

"Good night," Nick says again and takes a step down off the porch. My arm extends towards him until my fingers slide from his like some cheesy music video moment. I get why those moments exist. I'm having one right now.

Nick walks down the steps and stands by his door, waiting for me to go inside. I finally unlock the door and wave one more time before closing it. I run straight to my room and watch Nick drive away. After his car disappears around the corner, I fall onto the bed with a loud sigh. I just went on a date with Nick Marino. He said I was beautiful. He kissed me goodnight. I don't know how I will sleep tonight or work tomorrow. I already miss his touch, his smell. I'm already completely addicted.

Forget flying under the radar. Fuck the radar. I'm going to fall in love with Nick Marino.

I'm in the bathroom washing my face when the doorbell rings. It's late, and Lucy wouldn't ring the bell. Whoever it is must have seen Nick drop me off. They know I'm home alone. I creep into the hall and look down the staircase to see if I recognize the silhouette on the porch. The doorbell echoes through the empty house again. For the first time since the night of the accident, I'm scared. Lucy calls it an accident, now I'm doing it. I guess accident rolls off the tongue a lot easier than the truth. I look at the phone in the hall. I could call Johnson. He's home in Arcata. That's at least twenty minutes away. I could be dead by then. Now I sound as paranoid as Lucy. I'm safe here. Lucy, Johnson, even the police seemed convinced that Eureka was the safest place for me to be. I take a step to go downstairs when there is a loud knock on the door. I scramble back to the hall and pick up the phone, ready to call nine-one-one. What will I say? A stranger is knocking on the door? That's hardly an emergency.

There's another loud knock, then a voice yells my name. "Hey Dani, it's me." *It's Nick!* My heart does a happy dance while my stomach exits my throat.

I bolt down the stairs and open the door. "I'm sorry, I was in the bathroom." *Great, I just told Nick Marino I was using the bathroom.*

"That's alright." He smiles his Nick smile. "I just wanted to see if you felt like going to a party."

"Right now?"

"Yeah," he says apologetically. "I was going to ask you before, but you said you had to go home." He runs his hand through his thick dark hair. "I just really want to hang out with you a little longer."

I don't want this night to end either, but I hate parties. Especially parties that may include Heather King.

Nick runs his hand through his hair again. "So, do you think you can go?" His right eyebrow arches, and the hairs on my arm stand at attention.

No, no way. Lucy will freak out if she comes home and you're gone. You can't leave this house.

8
Matt

I hear cheering in the front room. Nick must be here—time to work. I splash water on my face and open the bathroom door. Two girls squeeze past me and slam the door. I don't know how long I've been hiding in there, but the line is all the way down the hall. After K's NASCAR-level driving from the beach to his house two blocks away, I was spinning. I felt better after dunking my head in a sink of cold water.

I find Nick in the kitchen with K. He pulls the bag of pills out of his pocket and opens it. "Tell Troy I said welcome home." Nick places half a dozen pills in K's hand. Troy is K's older cousin. He just finished his first year of college and is home for the summer. He's six foot two and close to three hundred pounds. He plays defensive end for Washington State. I don't think he's ever said more than five words to me that weren't:

Get the fuck out of my way.

Hey, fag, did your boyfriend pick that outfit for you?

Or my favorite: What are you buying me for lunch today?

Troy was the meanest bully Eureka High has ever seen. Everyone sleeps easier now that he's gone. From what I've read about thizz, I'm anxious to see how it will affect Troy's naturally volatile demeanor.

"Have you tried it?" K asks while pumping a beer from the keg in the middle of his kitchen floor.

"Not yet." Nick smiles at me and hands me a pill. I didn't realize I'd actually take one. I was so juiced about the music I forgot the real reason we were here. The pill is smaller than your average headache medicine and has a chalky feel to it. Each one is stamped with a dolphin. "That's sort of lame. Why not a shark or something? It might as well be a fuckin' goldfish." We laugh at Nick's lame association, but neither one of us take the pill.

"What are you bitches doing in here?" I freeze when I hear Troy's voice. He reaches around me for the freshly pumped beer in K's hand.

K hands him the beer. "Have you heard of thizz?"

"You punks never thizzed?" Troy scoffs. He stops laughing when K holds out his hand to show him the pills.

"Welcome home," Nick says to let him know he is to thank for the freebies. Troy never disrespects Nick, but he doesn't really like him either.

Troy nods to Nick as he swipes the pills from K. "Li'l bitches," he mumbles as he leaves the kitchen.

"Fuck him." K whispers so Troy doesn't hear. "Let's do it." K grabs a cup to pump another beer. Nick and I smile like we're ready, but I hesitate. I see Nick pause, too. K is about to pop the pill in his mouth when the doorbell rings. "I better get that." K palms his pill and hurries to the door before his cousins scare off the guests.

"We should wait for K," I suggest.

"Ok, but if anyone asks, it's the best shit you ever had." He winks as the kitchen fills with people. He leaves to go mingle and I stay behind to freak out.

I palm the pill and wonder if I can get away with not taking it. Once the party gets started, Nick will be busy making sales and fighting off chicks. I doubt he'll even care whether I take it or not. Tonight, I'll be an observer. I'll take notes on how people react to the pills, how long the high lasts, and I'll report it all back to Nick. I really don't know how else I can contribute to Nick's business. I'm not a drug dealer. Hell, I'm not even a user. None of us have ever done anything other than weed. In Humboldt County, the consensus is that marijuana should be legal, so it never felt wrong. Cocaine and meth are pretty much limited to the tweakers and freaks that live on the edge of town. Popping a pill is a whole new level for all of us.

9
Dani

I'm smashed between a couple of giggling girls and a massive guy in a dark hallway; we're all waiting for the bathroom. *Lucy is going to kill me.* I keep thinking about the note I taped to the inside of the front door. Lucy always puts the chain on when she gets home, so she won't miss it. I said I was invited to a party but I didn't tell her who I was with or where I was going. She shouldn't object to this. She wanted normal. I'm giving her normal. I mean, this is normal right? I look at the girls in front of me; they look normal. The guy looks, uh, huge. He catches me eyeing him and smiles. I look past him, down the hall like I'm looking for someone. I don't know anyone here except Nick. I don't even have to use the bathroom. I just felt overwhelmed walking into a house full of strangers wondering who the hell I am and how I ended up on the arm of Nick Marino. I'm still trying to figure that out myself.

The bathroom door swings open and Matt walks out.

Matt.

Something inside me lights up at the sight of him. Maybe it's just the idea that I know someone besides Nick. He stumbles down the hall and disappears into the living room before I even have a chance to call his name. He didn't look like he was up for small talk. He wasn't all that pleasant when I saw him earlier. He looks even worse now.

After I use the bathroom I walk back to the living room to find Nick. I really don't want to jump back into his spotlight, but he's the reason I'm here. The only reason.

"Hey, there you are." Nick pulls me into his arms and kisses my forehead. "This is Dani." Nick is beaming at me as if I'm the source of his light. I really do have him fooled.

"I'm K, welcome to my home." K shakes my hand. "Can I get you a drink?"

"Nah, she doesn't drink." Nick winks at me.

"I don't?" Do I look like the kind of girl that doesn't drink? How pathetic.

Nick looks flustered. "I guess…I just…you didn't want a beer at the bonfire, so I just thought you didn't drink."

Yeah, I declined a beer at the bonfire earlier, only because I wasn't sure one of the girls hadn't spiked it with poison. "I don't drink *beer*," I smile.

Nick raises an eyebrow at me. "Alright, get my girl a drink." He puts his arm around me and pulls me close. He seems happy to learn I'm not a non-drinking geek. I just hope he doesn't expect me to do shots or something. I've had alcohol—a glass of champagne on New Year's Eve, a sip of my mother's wine at a fancy restaurant. I've just never drank socially. I've never done anything socially, like go to a house party or a bonfire.

K disappears to get me a drink that isn't beer, and a group of guys bombard Nick. I know one of them. Nick shakes his hand then turns to introduce me. The way he does it feels like something formal. Like he's announcing I'm taken. It's sort of possessive, but it makes me feel special. "Dani, this is my boy, Arnie."

Arnie licks his lips and looks me up and down, like he's trying to place me. He is disgusting.

"We have English together," I remind him so he can stop staring. I don't offer my hand for him to shake like I did with K.

Arnie snaps his fingers and says, "That's right. You're the new chick." He continues nodding his head as if he's answering a question in his mind.

It's annoying. He is annoying.

"Can you really consider me new? I started school in February." I don't know why I'm challenging him. He isn't worth it.

"You'll always be the new girl." Arnie takes a gulp from his red cup and walks away.

His words sting a little, but he's right. I will never fit in here. I don't want to. I have a plan. I'm sticking to my plan.

This party is not in my plan.

Nick motions for me to follow him and we head out of the living room, down the hall, into a bedroom.

Whoa.

Nick closes the door behind us. My pulse races.

Nothing about this feels right.

There's a knock on the door. Nick opens it. K hands him a cup and smiles, then closes the door.

Holy shit, what is going on?

"Sorry, Arnie can be a douche sometimes." Nick hands me the cup and leans against a white wicker dresser with his thumbs in his front pockets.

I take the cup and sniff it. It smells like vodka and orange juice. Who knows what else is in there.

Nick wouldn't drug me, would he?

"Why don't you sit down?" Nick motions behind me to the bed.

He's crazy if he thinks I'm that easy. "I think I better go." I put the cup on the nightstand and reach for the door.

"Wait." He steps in front of me and I jump back. I don't know any self-defense, it's the one class my mother never signed me up for. But I know where to kick a guy to put him down. "No, oh no!" He opens the door. "It's not like that. I just thought we could...it's quiet in here. I wanted to talk. That's it. Just talk." He tries to take my hand, but I jerk it away. The back of my legs are up against the bed. If he wanted, he could knock me down and jump on me in a matter of seconds. If he wanted to. The thought sends a shiver up my back. I'm not exactly sure if it's the bad kind.

"I'm sorry. We can keep the door open." Nick pushes the door until the knob hits the wall. "I won't touch you." He backs away from the door and walks around the bed to the other side of the room. "See, you can leave anytime you want."

My cheeks flush. Of course Nick isn't a rapist. I bet girls line up to sleep with him. "I'm sorry."

"No, it's my fault. I shouldn't have brought you in here. It's just loud out there, and I really want to spend time with you. Without Arnie or anyone else bothering us."

I'm probably the only girl at this party afraid to be alone with Nick Marino. I should be grateful I'm even here. He could be in this room with a girl that wants to be ravaged by the hottest boy in school. Instead he's stuck with me, and from the look on his face, he's regretting it. I need to keep the façade going. I don't want him to see the huge mistake standing across the room.

I relax my shoulders and lean against the wicker dresser like I'm cool, like I belong here. Nick is leaning against the wall on the opposite side of the room. We're separated by the bed. Gulp.

"Whose room is this?" The bed is small, full-size at most. It's draped with floral bedding and matching throw pillows. Beside the bed is a small white nightstand with a seashell-covered lamp. It's the only source of light in the room.

"K's family rents it…" Nick stops mid-sentence and takes a sip of his beer. "These units come furnished."

"Your family owns this house?" I pick up my drink and sit on the edge of the bed. I smell it one more time and wet my lips with the contents.

"They own the block." *They* he says, not we. He really does disassociate himself from it all. "Look, I hate talking about my family." Nick sits on the other side of the bed. It's nice to know he's just as uncomfortable talking about family as I am. It's another thing we have in common.

"What do you want to talk about?" I take a sip of my drink and pretend it isn't burning my throat.

Nick runs his hand through his hair and smiles the sexiest smile I've ever seen. A smile that tells me the idea of being thrown on the bed and ravished by this boy is not what I'm afraid of. I'm not scared he will. I'm worried he won't.

"Have you ever heard of thizz?"

10
Matt

I lean against the wall in the living room, watching the crowd. The keg is flowing, blunts are being passed. I haven't seen Nick since the kitchen an hour ago. I wonder if he's hooking up with someone already. Part of me wants it to be true, and part of me doesn't. I don't want him to hurt Dani, but my life would suck a lot less if he did. I can't get her out of my head. The way she smelled when I hugged her. The pissed-off look on her face when I let her go. I'm a fucking idiot. She doesn't want me, she never did.

K puts on one of the CDs I made and cranks it up. During my thizz research, I found a bunch of songs about the drug and downloaded them from LimeWire. If the pills are a bust, I can probably make some money selling bootlegged CDs. The hard-hitting bass and raspy lyrics confuse the crowd. Only K's cousins and a few other people know the words and sing along. By the time the second verse hits, half the party is on their feet. Troy and the other cousins, who haven't moved from the sofa, are now socializing with the rest of the guests. The pills we passed out must be kicking in. Fifteen minutes ago this was a room full of strangers, now people are treating each other like long-lost friends. Lots of hugs and high fives going around the room. Hell, I'm even smiling, and I haven't taken anything.

The CD is on its second rotation when Troy turns it off to make a toast. He stands in the middle of the room, holding a bottle of Hennessy towards K. "Cuz, you're like a little brother. I can't tell you how much it means to have you throw this party for me." He pounds his fist against his enormous chest and looks to be fighting back tears. "I love you, bro." He reaches for K. They hug as the crowd oohs and aahs. Troy's brothers join them, turning the hug into a mountain of flesh and frizzy hair. Then one of them jumps back and says, "Let's get hyphy in this bitch!" They break apart and K turns the music back up.

Watching the crowd become overtaken by thizz isn't like watching someone chug a beer or take a shot. After a shot, your body shivers in disgust. When the thizz hits, everyone in the house looks like they are having the time of their lives.

I spot Nick walking into the kitchen and make my way through hands and bodies to reach him. I have to fight off two chicks that want desperately to make me the meat in their dance sandwich. I slap away their roaming hands and stumble into the kitchen. "Fuck! There are some aggressive chicks out there."

"I guess that answers my question." Nick laughs.

I look at Nick like he's speaking another language. "What question?"

"I was going to ask if you took your pill, but you wouldn't be bitchin about getting gang-raped by some wasted chicks if you did." Nick looks past me towards the girls dancing like strippers in the doorway. I realize it's the notorious Martinez twins—Alisa and Amy. They're not really twins, just cousins. They look like rejects from a rap video, grinding on each other in a way that I've only seen on cable television. Neither of them have ever looked in my direction; now they're all over me.

"What are you thinking? The one on the right?" The question is a test. I want to see how serious he is about Dani.

"Alisa Martinez, huh? She is hot." Nick grins and nudges me with his elbow. "She's all you, Matty."

"You're right, the one on the left it more your type." The girl on the left puts a lollipop in her mouth then takes it out slowly, letting the tip linger between her lips before sucking it back in. Even I'm getting turned on.

"Nah, I'm good." Nick turns back to the cup on the counter like there aren't two hot chicks ready to drop to their knees a few feet away. "Actually I wanted to tell you..."

He didn't bite, but he's sober. All of that will change once we take a pill.

"Let's do it." I take the pill from my pocket and hold it up. Nick stops talking and offers me the cup in his hand. I take a huge gulp and fight the urge to gag. "Oh, shit! Why the fuck are you drinking vodka?" I grab a beer from the ice chest on the ground and pop the top on the edge of the counter. I take a long drink, and fear starts to resonate over what I've just done.

"It's not for me. I was trying to tell you that I brought..."

Nick is saying something, but I can't focus on him. I just took a pill. A drug. An illegal drug. I'm freaking out.

11
Dani

Nick will be back any second, and I still haven't decided if I want to take ecstasy with him. I have no formal opinion on drug use. It's never been offered to me. I've never been invited into a group passing a joint back and forth. I guess if I did smoke, I'd just jump in line and wait my turn. See, I don't even know the protocol. Heather was right, this is not my scene. I was joking when I told her I went to book clubs, but I really wish there was a room full of book nerds out there discussing plot twists. Not a house full of teenagers indulging in drugs and dancing to rap music.

The door opens and Nick walks in the room. He closes the door behind him. Being alone with Nick is the least of my worries. He hands me a fresh drink and a little blue pill. "It's my first time too," he tells me. "It'll be like a milestone for both of us. Something we'll always remember."

I like the idea of sharing a milestone with Nick, but I was thinking more along the lines of first love. "I don't know." I look at the clock. "It's getting late." It's half past eleven. Lucy will be home soon. I'm not feeling as confident about the note I left her and the way she'll react when she gets home and finds me gone.

"Look, I'm not trying to force you into something you don't want to do." Nick places his hand on my knee and warms my entire body. "We can leave. I'll take you home before shit gets too out of hand. I don't know how hard it's going to hit me." It sounds like Nick is going to take a pill whether I do it or not. Which means someone else will replace me in this milestone.

I look at the pill and wonder what back-alley lab it was made in. Who knows what has been packed into this thing. "What is it exactly?"

"It's ecstasy. And I'm told it's pure. Real good shit." Nick looks at the pill in his hand. "Honestly, I have no idea what to expect, but everyone out there seems to be having fun, so I think it's safe, and I trust the guy I got it from." Nick seems confident about that. But whoever sold him the pill was just trying to push their product. I wonder if he's in the living room. Seeing who is selling these things might make me feel a little better about taking it.

"So, you're telling me you bought drugs from the world's only honest drug dealer?" Nick sucks in a breath, like I just punched him in the stomach. He sort of smirks and shakes his head. I think he's insulted, like I'm implying he's been duped. If a portal to an unknown land opened up in this room right now, I would jump through it and never look back.

"It's alright." Nick holds out his hand, he wants the pill back.

I close my fingers around the tablet. "I just meant...you can't trust a drug dealer."

Nick scoffs. "I wouldn't trust me if I were you either."

"Well, you're not a drug dealer, so I have nothing to worry about." I try to lighten the mood, but he seems even more distraught. Like every word out of my mouth is hurting him. I sound like the pretentious bitch Heather King labeled me as during my first week of school.

Nick runs his hand through his hair. He opens his mouth to say something, then stops when someone cranks up the volume on the music. He pushes his open palm towards me, waiting for me to give back the pill so he can offer it to someone else. Some slut that will consider taking a pill with Nick as some sort of honor. Nick looks at the door, then back to me. He's waiting for me to decide. It's my choice.

Do I go home and never see Nick again? Never feel his hand in mine or his eyes in my direction? If I leave I give up his touch, his smell, the way he smiles at me. Or do I stay, take this pill, and be linked in this milestone with him for all eternity? There should be another choice in there somewhere, but I can't find it. I don't want to take this pill any more than I wanted this drink or to be at this party.

But here I am.

Sitting on a bed with the most charming, totally terrifying boy I've ever met.

And I'm putting the pill in my mouth.

And I'm swallowing it with a vodka and orange juice I didn't want.

And he is smiling at me.

"You didn't have to do that."

"I wanted to," I lie. I think it's a lie. It's not a lie. I did it for him. I did it for me. I did it because I couldn't think of a reason not to.

I watch Nick pop the pill in his mouth and swallow it with my drink. He places the cup on the nightstand and turns around with a huge smile. "You're awesome." The look of admiration on his face is worth taking a thousand pills.

Nick and I sit side by side on the bed like a couple of old people watching the evening news. We talk about my job at the café and what plans we have for spring break while we wait to be overtaken by thizz. I have to admit, I'm not really scared. The pill was so small and insignificant, how much effect can it actually have on me?

"It kind of sucks that you have to work during spring break." Nick takes my hand, reinforcing my decision to take the pill. I can't give this up. Not yet.

"I don't *have* to work. I want to. It keeps me busy." I like the way my hand looks inside his. I just wish my nails were painted, or at least clean. I see little bits of coffee under my thumbnail. I hope he doesn't notice. Boys like Nick hold manicured hands, not stubby, dry hands like mine. I pull my unworthy hand from his and pretend to fix my hair. "What are your plans?"

Nick waits for me to finish fiddling with my ponytail, then takes my hand again. "You," he says confidently. "I plan on making you fall in love with me."

I think my heart just stopped. I seriously have no pulse. My heart has been ripped from my chest by those words. Nick's words. I look from my lap to Nick's awaiting smile. There isn't a hint of mockery on his face. He smiles with his whole face. His mouth, his eyes, he has the eyes of someone I want to love. Someone I will love. I should say something, but I can't. I can't speak or move. It's a miracle I'm even breathing.

The music in the other room is vibrating the whole house. It makes me lightheaded. I know I'm sitting on a bed, but I feel like I'm in an elevator shooting to the top of a sky scraper. My stomach is in my throat. My heart is floating somewhere above my head.

Nick is watching me.

Smiling.

A big, happy smile.

I'm smiling now.

A big goofy smile.

My heart beats rapidly. A beat I've never felt before.

I take a deep breath and exhale slowly.

This is it.

This is me falling in love with Nick Marino.

No. This is thizz.

12
Dani

Ho-ly shit.

This is amazing. Thizz is amazing.

Nick stands, and I stand too.

He takes my hand and kisses it, then pulls me into his arms.

We laugh. At nothing. At everything.

He asks me if I'm ready.

I nod, but I don't know what I'm agreeing to.

I stop caring. I just go.

He leads me into the party.

There's a party going on!

The living room is vibrating.

The bass from the stereo pumps through my chest in place of my missing heart.

It feels good.

My head bobs to the beat of a song I don't know. *But I love it!*

Nick looks back at me and smiles.

Those eyes. That mouth. I lean towards him and push my mouth onto his.

I'm kissing him.

I feel him smiling as he kisses me back.

Cheering. People are cheering.

Nick breaks away and high fives K.

They hug, then he hugs another guy, and another guy.

I stumble into the kitchen and see fresh red cups.

A dark-haired girl with a red tank top and white jeans offers me a drink.

I thank her. Her name is Alisa. She's nice. She has a cousin named Amy. She smiles at me with a big, goofy grin.

We sip from our cups and smile at each other, at the room, at life.

I feel amazing.

13
Matt

I'm still trying to convince myself I'm not going to die as I fall out the front door. I lean on the porch railing and look into the empty street.

How are you going to sell this shit, if you're too scared to take it?

"You ok?" I hear a female voice coming from the shadows.

Haley is sitting on the porch swing.

"I'm good." I try to regain my composure.

"Come and sit."

I don't want her company, but I do as she says. I don't want to be alone in case I start to die or something. "You gotta joint?"

"No, sorry," she says and offers a bottle of water. "Did you take a pill?"

I wave the bottle away. "No, yeah. I mean, I just took it."

"I took mine like two hours ago. I'm so fucked-up right now." Haley tosses her head back and closes her eyes.

"You look totally sober to me." As soon as I say that, I see her jaw tighten and release like she's chewing on something.

"Believe me, I don't feel sober. I feel fuck-ing amazing!" She grinds her teeth and kicks off the porch, forcing the swing into motion.

I laugh at the enthusiasm in her voice, but the swinging makes me nauseous. I drag my foot to slow it and then stand up. I lean on the porch railing and watch her chew on imaginary gum. I feel something different in her demeanor. She isn't herself. She's softer, happier than she was at the bonfire.

She stops the swing and says, "You know I used to totally crush on you in the seventh grade."

I knew she liked me back then, but she was still in her awkward phase. When I was twelve I was in love with Jessica Alba and Angelina Jolie, and girls from school couldn't compete with that. I shrug and kick her foot out from under her. The swing moves again.

"You're the nice one. That's what all the girls say. Matt's the nice one and Nick's the hot one." She wets her lips with water and smiles.

"Whatever." I snatch the water from her and take a drink. My mouth suddenly feels dry. Haley is watching me. It sort of makes me uncomfortable. "Thanks for the swing," I say and hand her the water bottle.

She grins and runs her hand along mine before taking the bottle. "For what it's worth, I think you're hot." She grabs the front of my hoodie and kisses me. Against my better judgement—I let her.

The tingling sensation starts in my feet and works its way up my legs until every nerve in my body is vibrating. I fall onto the swing with a thump. The kiss ends as abruptly as it began, and Haley goes back to swinging as if nothing happened. The swing is moving back and forth, back and forth. Haley sits quietly beside me. I close my eyes and literally feel my entire body go numb.

"DUDE!" Nick yells from the doorway. "This is fucking awesome!" I spring to my feet, and it feels like the first time I hit a home run in little league, pure exhilaration. "Thizz is going to change everything!" Nick screams into the empty air.

I'm bouncing on the balls of my feet in front of Nick. He mimics my movements and we mock fight on the porch. Haley squeals with delight on the swing. I leave Nick and scoop her into my arms. I squeeze her like I did Dani earlier, but Haley squeezes back. She even kisses my neck before I set her down.

"Dude, we are going to make so much fucking money!" Nick grabs my hand and pulls me in for a bro hug. "Fucking Stanford, dude!" Nick knows how badly I want to go. The fact that he brought me in on this shows what a good friend he is.

"Thank you, man," I say with more sincerity than I've ever felt in my life. I hug Nick and pound his back.

"You're my boy, Matty. Always have been, always will be. Nothing comes between this." Nick points to the space between us.

"Nothing." I look him square in eye and think of Dani. I have to ask. I have to know if his feelings are real. I need to know he cares about her. If he does, I'll let her go, I think. "What's up with you and Dani?"

"Ah, man. She's the shit." He gives me his stock answer, then he pauses. He really seems to think about his feelings for her. "I've never met anyone that didn't judge me because of my family. She doesn't grill me about being a Marino, she doesn't even give a shit. Dani likes me, for me. I think. Fuck, I don't know. I hope she does." Nick runs his hand through his hair, his nervous tick.

I can't stand to see my best friend fret over a girl. Even if it's a girl I sort of believe is amazing too. But she obviously doesn't want me, and I'm not a cock-blocker. I won't stand in Nick's way if he really does care about her. He deserves someone like Dani. We all do. I don't know why, but I suddenly want them to be together. "You're Nick fucking Marino, of course she loves you!" I punch Nick in the arm and he pretends to be hurt. The moment lightens and we start play-boxing again. Boxing turns into wrestling. We fall onto the lawn and Nick concedes. He must be high if he let me win. The grass is damp from the ocean air. I feel moisture seeping into my jeans as I stare at the stars.

"I like her," Nick says quietly.

I think about the way she smiled at me when I walked into our computer class. My heart feels like a rock skimming across the top of a still lake. I have to let it go, let her go. I can't have her, not that I ever could have.

"She's here." Nick stands up and cleans off his pants. "I tried to tell you earlier, but you were pretty fucked up."

Wait, what? Dani is here. With Nick.

Nick looks into the house. I stand up and follow his line of sight.

I want to see her. I don't want to see her.

"What's up, dude!" Nick yells to Arnie, who is racing down the steps toward us. Nick says dude this is awesome. Arnie tells him he's in love with thizz. Nick says dude I love you. Arnie pulls him in for a hug and says dude I love you too.

I walk away. I'm looking for her. I'm not looking for her.

I see her in the kitchen. She's sipping a drink. Haley's a liar. Why are girls liars? I hate girls.

"What's up, Matty boy." K pushes me into the kitchen and drags me towards the keg.

Towards Dani.

14
Dani

I see him, and I don't know why I'm smiling, because he isn't.

He looks at me like I just ran over his puppy.

He looks at me like I just stole his best friend.

I continue to smile at Matt. He doesn't smile back, and it breaks my heart.

I watch him get a beer, he watches Nick kiss my cheek.

I watch him stumble out of the kitchen when Nick takes me in his arms.

I'm confused. Matt confuses me.

He looks hurt. Jealous. Mad.

Why? He didn't want me.

Nick wants me.

I want Nick.

I'm sorry, Matt.

15
Matt

She looks at me and smiles. A big, unnatural smile. It's not her smile. It's not the small, shy smile that I've seen in my dreams. This smile isn't for me.

Nick pushes past me, straight to Dani, like he's a bungee cord retracting into place.

That smile is for Nick. That is Nick's smile.

I need to get away, far away. Before I do or say something I'll regret.

"Dude, you're fucked up!" K shoves a beer in my hand and drags me back into the living room.

I feel like I'm floating above the ground. Not so high that everyone can tell, just enough to where I don't have to use my legs to move. I glide towards the front door and hit a wall of flesh. Troy's brother, Paul, appears in front of me and says, "Get hyphy!" He shakes his long frizzy hair in a circular motion.

"What's hyphy?"

Paul falls onto the couch in hysterical fits of laughter. "Ah boy, you know, getting hyphy or goin' dumb." He starts laughing again when I shake my head. "Troy boy, go dumb," Paul yells to his brother.

Troy holds his arms out as if he is trying to balance his weight as he bounces his body up and down, or is it more of a circular motion? I can't tell by just standing here watching. I have to try it myself. I don't have the long hair or dreads that Troy wears, but I shake my head like I do. Troy and his brothers dance around me, laughing and clapping as I get hyphy with them.

The song ends and I come up for air. I turn towards the door and find Dani watching me. *She's so fucking beautiful.* If Nick wasn't guarding her like a god damn German Shepard, I'd be next to her. I'd be the reason for her smile. I'd be the one kissing her cheek, whispering in her ear, making her laugh. Nick pulls Dani's hand towards the door. She starts to leave then turns around. She walks to the center of the room and stops in front of me. I reach for her, then force myself to hold back. I can't touch her. If I touch her I'll never let her go. If I touch her, I will fall in love with her.

"That was amazing!" She lifts her arms and wraps them around my neck.

Too late. I put my arms around her waist and bury my face in her hair. Touching her gives me goose bumps. I want to pull her closer, I want to feel her against me. I look up and see Nick. I don't want him to think I'm enjoying this in any other way than pure friendship. My jeans would beg to differ. I back away so she doesn't feel anything she shouldn't. She lets me go, but not before she kisses my cheek. My entire body breaks into a sweat. I look over her head at Nick, and he nods to me like I should let go of his girl. I nod back and shrug. I'm not doing anything—but I'm thinking it.

"Where did you learn to dance like that?" Dani fidgets with the cup in her hand and vigorously chews on a piece of gum.

"From these guys." I point to Paul and Troy, who are dancing with a couple of girls behind me. "Do you want me to teach you?" I take a step back and hold out my arms. K sees me about to get down and yells, "Go Matt." Before I know what's going on, the entire house is chanting my name. Dani takes a step back with a huge grin on her face. *I can't fuck this up.*

I start to bounce up and down. I pinch the collar of my shirt and then flick it away to the beat. I repeat this to the other side. Troy and Paul join me, and we perform a little trio, taking turns in the spotlight. The house explodes when K jumps in and starts to pop. It's fucking awesome. I look through the crowd and find Dani. She gives me a double thumbs-up. I dance my way over to her. She does that girl thing where she looks like she's dancing, but really she's just swaying in place. It still looks incredibly hot. Yeah, she does that and I dance in front of her, like we're dancing together, but not really. Everything is all good until she throws her arms around me. I feel my heart swell with more force than my jeans.

"You have some skills," she yells in my ear. She doesn't really need to yell. I can hear her just fine, but having her close feels too good to care about my damaged eardrum.

"Thank you," I say softly in her ear. It would be so easy to just kiss her, kiss her ear, her neck. My lips are so close. One millimeter closer and they'd be touching her skin. Then suddenly, she's gone.

I look up and see Nick pulling her from my arms. He's taking her outside. He's taking her from me.

16
Dani

"Let's get some air, it's hot in here," Nick says.

I don't want to go. I want to stay inside *with Matt*. But I go anyway.

I step onto the porch—the cool air feels so good. *I'm never going back inside that house again!*

I follow Nick off the porch. He kisses my cheek and a chill ripples through my body.

"Come here." Nick sinks to the ground and I follow him. We lie on our backs in the grass and stare at the stars. I feel his hand search for mine, and I move it towards him so it's easy to find. He grips my fingers and traces his thumb over the back of my hand, and I can't stop wishing he was tracing other areas of my body. I don't consider myself a very sexual person, but Nick has turned me into a raging slut. In my mind anyway.

"What's your favorite movie?"

I look at Nick through the darkness and laugh. If he only knew what I was thinking right now, he wouldn't be making small talk. I'll play along. Anything to clean up the smut. "Um, I have a few."

"Ok, your favorite drama." He squeezes my fingers and sort of laughs.

"That's easy, *Butterfly Effect*." I was so addicted to that movie last year. I loved the idea of jumping to different times in your life and changing them. I think about what would happen if I could go back, change something from that night. Had we made the light at Brannan Street or sat in thirty seconds of traffic on the bridge. If any one of those things happened, I wouldn't have had to leave my home and move in with Lucy. I wouldn't have met Matt, and I wouldn't be here right now with Nick. My stomach twists at the thoughts in my mind. I'm happy here; does that mean I'm glad I'm not back home with my parents? As if that were an option.

"My favorite drama hands down is *Scarface*," Nick volunteers. I forgot he was even lying beside me. I focus on him, his words, his smell, the warmth emanating from his body. "*Goodfellas* is a really close second." I can't help but smile as Nick rattles off a bunch of gangster movies. I'm starting to see a theme here. *I wonder what Matt's favorite movie is?* Thinking of Matt causes another feeling altogether. Something I shouldn't feel at all. "I also like *Forrest Gump*." Nick rolls onto his side to face me and rests his head in his hand. "Don't tell anyone."

"About *Forest Gump*? Why?"

"Cause the guys will fuck with me." He sounds a little vulnerable, like he just confessed a secret. Is his image so important he can't admit he likes a movie that doesn't involve drug dealing and mass murders?

"I like *Forest Gump*. Stupid is as stupid does," I say in my best Gump voice.

"Life is like a box of chocolates…" Nick chimes in with a laugh and makes a face that reminds me of Matt. They have the same mannerisms. The way they nod their head when something is funny, like they're agreeing with the universe. Matt even held me the same way as Nick when he hugged me at the bonfire. Being in his arms felt good. Just as good as Nick's.

"Does Matt like *Forest Gump*?" I don't know why I asked him that. I can't help it. He's on my mind. Part of me wishes he was lying on the other side of me right now. *Oh God, I've reached official slut status.*

"Yeah. We watched it like fifty times." He falls onto his back.

Oh no. Why did I have to ask that stupid question about Matt? Matt doesn't want me. He set me up with Nick. He wants me to be with Nick.

I need to do something, say something to let Nick know that I want to be here with him and nobody else. I move closer to him, and he wraps his arm around me so my head is resting in the crook of his arm. "What's your favorite ice cream flavor?" I ask.

"Butter pecan." Nick moans softly as I drag my hand across his chest. I'm so focused on the movement of my hand and the way Nick is reacting to it that it takes me a minute to realize what he just said.

"Did you say butter pecan?" I sit up to look at him in amazement.

"I know it's like an old-lady flavor, but I like it." Nick places his left arm under his head. The muscles in his arm bulge like he's flexing. My hormones rage, or maybe it's thizz. Something is making me want to do unspeakable things to this beautiful butter-pecan-eating creature.

I lean in close to his face until our lips are almost touching. "I. Love. Butter. Pecan." I drag out each word.

"You know what that means?" He places his hand on the back of my head. "We were meant to be." He pushes me slowly towards him until my mouth is on his. Nick rolls me onto my back and drives his mouth, his entire body into me. Every breath becomes a movement, every movement a new desire. I pull at his hair, squeeze the muscles in his arms, and pull him to me all at once. We are like this for an infinite amount of time. It could have been seconds that felt like minutes or minutes that seemed like hours. I don't know how we started or why he stops. Nothing makes sense and it's fucking awesome.

Nick lies next to me and entwines his fingers with mine. "Do you like pizza?"

It's the most random question anyone has ever asked me. "Of course. Who doesn't like pizza?"

"Matt," Nick says flatly.

My heart skips a beat when he says his name. *Who cares about Matt? Certainly not me.* "What a freak." I sit up and kiss Nick. He smiles against my lips then pulls me on top of him.

"I really like you, Dani," he says softly. "I just thought you should know."

I don't know why Nick's confession feels like bad news. Isn't this what I wanted? Why I accepted the ride home, why I came to this party—because of Nick, not Matt. I have three months left of high school, so I might as well make the most of it. Nick kisses me softly. His lips move tenderly over mine and a new sensation floods my body. Dread, excitement, love. I don't know what I'm feeling, but I like it. I like Nick.

17
Dani

I take a small bite of scrambled eggs, washing it down with a gulp of water. *Who knew teeth could get this sore?* I try to hide the pain as I force myself to chew a piece of toast. I don't know if it was the gum chewing or the teeth grinding. Maybe both. I can barely open my mouth, let alone chew.

Lucy hasn't said a word since I sat down. I know she's dying to ask me about the party. I don't even think it's a matter of her scolding me for coming home late. She probably just wants to know if I had fun. Lucy is only eleven years older than me. She used to call herself the cool aunt. I'm not sure that title applies now that she's my legal guardian. Was my legal guardian. Now that I'm eighteen, I'm the boss of me. I don't need her permission to go out or date Nick, but knowing she cares keeps me from feeling utterly alone in the world.

I take another bite of the cold eggs and accidently bite my cheek. I make a small noise, which draws another look from Lucy. She drops her fork onto her plate and glares at me from the other end of the table. It catches my attention. I'm wrong. She's not curious, she's pissed. Her face is a mash of disappointment and anger. It's so not her. She's always smiling and putting a positive spin on everything. My father used to call her disgustingly optimistic.

"Look, I don't want to pry. But you sort of suck." I inadvertently smile at her lack of parental vocabulary. "I'm serious." Her back straightens like she's role playing the angry parent. "You can't just stay out all night and not tell me anything."

"I didn't plan on staying out that late, but my friend was drinking and didn't want to drive." That's the best I could come up with at three in the morning. "I'll call Patty and tell her I'm sorry for missing work." I was supposed to open the café this morning. When I didn't show up, Patty had to rush over and open two hours late.

"Don't bother, I told her you'd be there in an hour." Lucy lifts her coffee mug to her mouth, tapping the side with her fingernail.

I let out a long sigh. I guess going to work at nine is better than six a.m. I was in no condition to get up when my alarm went off at five-thirty this morning.

"So, the boy that dropped you off." Lucy smiles from behind her mug.

Here we go.

I put on a little show, like I'm embarrassed. I'm not, but I think it will make Lucy feel more parental. "That was Nick Marino, but I'm sure Patty already told you that." I sip my water and add an eye roll for dramatic effect. The old Lucy would ask me if Nick was a good kisser or something just as embarrassing. That is something a cool aunt would do, not my guardian. I don't want her to think Nick is irresponsible, so I tell her he had a beer at the party and didn't feel comfortable driving me home. "He felt really bad and thought I should call you to pick me up." It's sort of true. Nick waited until he felt the effects of the thizz starting to wear off before he got behind the wheel. Even I had started to come down. As soon as the euphoria subsided, I kind of freaked out about the time and what Lucy was thinking, so Nick drove me home.

Lucy's brow furrows. "Why didn't you call me?"

"Well, I don't have a cell phone." I state the obvious. "And, I didn't want to leave. I was having fun." Lucy's face brightens. I'll let her think her pep talk about socializing worked. "Am I in trouble?"

Lucy glowers at me for a second and sets her mug down. "I guess not. Please call me next time and let me know you're ok." She takes a bite of her eggs and smiles. She looks happy now. She looks like my mom. They're only half-sisters, but they share the same dark hair and light blue eyes. That's all they share. Lucy is the polar opposite of my mom. Lucy is the kind of person that dances at street fairs and wears elf ears on Christmas. My mother was refined, and took herself way too serious. Sometimes I hated that about her. When I was little, I used to wish Lucy was my mom. I hate that about myself.

The walk to work feels quicker, the customers seem friendlier, and even Mary is less annoying. She flips her hair in my face as she places three empty mugs on the counter. Ok, maybe I'm wrong about Mary. She isn't working, she's just here to torture me after spending the morning at her mother's salon. Mary is in full-blown makeup, fake eyelashes and all. Her dark brown hair cascades down the back of her pink sweater in perfect chocolate waves.

"Dani, sweetie, can you make Mrs. Montgomery one of your hazelnut lattes?" Patty is sitting at the gossip table in the corner. Every now and then I hear the name Marino. I don't know if they're talking about Nick's grandmother, Mariann, or their business in general. Just hearing his name, in any context, sends my heart into overdrive. I want to jump on the counter and yell: *I kissed Nick Marino!*

"Sure." I pull a large glass mug from a hook under the counter. I pump two squirts of hazelnut syrup into the glass and place it on the espresso machine. I'm preparing the milk when the bells above the door jingle. I pull the milk from the steamer, pour it into the glass, and realize the room has gone silent. I look around the espresso machine and find Nick standing at the counter.

He smiles so big his eyes turn into tiny slits. "Hi." His voice is hoarse, like mine, from talking all night.

I jump back and freak out at the status of my hair. I showered this morning, but I'm a sweaty mess now. I wipe my face with a semi-clean towel and sprinkle a little cinnamon on top of Mrs. Montgomery's drink. I place the glass mug on the counter. "Hazelnut latte."

Nick smirks at my lack of enthusiasm. It has nothing to do with my feelings for him. I have to suppress the urge to jump over the counter and into his arms. I don't want Patty to have a heart attack. I peek back around the espresso machine and offer a smile. "Small latte?"

"Extra foam," he adds and places four dollars on the counter. Two more dollars than the price of the coffee. *Is he actually tipping me?*

I make Nick's latte in a ceramic mug, and I make the milk extra hot so he will have to wait for it to cool down to drink. Sneaky barista trick. "What are you doing here?" I ask as I slide his drink across the bar with two packets of sugar.

Nick rips open the sugar and pours it into his mug. "I'm starting my plan." *His plan?* I look at him, confused, and he arches his eyebrow at me. Holy hell, he was serious about making me fall in love with him. He is crazy and unbelievably adorable. Nick leans against the counter with his mug in his hand and looks around. Mary practically chokes on her bran muffin when he smiles at her. "Morning ladies."

"Good morning, Nick. You're out and about early," Patty says in a disapproving tone.

I look at the clock; it's ten thirty, not that early. Lucy must have called Patty and told her I didn't get home until three in the morning because Nick was boozing it up at a party.

"I was just craving some coffee." He winks at me. His comment causes a buzz at Patty's table.

"How is your grandmother? I haven't seen her in a while. Tell her to stop by and say hi."

Nick's face tightens at the mention of his grandmother. "I will, Mrs. Murphy."

I've never heard anyone call Patty by her formal name. Even Patty is taken aback. She glares at him over the top of her glasses like he just made a smart remark.

"Patty, I'm going to take a fifteen-minute break." I untie my apron and toss it on the counter. Patty checks the clock as if she's actually going to time me.

Nick walks to the door and holds it open for me. He's so sweet. Can't Patty see that?

I choose a table farthest away from the main window and all of the curious eyes. Nick doesn't seem to mind or even notice that we are the object of everyone's attention. You can't look like he does and expect people not to stare. If I'm going to be with him, it's something I'll have to accept. I just wish I had on some lip gloss or something, and it would be nice if I didn't smell like bleach and coffee. I'm going to have to make an effort to look better.

"You look beautiful," Nick says, as if he's reading my mind. I roll my eyes. It's a knee-jerk reaction. "I'm serious." He runs the back of his hand down my sweaty cheek. "How do you feel?"

I felt better after I ate breakfast, but I've had two cups of coffee since I started my shift and I think the caffeine reignited my buzz. I'm definitely not normal. I tell Nick I feel fine.

"That was some good shit, right?" Nick takes a sip of his coffee and leans back in his chair. He looks proud, like he made the pills himself.

"It was my first time, so I don't really have a frame of reference." I tilt my head towards Nick and smile. See, this is not normal Dani. I'm not flirty, and this is definitely flirty.

"You're right. We should try it again just to make sure it wasn't a fluke. How about tonight?"

I can't tell if he's joking, but the thought of taking it again excites me. Lucy is working a double, she'll be gone all night. As far she knows, I'll be home, sleeping. Because that's what good Dani does. She stays home, alone, and sleeps. "We could do it again, but the results won't be accurate. We need another source. Do you know any other honest drug dealers?" I'm totally joking, but Nick looks flustered. I don't know why I even speak. Nothing I say comes out right.

Nick clears his throat and takes another drink. His cheeks look flushed. I can't tell if he's blushing or if it's just from the steam rising out of his mug. "What do you have against drug dealers?"

I hate that he isn't getting my sarcasm. My father dedicated most of his career to helping drug dealers get a fair trial. He was always quick to defend his clients to anyone who challenged him. He said it wasn't always about flashy cars and power. Most of them were just trying to feed their families. He also said it was a business built on desperation, fear, and violence. Drug dealers are one-dimensional, it's all about the money. It has to be. It's the only way they can live with the consequences of their product. Turning their neighbors and family members into addicts was a necessary evil. My father never claimed his clients were innocent. His job was to make sure they were treated fairly. That was their right, regardless of the crime. That's the only way he could live with himself. My mother hated it. Not just because he worked the cases from a home office and had some pretty shady clients visit every now and then. She hated that he offered his services for free. My father said it offset all the shitty things he had to do for his day job. He worked as in-house counsel for a consulting firm. He hated the corporate culture, the elitist attitudes. His pro-bono work was always straight forward. No bullshit. They knew what they were getting with him. He didn't have to play any games. He said most of his pro-bono clients were good people in bad situations. I loved that about my father. He always saw the good in people. No matter how horrible their crimes were.

"Maybe they aren't all that bad." Nick smiles a crooked smile. "You never know, you might even fall in love with one."

I make a noise that's a cross between a laugh and a snort. "You know a drug dealer that's looking for a girlfriend?" I laugh at my ridiculous question, but Nick doesn't join me. He looks at me like I'm the pretentious bitch Heather King said I was. "I'm joking, Nick. I get it. Drug dealers need love too." I break into a grin. "I'm sure the guy you bought the pills from is really nice, but I'm not interested in dating him."

"Who are you interested in dating?" A playful grin spreads across Nick's face, causing my heart to beat like I just took a pill. I'm hoping it's some kind of Morse code cluing me in on who it is I actually want. What I feel for Matt is nothing compared to what Nick is doing to me right now. Feeling his eyes on me is almost as good as his hands. They move over my face like the soft trace of a finger. They scan my body like he's memorizing every curve. Nick's eyes are like a laser, piercing through me and engraving his initials on my heart. Branding me as his.

Nick takes my hand and something amazing happens to my body. It's like a chemical reaction, like pouring peroxide on an open wound. He feels so good it hurts.

Fear, embarrassment, self-doubt—it all diminishes when we touch. I know exactly what I want, who I want. "You," I say. "You are the only person I want holding my hand." Nick squeezes my fingers. "You are the only person I want to kiss." He smiles his sexy smile and reaches for me with his perfect lips and presses them to mine.

I want to fall in love with Nick Marino and I want it to happen right now. I just need that little blue pill to help guide me in the right direction.

We break away and Nick straightens up in his seat. He takes a drink from his now lukewarm latte and says, "Tell me something about yourself, something nobody knows."

My heart stops then starts to beat rapidly. "What do you mean?"

"Don't you have one thing you've never told anyone, but you want to?" Nick leans his face close to mine, like I'm going to divulge my darkest secrets to him.

"I don't have any secrets," I lie. I know I will have to tell Nick about my parents eventually. This isn't the time or the place. I haven't told anyone. He will be my first. Just not now.

"Come on, don't be shy." He rubs his hand on my thigh. I don't care how charming he is, there is no way he's getting a single word out of me. I check my watch. Nick places his hand over the face to prevent me from seeing the time. "I'll go first." He smiles like I've agreed to something. I don't want to divulge my secret, but I'm not going to stop him from telling me his. He lifts my hand to his lips and kisses my knuckles. He runs his hand through his hair then launches into a story about a basketball game in Arcata.

"So, we win the game and Coach takes us out for dinner at this fancy restaurant. The bartender ended up being an old family friend. He spiked our Cokes with rum all night. Coach had no idea we were all wasted. The last thing I remember was getting on the team bus to head home." He pauses and sips his latte. I can tell by the smirk on his face, he's getting to the good part. "Keep in mind, I drank a lot." He looks so damn cute it's hard to focus on his story. "I woke up the next day and my bed was soaking wet." He begins to laugh so hard he can't finish his story.

"Why was your bed wet?" I ask, then I see the red in his cheeks. "You peed the bed?"

He nods and pretends to be humiliated, but I can tell by the coy look in his eye that he is impervious to humiliation. Nick Marino is too confident to be embarrassed. Hell, I don't even care that he wet his bed. I think it's cute.

"Your turn." He reaches for my hand and leans his head towards me. His fingers are unnaturally warm from the hot coffee.

The bells above the café door jingle and Mary pokes her head out. "Your break is over," she says in her toddler voice, then closes the door. I've never been so happy to see Mary.

"Ok," I tell her and turn back to Nick. "I have to go." I look down at his hand wrapped around mine. We fit so perfectly together.

He kisses my hand, then leans his head towards mine so our foreheads are touching. I know my parents loved me and I know Lucy loves me, but I've never felt this kind of affection before. The way Nick smiles when I smile, the way he holds my hand and kisses my cheek, is something new and amazing. It's something I never knew existed and will never be able to live without.

"I better go." I try to scoot my chair out, but Nick grabs the seat and pulls me to him instead. The metal legs screech against the cement until our knees are touching, then Nick spreads his legs and pulls me even closer. The faint smell of jasmine and exhaust mixed with the coffee on his breathe makes my heart flutter. I inhale him and close my eyes. The next thing I know, Nick's lips are on mine. He kisses me softly as his hand caresses the side of my face. My lips part and we kiss deeper. His tongue gently invades my mouth, and I let out a slight moan. I'm holding my breath, afraid to come up for air. I don't want to pull away, but I'll pass out if I don't. I end our kiss, and Nick seems to snap out of a daze. His breathing is rapid, like he just resurfaced from under water.

"I have to go," I whisper into the space between us.

He kisses me one more time and releases my chair. "I'll wait here until you get off."

I look into the café and see Patty standing behind the counter with her arms crossed over her chest. I don't know if I can take two hours of her scowling at me. "I don't get off until one. You don't have to wait. I can walk home," I tell him, but I don't mean it. I want a ride home. I want to spend every waking minute with him.

Nick stands and walks me to the door. He moves a loose strand of hair behind my ear and kisses my cheek. "I'll be back at one. My girl doesn't walk anywhere."

I open the door to walk inside and he calls my name. "Dani, wait." He smiles. His Nick smile. "Is my plan working?"

"Yes." I blush. *Your plan is working and mine is out the freaking window.*

18

Matt

Ice Cube's "Today is a Good Day" pulls me from sleep. I peek from under my pillow and see Nick dancing in front of my desk. "Who the fuck let you in?" I pull the pillow over my pounding head and moan.

After Nick took Dani home, he came back to the party and picked up me and Arnie. We drove to a frat party in Arcata and sold half of the pills Will gave us. One hundred pills in one day. I even sold a couple of my bootleg CDs. We popped a pill when we got to the frat house, then popped another one a few hours later. It was off the hook. I think my favorite thing about thizz is how friendly everyone is. Most parties end in fights because some drunk asshole can't handle his liquor. That doesn't happen when people are thizzin. It's all sunshine and fucking rainbows.

"Come on, Matty!" Nick yanks the comforter off my bed. "Ash let me in before she left with your parents. She said they were headed out for your mom's birthday. Shouldn't you be going with them? What kind of son are you?"

I know Nick is fucking with me, but it hits a nerve. It isn't like I would've gone, but damn, they could at least ask me. Things have been screwed up between me and my parents for a long time. I don't know if we can ever make it right. I was just a kid when Ashley was diagnosed. I didn't know how to handle it. I started acting out, breaking shit, and fighting. I refused to visit her in the hospital. Death was foreign to me. I was only eleven. Ashely's forgiven me, but I don't think they ever will.

Nick turns the music off to answer his phone. I hear the one-sided conversation and I can tell he's talking to Will. Nick hangs up and sits at my desk. "Arnie's coming over; we have some details to discuss about business. Get the fuck up!"

Arnie and Nick are playing Xbox in my living room when I get out of the shower. Nick turns off the game and fills us in on what's next. "Will is coming up sometime this week to drop off a boat. That's a thousand pills. We should be able to unload it in a month."

"A month, more like two weeks." Arnie reaches over and high fives me. "I'm ready to pop another one right now." Arnie's right, there is nothing like that rush. I wouldn't mind popping another pill if it will cure this headache.

Nick sits on the edge of the sofa across from me and Arnie. He runs his hand through his hair. "Look, Will's fronting us on this, so we're only getting eight bucks a pill. We gotta be smart."

Arnie makes a disapproving snort. "That ain't shit, bro. We're putting in all the work."

"Yeah, well, once we have enough capital to buy the pills, we'll get a better cut." Nick sips a bottle of Gatorade and paces the room.

My mind is processing numbers like an adding machine. We stand to make eight grand off the boat, while Will makes twelve. "When we get the money to buy the pills upfront, what's our cut then?" I have to focus on the money; it keeps me from feeling like a criminal.

Nick stops pacing and sits on the end of the sofa. "It depends.

Everything is negotiable, but Will said once we get rolling, we can pick up a boat for three to four grand."

"That's what I'm talking about!" Arnie leans over and high fives Nick. "And how are we cutting our shares?"

Nick looks at us and smirks like he's offended. "What, you think I'd burn my boys?" Arnie sort of shrugs, but I know Nick wouldn't fuck us. "We split this equally, three ways. We're in this shit together." Nick holds out his fist and bumps it with mine, then Arnie's. "We gotta be smart though. You're responsible for your stash. Will warned me about getting high when we should be selling. We aren't a bunch of tweakers. We can party, but when we're working, we gotta be cool. We can't be abusing this shit, you feel me?" Nick takes another swig of his Gatorade, and I wonder if he even slept. He still looks wired.

"Does this mean we can't kick down a few freebies every now and then? I mean shit, you know the chicks are all over this!" Arnie grabs his crotch and pumps the air. "I had my pick of the honeys last night." Arnie reaches up for a high five.

Nick slaps his hand. "Let's play it case by case, alright?"

Arnie nods, but we all know he'll do anything to get laid. The Nick I know would take full advantage of this new power. Well, the old Nick. After the way I saw him looking at Dani, I can tell he cares about her. I can almost guarantee she's in love with him. It doesn't take long for girls to fall for Nick. He's got the whole rebel-without-a-cause thing going on. He's got the car, the name, not to mention money. He plays ball, he has good teeth, and now he has thizz. Hell, if I was a chick I'd love him too.

I tried to keep my distance from Dani at K's party. When she was in my line of sight, I couldn't take my eyes off of her. I had to fight every urge in my body not to go to her, or even to talk to her. I didn't want to risk crossing a line or saying something out of pocket.

Something like, I saw you first. Why couldn't you look at me the way you look at him? Why didn't you choose me?

"What about Dani?" *Where the hell did that come from?* "I mean, does she know you sell thizz?"

"Who's Dani?" Arnie asks.

"You know, the chick from the party. She's Nick's girlfriend." Saying it out loud feels like a knife in my chest.

"Damn, Matty. You dropping the g-word already." Arnie looks at Nick incredulously. "They just hooked up once. You know our boy just one-night's them." Arnie lifts his hand to high five Nick, but Nick leaves him hanging.

It pisses me off that Nick isn't speaking up about her. Last night she was the best thing that ever happened to him, and now he won't even say her name. I pick up a Nerf football and squeeze the shit out of it. "It ain't like that this time. Nick's whooped." I toss the football to Arnie, and we look at Nick to see his reaction. He's too lost in thought to say anything.

"We can't tell her," Nick finally says. "I don't want her to know we sell thizz or weed or fuckin' anything." He looks worried, like her knowing will be an issue.

"Why not?" Arnie tosses the football back to me.

"She said some shit about drug dealers that wasn't cool. I don't want her to think I'm a fucking sleazeball." Nick runs his hand through his hair.

"Fuck her, if she does." Arnie waves his hand in the air, dismissing Nick's self-deprecating comment.

I fire the Nerf ball at Arnie's head.

"What the fuck, Matt!" Arnie rubs his temple and looks around for the ball.

Nick snatches it from the floor before Arnie can grab it then leans over and high fives me. He points the end of the ball at Arnie. "Don't you ever talk about Dani like that." He fires the ball at him. It bounces off the side of his head and back into Nick's hand. I've never seen Nick stand up for a girl. He must really like her. Fuck.

Arnie rubs his head and sits on the couch with his arms over his chest. He's such a cry baby.

Nick starts pacing again. "Matt, you're friends with her, right?"

"I guess." *I don't know what we are.*

"Alright, then you keep her busy. You know, divert her attention when we're out and someone wants to by some shit. Can you do that?" Nick looks desperate.

It seems impossible to hide the fact that we sell thizz from Dani, but if anyone can do it, it's Nick. I'll do everything I can to make sure she doesn't find out about it either. If Nick is worried about what she'll think of him, then I know it will be far worse for me. He's Nick Marino. I'm nobody.

"I can do that." I hold out my hand and he pulls me in for a bro hug.

"You're my boy, Matt."

Nick and I have been best friends since first grade. I don't think we've ever had a single fight. Not over a game, a toy, or a girl. When Ashley was diagnosed, my parents lived at the hospital. They sort of forgot about me. So, Nick invited me to stay with him. His grandmother made up a room for me, but I stayed in Nick's room. He had bunk beds and gave me the top, even though it was his favorite. He didn't make fun of me when I woke up crying for my mom and he never, ever, left my side. He's the kind of guy that will give you the shirt off his back or bring you in on a business that will make you a lot of money. I'd do anything for him. Even give up the girl of my dreams.

19
Dani

My alarm goes off and I slap the top of the clock. It falls on the floor and breaks. Fucking great. I stumble down the stairs to the bathroom and jump in the shower. I perform all my morning rituals on autopilot. I dress in whatever shirt and pants are on top of my laundry basket then I slip on my Vans. Ready for school. The walk is cold because I forgot to wear a jacket. I hate Mondays and Tuesdays, and any day that doesn't include me taking thizz. Being on thizz is the best feeling in the world. Being hungover is not.

I don't know how I make it to lunch, but I do. I've sat in the center of the quad every day for the last two weeks. I need a break from the bullshit and fake smiling. My nose burns from the battle of the body sprays at Nick's lunch table. I miss the oblivion. I don't want everyone to know my name. I don't care about who is dating whom, or where the good parties are going to be. I can't do popular today. I walk to my tree and sit down. I close my eyes and tilt my head to the sun. It feels good on my bare arms.

"What are you doing over here?"

A smile forms on my lips at the sound of his voice. I open my eyes and find Matt's silhouette standing in front of me. "I'm eating." I look down at my lap. I didn't get any food, just a can of diet soda. "I mean, I'm drinking."

Matt sits next to me and leans against the trunk of my tree. "I can't eat either. I'm still fucked up." We got high yesterday after my Sunday morning shift at the café. We started on Friday after school, then stayed in some state of ecstasy the rest of the weekend. Lucy is on doubles at the hospital. There is a stomach flu going around, so they're short staffed, which means no lies, nobody waiting up for me when I crawl into bed at dawn. It's usually just Matt, Nick, and me. Sometimes K tags along, or Arnie if we're going to a bonfire or someplace where there will be lots of people. I hate those nights. I hate being high in a crowd. I feel so exposed, although small talk is a lot easier when I've got tons of serotonin flowing through me. I'm almost fun to be around. Mostly it's just me and Matt no matter where we go. Nick is always off somewhere doing popular-people things. I really don't mind. Matt is fun to be around, high or not.

The yard is filling up. I see all the usuals at Matt's table. Heather, her minions, a few jocks, but no Nick. Matt must see me looking for him and volunteers that he had to meet with his counselor. As much as I adore Nick, sometimes I just need a time-out. Being Nick Marino's girlfriend is equal parts bliss and horror. I'm on the hit list of every girl that ever wanted to hook up with him. It's sort of like being hunted by terrorists. You never know when they will strike or how. The first couple of days were bad. I was pushed down a flight of stairs. Ok, the last two stairs, but still. Someone wrote slut across my locker, which Matt quickly painted over. And to top it off, everyone thinks Nick and I have slept together, because why else would he want someone like me unless I was the world's best fuck? Nick assures me that nobody has the nerve to mess with me now that we are official. Ok, so maybe I'm not going to get jumped on my way to school. But

I still have to deal with how I dress and the state of my hair on a daily basis. I don't know what's worse, having some random girl kick my ass, or having a group of girls laugh at me because I don't know how to apply eye shadow.

"Let's get out of here." I sit up and look at Matt. "I'm about to graduate, and I've never ditched school."

Matt just shrugs. Like finding out I'm a dork that's never ditched school doesn't surprise him. "I don't know. I kind of like your tree. I wish I would've noticed it sitting here a little sooner. This tree and I could have had some good times." He looks angelic and totally at peace as he closes his eyes and lifts his face towards the midday sun. I elbow him in the side and make a little whining sound. He opens one eye and turns his face towards me. "You're really serious?"

My heart does a double back handspring when I see the adorable look on Matt's face. I don't understand why things like this happen when I'm around Matt. I think it's because I've never had a guy friend. I confuse Matt's friendly smile, his innocent touch, with something else. Matt has never given me any reason to think he's interested in anything more than my friendship. The inappropriate thoughts that sometimes cross my mind when I'm high are just moments of weakness on my part. "I'm totally serious. Let's do it. Let's ditch."

"Alright, let me text Nick." He pulls out his phone and starts to type.

Oh yeah, Nick. Matt and I spend a lot of time together. Nick is always going off to run an errand for his grandmother or to say hi to a family friend. When we're high, Matt is my partner in crime. We go on adventures at the beach, searching for starfish or talking dolphins. We have philosophical discussions about the amount of water left on the earth, the utter failure of our judicial system when it comes to white-collar crime, and the best way to eat ice cream. I say cup, he says cone. Not even a sugar cone; he likes the old-school flat bottom kind that are a cross between cardboard and Styrofoam. I always have fun with Matt. I feel like I can let loose and be myself with him. My real self. When Nick is around, everyone is always so serious. Nick brings out the grown-up in all of us. Don't get me wrong, I love being around Nick, especially when we're alone. When Nick and I carve out some time on your own in the dark, talking and goofing around is the last thing we do. Soon the rumors about me sleeping with Nick will become justified. I just hate that my sex life is something people are placing bets on. If this is what it's like to be popular, then I consider myself lucky to have lived in the shadows as long as I did. I would happily return there, if Nick would join me.

Nick texts Matt right back. "It's on. We're meeting him in the parking lot in ten minutes." Matt stands and helps me up. "Be cool, I don't want Arnie following us out." One thing thizz hasn't changed is my feelings for that jerk. I try to walk through the quad like nothing is up, but the excitement of cutting school feels kind of like a thizz rush. It makes it impossible to wipe the smile from my face.

We're almost to the door when Arnie spots us. "Hey Matt, where you going?"

I swear the entire yard goes silent.

"Nowhere." Matt shrugs. "I'll be right back." He pushes me forward and I stumble into Heather.

She turns around with a murderous look in her eye. When she sees me standing behind her, she steps back and smiles. "Sorry, Dani," she apologizes. Heather King is apologizing like she was in my way and not vice versa. What planet are we on?

I step around her, waiting for one of her minions to grab me by my ponytail and swing me across the quad. Instead they offer identical smiles in their matching Eureka High Cheer uniforms. They look like three smiling, cheering, blonde-bots whose mood switches have been set to nice. It isn't just Heather and her clique. Everyone is always smiling at me, saying good morning, offering me gum. All of sudden I exist. Not as myself. I am Nick Marino's girlfriend. Most days I don't mind playing that role.

Matt pulls on my arm and I follow him into the building. I don't have time to process how I feel about my newfound popularity. I have school to ditch. "Let's go." Matt breaks into a jog and I keep pace beside him. We run through the main hall, towards the parking lot, and right into Principal Leigh.

"Mr. Augustine, where are you off to?" She steps towards us, wearing a drab gray pantsuit and granny heels.

"Uh, nowhere, just going for a run." Matt looks at me and we burst into laughter.

Principal Leigh does not. "Well, there's no running in the halls. I suggest you go back to the quad."

"Yes, ma'am." Matt starts back to the yard and I follow behind him.

We walk into the yard, unnoticed this time.

"That was an epic fail," I say as I plop back against my tree.

Matt sits beside me. "You suck at ditching."

"That's probably why I never tried it before." I crack open my diet soda and take a sip, then offer it to Matt. He takes a drink, hands it back, and says he better text Nick and tell him to abort the mission. *Oh yeah, Nick.*

Tuesday is a little better than Monday. By Thursday I'm almost back to normal. It doesn't matter, because today is Friday and we are starting all over again. I hop out of bed fifteen minutes early and take a quick shower. I can't wait to get this day started. Friday is thizz day.

I dry my hair using something Lucy calls the scrunching method, where I crush my hair in my hand like a stress ball. It brings out the natural waves in my hair. Weird, right? But it works. I open my new bottle of foundation and dab little dots on my face. Lucy was off on Thursday night and Nick had some family business to deal with, so I let my shopaholic aunt take me to the mall. We spent an hour at the make-up counter, where the quirky sales girl guaranteed the hundred dollars' worth of product we bought would give me the fresh, natural look I was going for. I also bought new jeans and a couple of tops that looked good on the mannequins (on me they're alright). I've lost about ten pounds since I moved here. Lucy calls it a stress diet. Johnson calls it bad cooking. My new body is still curvy, but in the good way now. Caring about my appearance has taken some getting used to, but, hello, Nick Marino can't have a slob for a girlfriend. If that means upping my personal hygiene game, then I'm all over it. The hair and make-up aren't just for Nick. Giving a shit about my appearance makes me feel better about myself in a totally non-superficial way.

It's a miracle I haven't gained any weight back since Nick insists on driving me everywhere, and I let him. Except to school. I like walking, it helps me prepare for the day. Although the days are getting a lot easier. There are less death looks and more smiles thrown my way. I'd like to think it's me—the hair, the eyeliner—but I know it's Nick. They accept me because of him. I try not to think about what would happen if Nick and I weren't together. It's strange, but Nick doesn't have any ex-girlfriends at school. Matt said he never officially dated anyone before. There are girls he's hooked up with, whatever that entails, but none of them were special to him the way I am. Knowing this has changed me. It isn't just being on everyone's radar, having them notice me, watching my every move. I also want to be the girl Nick deserves. Someone he can be proud to have hanging on his arm. I walk through the doors of Eureka High with a smile on my face. For the first time since I moved here, I'm excited to see where the day takes me. Who am I kidding? I know exactly where this day is heading—to thizz.

I see Nick between second and third period; he tells me he missed me while three girls from my gym class follow us down the hall. They say good morning to me and smile at Nick. He nods at them and I wonder how genuine their interest in me really is. *Does it matter?* There are only two months left of school. At least I'll get to end high school on a happy note.

Nick, Matt, and I have lunch under my tree, discussing where we will party tonight. Nick wants to go to Gold Beach since the weather is nice. Matt agrees and tells Nick he will let K and Arnie know. When the bells rings, Matt heads to his locker, leaving me and Nick alone. The courtyard empties quickly, but Nick and I stay until the birds in the tree above us are the loudest thing in the yard. He cups my cheek with his hand and stares into my eyes. "Is it working?" he says in almost a whisper. I watch his hazel eyes smile as I whisper yes into the space between us. "Good, because I'm falling for you, Dani." Nick looks nervous, like he wasn't planning on divulging this information. I'm a little surprised that he's telling me this now, here. Sober. Affirmations like this are usually disclosed when we're high.

I'm not exactly comfortable with this level of intimacy, so I smile and pretend his declaration is no big deal. "You better be." I stand on my toes and kiss his cheek.

Nick scoffs when I don't respond with my own declaration of love. I think he likes that I'm not some sappy, love-sick idiot. He likes a challenge. "Oh really?" He picks me up and spins me around. The weightless, carefree feeling reminds me of thizz. I can't help but think how this moment would have felt if I was high. Kisses, touches, laughs, smiles, words—they're all enhanced by thizz. It's like the icing on a cake, the hot fudge on top of a sundae. It makes everything better.

"Hey, Dani. Wait up." I turn and see Matt jogging towards me. "Nick ditched sixth period. He's going to meet us in the parking lot after school." Unlike me, Nick ditches a lot. Matt says it's all family stuff. For someone who told me he doesn't associate with his family's wealth, he sure is invested in its business. Nick and I don't talk about family—mine or his. So I don't know why he's always running errands for his grandmother, but it really isn't my place to ask.

Matt and I walk into computer class and take our seats in the back. It's the Friday before spring break, so I'm surprised to see an assignment on the board. The rubric says we have to build a three-page website. One family, one hobby, and one free page. The free page can be a dedication to a favorite band or the college we are attending in the fall. That reminds me, letters should be going out soon. The thought of leaving Eureka, leaving Nick, causes a sick feeling in my stomach. "Did Nick apply to school?" Matt is my go-to for all things Nick.

He sort of shrugs and keeps his focus on his screen. "I don't think so."

Nick mentioned something about moving to San Francisco after graduation. I hope that's still his plan. That makes my plan suck less. What Nick Marino plans to do after graduation shouldn't concern me, but it does. We've only been dating three weeks, but it feels like a lot longer. When you're thizzin, seconds are minutes, minutes are hours, and hours are days. Each time we take thizz it feels like a year has passed by the time we come down.

I peek at Matt's screen to see what he's so interested in. He's already starting on his page. His background is Stanford-burgundy. Matt wants to get into Stanford just as badly as I want CAL. It's all he ever talks about. Nick and I never talk about the future. We live in the moment, and the moments we share are more than enough—for now. I don't ask him about his plan, and we never talk about mine. Nick knows I applied to CAL, he knows I'll leave if I'm accepted. Neither of us are ready to deal with what happens when that day comes. We have now, and now works for us.

Matt finally looks up and glances at my blank screen. "Do you need help with your page?"

"No, I got this." I open a browser and search for the CAL logo. At least I have one page I can work on. I don't know what I am going to do about my family page.

When the bell rings, I'm almost done with my first page. The background is royal blue, and I added some text from the CAL student life page. If I get my acceptance letter, I may add a picture of it, for personality points.

After a quick trip to Matt's locker, we head outside. Matt opens the door and I spot Nick across the parking lot. He's smiling at someone who isn't me. I watch her bouncing blonde hair as she leaps into his arms. It's just a friendly hug, but the smile in his eyes when he sees her infuriates me. I follow Matt to Nick's car, trying to keep a stoic expression on my face.

"Hey, babe." Nick smiles and shoves Heather to the side. He reaches for my hand and pulls me into his arms. "Did you miss me?"

I answer him with a long, deep kiss. When I open my eyes, Heather is rolling her eyes.

"I missed you too." Nick whispers in my ear. "Have I told you how beautiful you look today?"

I blush and kiss Nick's cheek. "Yes, twice." Heather makes a snorting noise beside me.

"Just wanted to make sure you knew that." Nick takes me in his arms and I melt into him. I can't wait to take thizz. To enhance everything I feel right now times a thousand. Someone honks the horn inside Nick's car and I jump back. I look into the car and see Arnie sitting in the front seat. My seat. I look at Nick in protest. "Hey, you guys need to work it out." Nick walks me around to the driver's side and opens the door. He refuses to get in the middle of the constant battle brewing between me and Arnie. Conveniently, Nick's phone rings, and he answers it before I can state my argument for why Arnie should sit in the back.

"You suck," I say to Arnie, who is triumphantly smiling from my seat.

"Nick wishes you did," he whispers, so only I can hear the insult. Nick won't pick between me and his friend, but he doesn't let Arnie tease me. I don't mind being a tattle-tale whenever Arnie tries to take a dig. "What did you say to me?"

Nick looks into the car with his phone to his ear and glares at Arnie. Arnie gives one of his disgusting smiles and says, "Bros before hoes, dude."

Nick shakes his head like a disapproving parent and closes the car door to finish his call. Nick is always talking on the phone or texting. I don't think Matt would lie to me about the nature of the calls. It isn't like Nick has time to see other girls; we're always together.

Suddenly Heather's face appears at Arnie's window. "What's up, girl." She leans in and he kisses her cheek. "You ready to hang with us tonight?"

My heart stops beating.

Heather looks at me with a wicked grin. "Sure, if you think Nick won't mind."

I mind. Heather is the only thing that can ruin my thizz high. I've already had to wait five days, and now my night is about to be ruined by this snarky blonde. Arnie asks Nick if Heather can tag along, and of course he says yes. There are so many reasons to hate Arnie. He pouts like a baby when he doesn't get his way, he's a pig when it comes to girls, and he's a chronic high-fiver. Inviting Heather King to hang out with us is an entirely new level of douchebag.

Twenty minutes later I'm sitting between Matt and Heather King in the backseat of Nick's car, headed towards Gold Beach. We haven't said a word to each other the entire drive. Nick pulls off at a 7-Eleven and the guys head inside, leaving me and Heather in the car. It seems ridiculous to ignore her when we're about to get high together.

"When was the last time you took thizz?" I ask in my best fake girly-girl voice.

"This is my first time." It sounds like it pains her to admit this.

"Really? I thought since you like to party that you would have done this before." It feels good to rub it in her face.

"Arnie wouldn't let me," she says softly. Arnie is the last person I would suspect of being protective. Maybe he likes her, and that's why he invited her out with us tonight. The thought makes me feel better.

Heather and Arnie will be too preoccupied with each other to annoy me.

The guys return from the store and I start to get excited. An hour from now I won't care about Heather King or Arnie or anything. In sixty minutes I'll be high and my world will be perfect.

20
Dani

One minute I'm dancing with Nick, the next I'm running down the beach with Heather. Or am I dancing with Heather and running with Nick? Who cares. I'm high, and nothing in the world matters. I pause to watch the sun slip into the Pacific Ocean, and I have this overwhelming feeling that this is where I belong. I wouldn't trade this moment for anything in the world. Not even my old life. That sounds like a shitty thing to say, but it's true. Does it mean I'm glad my parents are gone? I wrap my arms around myself and shiver at the thought. *No.* I'm just happy to have found happiness. They would be too.

"What are you thinking about?" Nick slides his arms around me and kisses the top of my head. We watch the last sliver of light dip below the horizon, then I turn around and snuggle up to his chest.

"Nothing. Everything. Me. You. Life. The future. The past. Where the bathroom is."

"See, that's what I love about you." Nick squeezes me to him. "You don't have to say anything, and I get you."

"I'm glad, because sometimes I don't get me."

"I got you, Dani. No matter what." Nick kisses my head again and I close my eyes. I can't imagine not having this in my life. This feeling. These moments with Nick. Or is it the rush of emotion, the euphoria that makes my skin tingle that I will miss? You know that saying, which came first, the chicken or the egg? In my case, it's which came first, my feelings for Nick, or thizz? Would one exist without the other? Can I exist without either one?

I wonder where we'll be six months from now. I want to ask him about school, what he plans to do after graduation. Will I see him, have access to his mouth, his kiss, his pills?

"You know why I think you're awesome?" Nick squeezes me to him.

"No fucking clue."

"You don't care about who am I or what I'm supposed to do with my life. You live in the moment. Who gives a shit about tomorrow?"

Maybe now is not a good time to ask him about his plans. He's right. I do live in the now. This is all I have, all we have, because nothing in the future is certain. I know I want Nick, that I need thizz, and that I like my life. That's ok for now. "We don't know what will happen tomorrow. I learned the hard way that I need to appreciate what's in front of me."

Nick pulls me away from his chest to face him. "I know one thing that will happen tomorrow. I will wake up and have you. You can always count on me, Dani. Always." His dilated pupils ping-pong back and forth. He's high as fuck. I wonder how much of what he's saying is the thizz talking. I don't want to know. I don't care. Not right now.

"Do you promise?" I whisper almost to myself. I don't want to need him, but I do. I refuse to think of myself living anywhere without him.

Nick presses his forehead to mine. "I promise," he breathes into my mouth, as if he's giving life to me with his words. I close my eyes and feel them travel past my lips. I breathe them in. My heart rate increases and my breathing hitches. *I believe him.* Nick kisses me with more want and need than I'm ready to accept. He leans into me and I lose my balance. Nick catches me around the waist and gently lowers me to the ground. Our eyes stay locked on each other, trapped in this moment. Seeing him hover above me drives my body insane. I pull him closer and he drops onto his elbows. We kiss, and I feel him wanting to go farther, push harder. He's cutting off my air supply, but my body is screaming for more.

"Get a room," Arnie yells from the darkness. Leave it to Arnie to ruin a moment.

I feel Nick smile as we kiss. "To be continued," he whispers and pulls away. I don't want him to stop, but I don't really like making out with an audience. Nick sits up on his knees just as K yells heads up and a football comes spiraling at us. Nick catches it then jumps up and starts running with the ball. K takes off after him. *Boys.*

Arnie plops down beside me with his big thizz smile. "How you feelin', D?" He nudges me with his elbow, but doesn't take his eyes off Nick and K running football drills in front of us. Asking someone how they feel is a common question while on thizz. Your feelings become very relevant to everyone around you. There is a need, a desire, for everyone to feel like you do.

I'm high and no longer feel stifled with self-doubt or embarrassed to say what's on my mind. I use that to my advantage and call Arnie out for treating me like crap. "Why do you hate me?"

Arnie looks at me like I'm crazy. "I don't hate you. Shit, I thought you were hot when I first saw you. I was going to ask you out, but

Nick beat me to it." His eyes look as if they're about to shake loose from their sockets.

I smile at his attempt to compliment me, even though I know he's lying. I've sat behind Arnie for almost three months, and he never looked at me once. I was invisible until the day Nick noticed me. Invisible to everyone except Matt. He was always there. Where is Matt?

"Nick's never had a real girlfriend, so I was surprised when you started hanging out with us every day and taking *my* seat. I'm a little jealous, I guess. Nick's my boy. I'd die for his dumb ass. So, you better treat him good!" The sincerity in Arnie's voice changes my perception of the situation. He has feelings, and I'm hurting them.

Thizz heals all wounds.

"I get it. I'll let you have shotgun sometimes." I really mean it. Arnie and Nick have been friends for years, and they'll be friends long after I'm gone. Arnie holds his fist out to me. I bump it with mine and laugh at the silliness of it. "I have one more question." I try to keep a straight face.

"Shoot," Arnie says and turns to give me his full attention.

"Do you still think I'm hot?" It was meant as a joke, but Arnie actually takes the time to check me out before he answers.

"All I can say is, you're lucky I love Nick, because the way I feel right now…" Arnie lifts his eyebrow at me.

"Don't be a jerk!" I laugh and sock him in the arm.

"No, but really, I think you're beautiful—inside and out."

I blush at Arnie's sincere compliment. "I'm so glad we had this talk." I lean over to give him a hug. He wraps his arms around me then pulls me on top of him. I squeal and try to break free, which only makes his grip stronger.

"Nick! Your girl is raping me, dude!" His breath smells like beer and weed.

My incessant laughter weakens me. I have no control over my limbs as Arnie tosses me back and forth. He lets me go a split second before Nick jumps on top of him. I try to get up, but my legs feel like Jell-O, and standing seems like a monumental event. I crawl away and spot Heather across the fire. Her arms are wrapped tightly around her legs. "Are you cold?" I ask, looking around for my discarded hoodie.

She stares blankly into the fire, gripping her knees. "Do you like it?"

It takes me a second to realize she's referring to the drugs. The euphoria feels so natural I often forget it's artificial. Heather doesn't look as euphoric as she should. She looks a bit freaked out. I don't want to say or do something to make it worse. Matt walks up behind Heather and sits between us. He's wearing his Stanford sweater. He must have went back to the car to get it. I wish I had my CAL hoodie so we could play my school is better than yours.

Heather reaches around Matt to give me a hug. "I love you, Dani." My body stiffens as if it's waiting for a knife to puncture my skin.

Matt leans back and represses a laugh. She's rolling hard, so I just go with it. "I love you, Heather." The words don't feel like a lie, but I know the feelings I have for Heather, and they are not love.

Matt clears his throat, his blue eyes a glimmer of light in the darkness. "What about me?"

I reach over to hug Matt, and Heather joins me. "I love you too, Matt." That definitely doesn't feel like a lie. I have a lot of feelings for Matt. Most of them I can't define. He's my best friend, for sure. It's the other feelings, the tingles and warmth that he creates when we touch. Sometimes I think it's just me, my ego, or my imagination making up things that aren't there. Matt is just being nice to me. Just being my friend. I've never had a male friend, so I don't know how to differentiate platonic feelings and real love.

His warm hand moves under my shirt. He caresses my back, causing tingles to shoot up my spine. I sit up and we lock eyes. For a brief moment, I see the boy I met last February, the boy whose warm smile slowly chiseled at the block of ice inside my heart. *My Matt.* I shake the thoughts racing through my drugged-out mind. He was never mine. He didn't want to be. Thizz is making me think there is something in Matt's touch, his look, his smile. But it's all in my head. Matt doesn't want me. He never did.

"Hey, what the hell's going on over here?" Arnie is standing over us.

"While you guys are wrestling each other, I'm keeping the girls company." Matt leans on his elbows with an evil grin. Heather punches his arm and rolls away. Matt returns fire by slapping her ass.

"Ouch!" Heather leans into me. "Help, Dani!" I grab her hand and pull her away from Matt. Maybe Heather isn't so bad.

Nick sneaks up behind me and pokes my sides. I spin around and give him a big hug. The joy and love emanating from our group is unlike anything I've ever experienced. I can't put into words the way I feel laughing and dancing with my friends.

My friends.

I kiss Nick, hug Heather, high five Arnie, and fist bump K. I keep my distance from Matt. We don't need to do or say anything. Everything I need to know about him, I read in his eyes. Nick is my first love, but Matt is my first real friend. He liked me when nobody knew my name. I'll always have a special place in my heart for Matt.

"Hey, I have an idea." Heather jumps up to address the group. "Let's play a game."

21 Dani

We assemble around the fire and Heather explains the rules. "Ok, this is just like truth or dare, but you flip a coin. Heads—truth, tails—dare. Then we spin an empty bottle to see who gets to ask the question or give the dare. Everyone got it?" She doesn't wait for a response. She flips the coin to go first.

I'm sitting next to the fire with Nick on my left. Matt is next to him. Arnie and Heather sit directly across from us. The fire is our sixth player, since K decided to be the referee. On the outside I seem super excited to play Heather's game, but I have a knot in my stomach the size of a grapefruit. I hate games. Especially ones with the words truth and dare in them.

"Truth," Heather announces.

The empty beer bottle makes two quiet rotations in the sand before stopping in front of Nick. I do a happy dance inside, thankful it's just a question she is getting from him.

"Do you think Matt is hot?" Nick asks while punching Matt in the arm.

"Cop out!" Arnie calls through his hands.

"Yes," Heather answers flatly. She holds the coin in front of me and says, "Clockwise."

I flip the coin low and catch it. It's hard to focus on the images. The more I concentrate, the more my eyes ping-pong from side to side. Nick takes my blindness as hesitation and rubs my back. He leans into me and kisses my cheek. I giggle when his warm breath tickles my neck. I'm lost in the euphoria of Nick. His smell, his hands on my bare skin. *This feels nice.*

"Ahem." Arnie clears his throat. "Can we get back to the game?"

"Tails," Nick calls to the group as he continues to kiss the space behind my ear.

Oh shit, tails.

Nick hands me the bottle. "Spin it," he says with an encouraging smile. It spins once, twice, three times, before stopping in front of Matt.

"Dude! You better make it good!" Arnie warns him.

The wicked look on Matt's sweet face is misplaced. I know he wouldn't do anything to embarrass me. Would he? "Dani," he clears his throat, "I dare you to let Nick..."

I exhale when I hear Nick's name.

"Fuck that," Arnie interrupts. "You can't dare her to do something with Nick. That's not fair."

"Shut the fuck up, Arn! You don't even know what I'm going to say."

"It doesn't matter. I know it's going to suck!"

Matt flips Arnie off with both hands just inches from his face.

"Just go!" Heather yells, bringing their focus back to the game.

Matt elbows Arnie, who is steadily tossing sand in his lap.

"Ok Dani, I dare you to let Nick kiss your chest." Matt seems very pleased with himself.

That doesn't sound too bad. "Over my shirt or under?"

"Under," Arnie answers for him.

My bra is black with little silver stars; it looks just like a bikini top. Considering we are on a beach, it's very appropriate. I start to lift my t-shirt when Heather yells for me to stop.

"No, no she doesn't have to take off her shirt." Heather is the only one brave enough to stand up to Arnie.

Heather, my new friend. I can't believe I was about to strip in front of the guys. *Damn you, thizz.*

After a few minutes of bickering, Matt restates the dare. "She has to lift her shirt, but she doesn't have to take it off."

I smile thankfully at Heather. She really is a great friend.

Nick scoots closer to me. His head is lower than mine, so I can't read the look in his eyes when he lifts my t-shirt. This is the most intimate we've ever been, and we have an audience to witness it.

"Wait!" Arnie shouts. "What about her bra?"

"Matt said chest, not breasts." I look to my new ally—she nods her head in agreement.

"That's bullshit," Arnie exclaims. "You're cheating. You meant *breasts,* right Matt?" Arnie makes air quotes when he says the word breasts. I think it's probably the first time he's used the term to describe a girl's anatomy.

Matt squirms uncomfortably beside Nick. I know he's trying to choose between the lesser of two evils: humiliate me, or piss off Arnie.

I don't care how messed up my brain is right now. I draw the line at nudity.

"I said chest, but technically, that means breast," Matt reiterates. He also air quotes the word breasts.

"No, it isn't the same thing," Heather argues.

"K, we need a ruling," Nick finally calls over the fire.

"Chest is *not* breast," K declares. We all giggle when K makes over-exaggerated air quotes.

"Yes!" I cheer, lifting my hand to Heather, flaunting the high five in Arnie's face.

"Ok, just do it," Arnie hisses.

Nick lifts the front of my t-shirt. I feel his warm breath on my skin as his lips move over my bra. Although the fire is scorching my back, cold chills run through my body. I look up from the top of Nick's head at Matt. He isn't even watching. His eyes are focused on the beer bottle in his hand.

"Enough," I say, pushing Nick away.

Arnie's hands are already up in the air for a high five when Nick returns to his spot.

I hand Nick the coin and lower my shirt. Nick flips it so high I lose sight of it. It is becoming increasingly difficult for me to focus. Nick announces he has truth and spins the bottle. It lands between me and Heather. After some deliberation on whether it means he should run through the fire, K decides he should spin again. Nick's second spin makes one perfect rotation and stops in front of me. I know exactly what I'm going to say, but I can barely contain my laughter long enough to get the words out. "Nick, have you peed the bed in the last year?"

He looks at me, stunned that I would reveal his secret. "Yes—but let me explain," he yells. It's too late, the guys are already rolling in the sand, calling him piss-head.

I laugh until my stomach hurts.

"I can't believe you told my secret!" Nick grabs me in a bear hug. "That reminds me, you still owe me a secret."

I can't tell him my secret, not now. Not when I feel this good. This truthful.

"I know." I kiss him. It's a long, deep kiss. The kind of kiss that makes you forget what you were talking about.

"Alright, guys. Let's play." Heather brings everyone's attention back to the game.

Thank you, Heather.

Matt flips the coin next. "Truth." His bottle spins at least four times before finally landing on Heather.

She claps her hands and sits up. "Matt, who do you think is prettier, me or Dani?"

Matt doesn't hesitate, he just blurts out my name. Heather smiles, seeming satisfied with his response. Her reaction is odd to me, even with my flawed senses. Why would she want Matt to choose me over her? Heather isn't the type of girl that likes to lose.

Arnie snatches the coin from Matt and flips it high in the air. It seems to be lost in the stars until Arnie yells, "Tails baby!" He jumps to his feet and dances in the sand.

"Come and spin, dumbass." Matt rolls the bottle to Arnie.

Arnie squats down and focuses on his spin. He lines up the neck of the bottle so it points directly into the fire and gives it a hard, firm spin. We wait breathlessly for it to stop. There is a collective sigh of relief when the mouth of the bottle lands in front of Arnie.

"I get to choose my own dare," he declares. As if any of us could come up with something outrageous enough for his standards. "Let's see." He taps a finger to his chin while surveying the group. I notice I'm not the only one trying to avoid eye contact, fearing he will take it as a request to join him on whatever he is scheming. "I dare myself to jump in the ocean—naked!" he says, then takes off running towards the water line.

"You're a fucking idiot!" Matt screams as he jumps up and follows him.

Arnie stops a few feet from where the surf cuts through the sand, takes off his shirt, and drops his pants and boxers in one quick motion. Even from where we stand, we hear his muffled scream over the roar of the ocean when his naked body comes into contact with the freezing cold water. He splashes frantically, fighting to get back on his feet as the waves crash around him. I almost feel sorry for the idiot.

The guys finally make their way back to the circle, and Arnie regales us with the details of his swim. If I didn't see it for myself, I might have actually believed his distorted version, which included spotting a shark fin.

Matt leaves the guys standing at the fire and sits down next to me. "How you feeling?"

"I'm great!" I get a nice surge of adrenaline as I suck down half a bottle of water.

"Are you mad at me?" Matt looks at me with his crystal-blue eyes and I swear I see dolphins swimming in them. His eyes. Those eyes. Those secretive, curious eyes.

I shake my head, because I'm at a loss for words.

"Good." He smiles, and my heart kicks back into motion.

"Why would I be mad at you?" I clear my throat and try to gain some composure. It's really difficult to pretend that the look on Matt's face doesn't knock the air out of my lungs. That the touch of his hand on my leg doesn't send my pulse into hyper drive.

"Because of the dare."

"No, it's just a game." I lean into his shoulder. "Just wait until you see what I have planned for you." Matt gives me a curious smile and bites his lip.

Oh my God.

All conversation stops when we hear Nick's cell phone ring. He answers it and walks away from the fire. Matt leans over and turns the music louder, which seems weird to me.

"Who is Nick always talking to on the phone?" I've asked Matt this question before, but maybe one day he'll tell me the truth.

"It's just family business." He shrugs.

I look at my watch. "What kind of family business does he need to take care of at midnight?"

Matt fidgets with a bottle cap before tossing it in the fire. "He has a lot of family obligations, you know what I mean?"

"No, not really." Nick told me he wants nothing to do with his family's business. Was that bullshit?

"His grandmother depends on him a lot to help with tenants and stuff." He places his hand on my leg. "You have nothing to worry about."

Matt's wrong. The tingles shooting up my thigh are definitely something to worry about.

Nick hangs up and walks back to the fire. Matt removes his hand and nudges me with his shoulder. "Hey, don't mention the calls to him. He hates talking about his family, you know."

"I know," I assure him. I won't say a word.

Arnie stumbles in front of us and I lean towards Matt to avoid being trampled. Matt slides his arm behind me, cradling the small of my back with his hand. I want to blame the drugs, but I wasn't this tingly when Arnie held me.

Arnie grabs Heather and starts dancing with her in a way that could be considered sexual harassment. "Dude, get a room!" Matt yells at them, which only makes it worse. Matt's face, lit by the fire, is beautiful. I don't want to look away, but I have to. I have to be stronger than thizz. I don't know what's wrong with me tonight.

I turn my attention to Arnie and Heather. The obnoxiously red lipstick Heather had on has faded. Her wavy blonde hair and curvy shape form the outline of the perfect female body.

"Does Nick think she's pretty?" I wonder aloud.

Matt snorts next to me. "Nick loves you, Dani."

My heart is in my throat. I don't know if hearing Nick say it would have the same effect on me. Somehow Matt's words make it real. If the person that knows Nick better than anyone in the world can see that he loves me, then having Nick say it is unnecessary. Matt withdrawals his hand from around my back and grips his knees. He just told me his best friend is in love with me, and all I can think about is how badly I miss being in his arms.

The song ends and Heather drops to her knees in front of us. "My turn." She flips the coin. "Tails." She spins the bottle. It makes an entire rotation before stopping at Arnie. He jumps up and does a victory dance, kicking sand all over everyone. I open another bottle of water and take a long drink, swishing it around, replenishing the moisture that is missing from my mouth. Nick sits down beside me and I offer him the water.

"No, I'm good." He smiles and his jaw tightens. He rolls his neck and focuses on Arnie. He looks different to me somehow. Like Matt just peeled a layer of skin off of him and I can see something that wasn't apparent before. Or maybe I could and I just didn't want to believe it.

"Heather—I dare you to kiss Dani," Arnie announces with an evil grin plastered on his face.

I choke on a mouthful of water. *What did he just say?* My eyes shoot across the fire. "French kiss," he clarifies, so there will be no arguments.

I look at Heather. She seems unaffected by the dare, like she was expecting it. "I'm down," she proclaims.

Everyone's eyes move in my direction. I instinctively look to Nick, who's smiling at Arnie as Heather crawls over to me like a cat in heat. She arches her back and licks her lips in an effort to win over the boys. She stops in front of me and sits up on her knees. "Well, are you in?"

I look at the guys, who anxiously await my next move. I clear my throat and take one more sip of water.

"I knew she wouldn't do—" she starts to say, but before Heather can finish her sentence, I grab the back of her head and kiss her. Her lips are small and unsure. I am definitely the aggressor. She tried to one-up me, and I beat her at her own game! I hear a rumble of moans as I move my mouth over hers. She finally yanks free to a roar of cheers.

She recovers quickly and forces a smile. "You little slut," she sneers before crawling back to her spot.

I receive a high five from Arnie and a quick kiss from Nick.

"Your turn," Heather says and holds out the coin.

I snatch it from her and flip it in the air, watching carefully to make sure it lands in my palm. Tails—another dare. The group is silent as I spin the bottle. It makes two rotations before landing in front of my worst nightmare—Arnie. The guys get excited at the possibility of some more girl-on-girl action. My teeth chatter out of control as I wait for him to speak.

Arnie isn't smiling. He isn't laughing. He's so serious it gives me chills. "Dani, I dare you to kiss Matt."

Before I can respond, Matt is on his feet. "No way dude, that's just wrong!" Matt says all the right things, mounts the perfect argument. He says all the things I should say, but I don't say anything.

"If you want to be a punk, then you shouldn't play." Arnie looks directly at me. "K, back me up here."

K shakes his head. "No way, this is Nick's rule."

All eyes turn to Nick. His face is expressionless.

"Nick," I say quietly and reach for his hand. I need to know what he's thinking.

Nick pulls his hand free and runs it through his hair. "Arnie's right, we decided to play."

"That's bullshit," Matt yells. "Arnie made up his own dare!"

I reach for Nick again. This time he takes my hand and squeezes it tight before letting go.

Matt drops to his knees beside Nick. "Dude, it's not right."

Nick stares into the fire, rolling his beer bottle between his hands.

"Man up, Matt. Nick said it was cool. Hell, I'd kiss her." Arnie laughs as he punches Matt in the back.

"Then you should've kissed her instead of running around here naked, dipshit!" Matt chucks a handful of sand. Arnie turns away and takes the brunt of it on the side of his head. He doesn't respond to Matt's hostility. He just puts his arm around Heather and smiles. Heather might as well be screaming with joy, it's so obvious she wants this to happen. If I kiss Matt, all gloves are off. Anything goes. So much for Heather being my ally.

"Nick, you're seriously cool with this?" K isn't really buying Nick's calm exterior. Neither am I.

"Yeah, it doesn't mean anything, right Matt?" Nick locks eyes with Matt.

Matt looks at Nick then looks at me. "Nope."

My jaw drops. *Is this really happening?* I should object. I should say something. But I don't.

Nick turns to me. "Dani, don't worry about it." He pats my hand. "It's just a game."

I look from my hand in Nick's to Heather. She's got a front-row seat to my humiliation.

"Alright. Nick ruled—do it," Arnie demands.

My eyes dart from Heather's traitorous glare to Matt. He looks at Nick then back to me and suppresses a smile. He rubs his hand over his face as if he's wiping the grin away. My heart races at the small evidence of betrayal that crosses his face. *He wants to kiss me.*

I can pretend to be upset, disgusted, and embarrassed, but inside I have a small smile of my own. I make my away around Nick to kneel in front of Matt. The only sound in the air is the crackling fire and the pounding, relentless waves crashing behind me. Matt lifts his hand to my cheek and my lips part. I close my eyes as he leans in and places his mouth on mine. Glorious sensations flood my body. His tongue slips into my mouth and I open my eyes. It's strange to see someone other than Nick so closely, but I'm grateful it's Matt and not one of the other guys. After a few seconds, Matt opens his eyes and jerks away, like he just woke from a bad dream. We quickly break apart and look around, waiting for someone to speak. Nobody does. They looked stunned, like they can't believe we went through with it. I know I am. We return to our spots on either side of Nick. I don't have the courage to look at Nick. If he's hurt, I don't want to see it. If he's angry, I can't deal with it. I figure it's best to sit back and avoid any further despair.

The game is less light-hearted now. The fun and laughter are gone as we all silently plot our next move. Nick flips the coin—another dare.

How many dares is that now?

He spins the bottle; it makes two turns and lands on me. I look at Arnie, already feigning boredom as he leans onto Heather's shoulder and pretends to fall asleep. I don't want to be responsible for slowing the pace of the game. Other than having sex with Nick in front of everyone, I can't think of anything else I can do to make Arnie happy. I rack my brain for movies I've seen, trying to pull something from my subconscious. Unfortunately, my brain is mush at the moment. Then it comes to me. My heart sinks as soon as I realize what I'm about to say. I cover my face with my hands and grind my teeth.

I don't want to do this. I have to. I have no choice. It's just a game.

"Nick." I look at Arnie when I say his name, waiting for his reaction. He raises an eyebrow at me and snickers when I hesitate. "Nick, I dare you to kiss me and Heather at the same time."

Arnie's mouth forms an 'o', then he looks at Matt. They fall back into the sand, bulldozed by my dare. K even looks impressed. I finally turn to Nick. He runs his hand through his hair and smiles at the boys. His casual demeanor enrages me. His arrogant grin infuriates me. After he's done fixing his hair, he looks at me, leans in close, and whispers, "I love you."

My mouth falls open. *He loves me. Nick Marino loves me.* I don't even have time to respond. Heather quickly appears at Nick's side. I won't dare let her get the first move, not now, not with the boy who loves me. I kiss Nick on the cheek and slowly make my way to his mouth. Heather follows my lead on the other side. We time it perfectly and meet at Nick's lips. He makes a few movements with his mouth but lets us do the rest. Nick runs his hand down my back and pleasure floods my body, until I feel Heather slide her tongue across Nick's lips. I back away in disgust, allowing her full access to his mouth. When I see his lips reach for hers, I pull Nick away. "That's it!" I point for Heather to move back to her side of the circle and resist the urge to slap the smug look off her face. Then I take Nick's face in my hands and give him a long, deep kiss. The guys whistle and cheer me on.

"Go Dani!" I hear Arnie say.

"You lucky bastard," K adds.

I sit back down, satisfied and somewhat heartbroken.

Nick squeezes my hand and kisses my cheek. "You're amazing, Dani." He puts his forehead to mine and my heart melts. I feel like I haven't spoken a word to Nick all night. I need to process everything that's happened, so I ask him to walk me to the bathroom. Arnie makes a disgusting comment about condoms and sex in the sand as we walk away. *He's such a pig.*

Nick tightens his grip as we slip into the darkness. "Are *you* having fun?" He burrows his face through my hair and kisses the back of my neck.

"I guess." I don't know if this can be classified as fun. I feel good. Thizz feels good. But that's it. There was nothing fun about that game. Not really. I kissed his best friend; did he think that was fun?

Nick stops just short of the lights in the parking lot. "Is it working?"

"Yes," I whisper into his mouth. I ready myself for a long kiss, but he backs away. He lifts my hands to his lips and kisses my knuckles, looking at me like he's waiting for me to say something. *Oh no.* It's my turn to say it. I bury my face in his chest and mumble, "I love you too." The sound of my voice saying I love you is so weird. It's like the first time I heard myself speak Spanish. The words just don't sound right coming from me.

"I've never felt this way about anyone before. I never knew I could." Nick lifts my chin and forces me to look at him. "I love you," he says again in plain, beautiful English.

Nick Marino loves me. And I love him. I think.

"You really aren't mad at me for kissing Matt?" I know he gave his permission, but it could have been the peer pressure of the group.

"No, no way," he assures me. "I know Matt would never do me wrong. I trust him with my life. *You* are part of my life." He kisses me softly on the lips, then pulls away too soon. "Why don't you ask if I'm mad you kissed Heather?" Nick raises his eyebrow in that sexy way he does. This time it has no effect on me.

I swallow hard and feel the hot, acidy tang of bile rise in my throat. "The last thing you *felt* when I kissed Heather was anger," I say and wiggle myself out of his arms. Nick refuses to let me go.

"Would you be mad if I kissed Heather?" Nick squeezes me to him as if he's trying to comfort me, but every word out of his mouth cuts me like a razor.

I try to block the mental picture, but it flies at me in 3D. Even hearing the words makes me want to puke. "You did kiss her." My stomach knots at the memory. That's a visual I'll have for the rest of my life. *Thanks, thizz.*

"No, I mean, you know, like you kissed Matt."

Someone has just stabbed me in the chest. I place my hand over my heart and check for blood. "Uh, yeah." I back away in case I actually throw up.

"Why? It's just a game."

I can't tell if he is serious. My eyes dance wildly, making it impossible to focus on his face. "Because, it's different. You know I don't like Matt." My tone is surprisingly firm. I even believe the words I'm saying.

"And you know I don't like Heather."

Ok, now he's twisting the knife into my heart. I don't understand why he is forcing the issue or why he feels the need to lead our conversation in this direction. He wouldn't be doing this, unless…*oh*

God. He wouldn't push for this, unless he wants to kiss her. He reaches for my hand and I jerk it away. Does he think I owe him now because I kissed Matt? A kiss for a kiss? Something that feels like reality is starting to creep in. I really wish I had another pill. I wonder if Nick has more. I wonder if he'd give me one if I asked.

"Why do you think I would do anything to hurt you? I've never felt this way about anyone before you." His words sound sincere, yet what he's asking contradicts the sentiment. "Don't you trust me?"

My anguish turns to anger in a matter of seconds. I know Nick's views on trust. He explained them to me a few days ago when I saw a voluptuous Greek goddess get out of his car. He caught me staring from the doorway of the café and rushed inside to explain, while the girl headed off in the direction of Lady Luxe. He said jealousy is for the weak, and I have nothing to worry about because he was just giving a ride to an old friend. There really wasn't much I could say. He was right. Jealousy is for the weak. And I am weak.

"I'm sorry. It's not you, it's her." I decide to focus my distrust on Heather, not Nick. That way he can't defend against my rage.

"She's your friend."

"She is *not* my friend." I break away from Nick and stomp towards the fire. How can he say she's my friend? Doesn't he know me at all?

I hear the sand sloshing behind me and I speed up. "Dani, stop." He grabs my hand and spins me around. "These are the only lips I want to kiss." He runs his thumb across my mouth. "Forever."

"Why?" I spit back.

"Why what?"

"Why me? What makes me so special?" I choke on the words. I'm getting emotional; it's so unlike me.

Nick must see the tears glistening in my eyes, because his reaction is unexpected. He rests his head on my shoulder then stands upright and wraps his arms around my neck, crushing my head to his chest. "I don't know. I just do." His voice cracks slightly. "When I look at you, something happens to me. Something new and amazing and scary as shit. I can't decide if I want to kiss you or run away." This is the most honest thing he has ever said to me.

"Thanks a lot," I joke. I don't do well with this level of intimacy, so I turn to laughter.

"It's not like that. I should run because I'm not good for you."

I snort in reply. "If anyone is unworthy in this relationship, it's me. I don't deserve you. Look at me."

Nick steps back with a serious look on his face. "Don't say that. Don't put yourself down, ever." I start to defend myself, but Nick won't let me. "There isn't anything about you I would change." He cups my face in his hands and rubs his thumbs down my cheeks and then across my lips. His eyes fill with desire as he leans towards me. I close my eyes, and half a second later his tongue slides into my mouth. Even though this is one of the most tender kisses we have ever shared, my mind wanders to another kiss. Matt's hand on my face, his mouth on mine, the heat of his body as we kneeled in front of each other. The intensity is unrivaled, even now as Nick holds me in his arms. I grab Nick's head and pull him closer, deeper into my mouth. He grips my hips and pushes against me. "I want you so bad, Dani," he breathes into my mouth. "Do you want to go to my car?"

Yes! I scream in my head. I want him right now. My body needs something. Maybe I don't need another pill. Maybe I just need Nick. We hear a yelp from the fire and turn to look. Arnie has Heather over his shoulder. I scan the faces around the fire and see Matt. I snap back to my senses. I can't do this; no matter how badly my body is screaming yes.

"I don't want to be the girl who loses her virginity in the back of a Chevy."

Nick looks like he's just been socked in the stomach, and my face turns ten shades of red.

"You're a virgin?" he chokes a little on the last word.

I'm so humiliated. Not because I am a virgin; it's the fact that Nick thinks I'm not. Three weeks ago he thought I didn't drink alcohol, so why is finding out I've never had sex such a shock? I don't know what to feel, but lots of feels wash over me, thanks to thizz, and sadness is the one that sticks. I put my face in my hands and try not to cry.

"It's ok, Dani." Nick pulls my hands away from my face. "I'm just surprised. Well, not really. I guess I'm...happy." Nick kisses my forehead like I'm a fragile piece of glass. "You're right, this is not the time or place." Nick looks as if he's just been given the key to a bank vault. He's giddy over the fact that I'm a virgin, which only makes me feel more like a freak.

Nick suggests we head back to the group since he knows he's not getting laid. He wraps his arm around my shoulders, and I feel a vibration in his pocket. His phone is always ringing, and he always answers it. Nick is more involved in his family's business than I thought. It makes me wonder, if we had gone to his car, would he still have answered it? The sad thing is, I know he would have. He always does.

22
Dani

We leave the beach a little before eight in the morning. Watching the sky turn from dark to light is a strange feeling when you haven't slept. It's like the world is working in reverse. It's disorienting. Or it could just be the thizz. Nick, Matt, Arnie, and I go back to Matt's house. K and Heather stay at the beach. K only lives a few blocks away, and he promised Arnie he would make sure she got home safe. Heather said her parents aren't expecting her home until after noon. She can't show up at dawn and have them actually believe she was sleeping at her friend's house. I'm the opposite. Lucy gets home from her shift around eleven thirty. I have to be home before then so she doesn't suspect I've been out all night. Only I don't want to go home yet. I hate being alone when I'm high.

I fall in and out of sleep during the drive, so I miss the conversation between Nick and Arnie that ended up with me staying at Matt's house while Nick drove Arnie home. I stumble into the house and plop on Matt's sofa. It feels good after lying in the sand all night. Matt brings me a glass of orange juice then disappears down the hall. It's too tangy for my current taste buds. I can't really stomach anything but water when I'm coming down. I place the glass on the coffee table and pick up the remote from the arm of Matt's sofa. Nick said he'd be right back. That was seventeen minutes ago. I need to stay awake if I want to beat Lucy home. She gets off at eleven and usually stays up a few hours before heading to sleep. I like to beat her home and pretend my day is just starting as she heads to bed. If I don't make it home, I'll have to swing by the café in case Lucy checks up on me. This way, Patty can say I was there in the morning and Lucy will think I was just out getting coffee. I have it all planned just in case things don't fall into place. I've been lucky so far. Lucy doesn't suspect a thing.

Just as my eyes start to shut, Matt walks into the room. "Come on, sleepyhead." He holds out his hand and I take it. He yanks me to my feet and tells me to go lie down in his room. I'm too tired to protest or worry about how that may look. I trust Matt. More importantly, Nick trusts him.

I stumble into Matt's room. My only choices are his desk chair or the bed. The chair is probably the safer, less comfortable option, but I don't care about safe right now. I sit on the bed and kick my shoes off. Matt walks into the room carrying an armful of water bottles and a bag of chips. He closes the door behind him and places the snacks on the desk. The only light in the room creeps between the slits of the window blinds. I watch it slowly climb the wall as the sun rises outside. I hope Nick comes back soon. Eureka is small, Arnie can't live that far away. Matt is settling in like I may be here for a while. He isn't acting like Nick will be back any minute.

"You want some?" Matt holds up a bag of chips without looking at me. Why won't he look at me? I don't want snacks. I need to stay awake and wait for Nick.

"No thanks." I know what I want. The question is, am I brave enough to ask for it? What if he doesn't have any, or worse, what if he says no? Quit being stupid. This is Matt. I can ask him anything. "Do you have any more pills?"

Matt stops shuffling CDs. His back stiffens then relaxes just as quickly. "Uh, I don't know…" He turns around with an answer on his lips, but nothing comes out. He just stares at me as I unzip Nick's hoodie. I slide it off one sleeve at a time, passing my orange juice glass from one hand to the other as I go. I watch Matt's eyes commit my body to memory before stopping at my mouth. He knows how my lips feel. I know what Matt tastes like—this is information neither of us should know. We're friends. Friends don't kiss. I can't believe Nick even allowed it. The more sober I become, the more awkward this feels. Thizz is the only thing to cure that. When I'm high, feelings like embarrassment and regret don't exist. Thizz makes the world an uncomplicated place.

Matt walks to the closet, pulls out a shoe box, and places it on the bed. He takes off the lid, slides opens a zip lock bag. He must feel the tension too, because he doesn't even hesitate as he hands me the pill.

"Thanks." I swallow it with a sip from my orange juice, and Matt goes back to his CD search. He finally chooses one and moves to his boom box to put it in. I take a peek inside the shoebox. My heart stops. Where did he get all those pills? I look at Matt. His back is to me. I reach in, swipe a handful, and shove them in my pocket. Adrenaline pumps through my veins. This is the first time I've ever stolen anything. I feel bad stealing from Matt, but then again, I don't. He has so many, at least a hundred. *Is Matt the dealer Nick was protecting?* How well do I even know him, or Nick for that matter? They know nothing about me. Who I really am. I don't even know who I am anymore.

A woman's soft, sultry voice suddenly fills the room. This song isn't something a drug dealer would play. If there is a drug dealer playlist, I guarantee this song isn't on it. This song is bluesy with a jazz feel. I'm actually surprised Matt would even have a CD like this. He's always quick to put on rap or hip hop in the car. This is a nice surprise. Matt adjusts the volume then sits next to me on the bed. I watch him crack every knuckle on his right hand. The same hands I watched typing in class. Those fingers typed a message once. The message that led me to Nick. That led me to this moment. Matt set me up with Nick. Boys don't play matchmaker with girls they like. Matt doesn't like me, not like that. But my fingers itch to touch him anyway. It's the drugs. It's not real. Some people crave touch when they're high. I never understood why until this moment. If there was a bottle of lotion in this room, I'd have it slathered all over my hands right now. I lie back and lock my hands behind my head. Music surrounds me, and a familiar tingle pricks at my skin. I have a million thoughts running through my head, but I can't think of a single word to say to Matt. My eyes wander around the room, looking for some safe topic of conversation. They land on the poster above the bed. "Are you serious?" I snort, gesturing to the bikini-clad model holding a fire hose between her legs.

"What?" he says with a little laugh. "It's a dude thing."

I turn towards Matt and find his blue eyes staring back at me. My heart feels like it's trying to claw its way out of my chest. This would be so much easier if Matt didn't have those eyes—that smile.

I stand up and walk to the desk. I need distance until this pill kicks in and we are back in friend-mode. I open a bottle of water and take a huge gulp, hoping the simple task of drinking will chill me out. I watch Matt over the top of the bottle. Our eyes lock when he reaches out to me and slides the bottle from my fingers. He gulps down a mouthful of water and then places the bottle back in my hand. There are two unopened bottles on the desk, but he took mine. He wanted mine. I take a drink to see if I can taste him, but it doesn't taste like anything but water.

I know what Matt tastes like. When we kissed, he tasted like beer with a hint of bubblegum. The fact that I've kissed him is something I should be embarrassed about, ashamed of, but all I keep thinking is how badly I want him to kiss me again. I can't think like that. I can't feel this way, about Matt or anyone. I'm with Nick. And if I keep telling myself I love him, maybe one day it will feel real. It felt real last night. I also thought Heather King was the sweetest girl I've ever met. Thizz really warped my perception. There is no way I will ever be friends with Heather, no matter how awesome I thought she was. Is it possible that my feelings for Nick are just as warped? When I'm sober it isn't Nick I want to be around, it's Matt. It's always been Matt.

"Can I ask you something personal?" Matt leans back on his elbows. "If you don't want to talk about it, I understand."

Yes, let's talk about something, anything. "Sure."

"I was just curious why you moved here. Where are your parents?"

As soon as the words leave his lips, I know I will tell him the truth. I want to. I need to.

"They were shot during an attempted carjacking," I say casually, as if Matt isn't the first person I've ever told. "I don't have any other family, except Lucy, and she lives here." I look away and wait for the obligatory apology and empathetic look that usually follows when someone learns about my orphan status.

"Damn," Matt mumbles. "Don't you miss living in the city?"

I swivel my head and look into Matt's crystal-blue eyes. I'm so happy he didn't make this weird. He smiles his sweet smile, and I can't help but smile with him. "Not really. Not anymore." I look at him and feel a fresh wave of serotonin flood my veins. My body melts into itself. Thizz is the reason I'm happy. Thizz has made Eureka tolerable.

I can make it through the day without seeing Nick or talking to Matt. Thizz is what I wake up for and go to bed with. And now I know who holds the key to keeping me happy. *Matt.* Had he showed up at the café that night, I'd be with him, not Nick. But he didn't, because he didn't want me. Love isn't always requited. Sometimes love is complicated. That's where thizz comes in.

Matt asks me trivial questions about my old neighborhood. I tell him about my favorite café and the best place to buy a burrito in the city. For the first time since I lost my parents, I'm able to talk about my old life with a smile on my face. The ache in my chest is dulled by the drug flowing through my veins.

"My father was a lawyer, corporate law. My mom was a lawyer's wife." I remember the way she stood beside him at parties. I don't know which of them was more proud. "She was a great party planner." I laugh about it now, even though I hated the superficiality of it all. "He had a day job, but he spent most of his time working pro-bono cases. My mother used to tell people he was trying to save the world one ghetto kid at a time." I know I'm rambling, Matt doesn't seem to care. It feels good to talk about them. To remember them.

Matt tells me his father is a lawyer and his mother does interior design. We have a lot in common. I like that. I knew Matt and I would hit it off. It just wasn't in the way I thought. Maybe we were just destined to be friends. I really need a friend right now.

"Does Nick know about your parents?"

My stomach does a somersault at the thought. "No, and you can't tell him. Promise me?"

"You guys have a lot in common," Matt insists.

Everyone knows Nick lost both of his parents. I don't want to have *that* in common with him. "You don't get it. People treat you different when they know. Please don't say anything—to anyone."

"Ok," Matt concedes. "I promise."

I hold out my pinkie and Matt hooks his with mine. There is a tiny spark hidden in his lazy smile. The way someone looks right before they tell the punchline of a joke. Matt fights it back by letting my pinky go and turning away. He tucks his hands under his head and stares at the ceiling. I lie on the bed beside him and a new song comes on, this one is even sultrier than the last. I wish Matt took another pill. I wonder if he would take one if I asked him to. I bet there are a lot of things I could persuade Matt to do for me. *What a fucking horrible thing to say.* I glance at Matt and catch him watching me again. We lock eyes briefly and then turn back to the poster. The poster is our safe place. Not that we need one. We're just friends. Any tingles or warmth I feel at the sight of him are drug-induced hallucinations. They aren't real. Our kiss wasn't even real. Just some stupid dare. Something he would have done with Heather or any other girl put before him. Nick is real. His kisses are real. He loves me and I love him.

Where the hell is Nick? "How far away is Arnie's house?"

"Why? You got a date with Arnie later?" Matt jokes.

"Because Nick said he was going to drop him off then come back."

Matt's eyes get huge, and it has nothing to do with thizz. He doesn't want to tell me where Nick is, which makes my imagination run wild. My adrenaline surges—not in the good way. "Where did he go?" Matt stays silent. "Is he really dropping Arnie off?" Matt sort of shrugs. *If he didn't take Arnie home, where would he go?* As soon as I think the question, the answer comes to me. My hands are shaking at the thought of him and Heather at the beach together.

"Did he go back to the beach?" I give Matt a serious stare, daring him to lie to me.

Matt has an internal debate before he answers. "Yeah, he's at the beach." Matt looks relieved that I figured it out on my own. Technically, he didn't tell me, so he won't be in trouble.

"With Heather?" I choke on her name. I would rather be choking her.

Matt's eyes pop out of his head, as if he forgot about Heather. "No, it isn't what you think. He was too amped up to be inside. They took too many pills last night and he's still wired."

Too many? I don't know if what I feel is jealousy because Nick is at the beach with Heather or the fact that he took pills without me. "How many did he take? Why didn't he give me one? Did he give one to Heather?" I think about Heather asking me if I liked thizz. She didn't look like she was having a good time. So why take another pill? Unless someone gave it to her. Someone who wanted to keep her up and alert and at the beach. I feel like I may puke.

"I don't know if she's at the beach." Matt looks sincere, but what do I know. He could be as good at lying as I am. "He just went back to hang out with K and the guys. They're going to play football, then he'll be back."

What a pathetic excuse. I stand up to get another bottle of water and spot Matt's cell phone on the desk. I pick it up and contemplate calling Nick. Matt puts his warm hand on mine to stop me from calling. His touch sends tingles through my body. *Tingles that feel real.* I pull my hand free and sit on the edge of the bed. I know I can't call him. I have to trust him. If we don't have trust, we don't have a relationship. Nick said he trusts Matt. Even with me. The question is, do I trust myself with Matt?

23
Matt

I fucked up. I shouldn't let her think Nick went back to the beach, back to Heather, but I can't tell her the truth—that he went to a party. It was a fraternity thing at Humboldt State. Arnie had a chick he knows sell pills for us last night so Nick could party at the beach with Dani. It kills him to lie to her, but we can't let her find out. If she finds out Nick sells thizz, she'll hate me for lying to her all this time. It's safer this way.

The girl from Humboldt called a few hours ago and said the party was still raging, and people were looking to buy more pills. Nick wasn't about to miss out on sales, so he brought me and Dani back here then took off for Humboldt State with Arnie. Nick was banking on Dani falling sleep. He figured he could come back in a few hours and tell her he was here all along. That isn't going to happen now that I gave her another pill. Not the smartest fucking thing to do, but I couldn't say no. Not to those desperate eyes. I didn't know Nick told her he was just taking Arnie home. What kind of lame-ass lie is that?

"Dani, you know Nick loves you. He just has to get it out of his system. He didn't want to leave you sleeping in the sand when you could come back here with a working toilet." That sounded like the right thing to say. "You said yourself that you could barely keep your eyes open."

"If he loved me the way he says he does, he would've given me a pill and let me stay awake having fun with him." She hands my phone to me and I shove it in my pocket. "Like you just did."

My heart crashes through my chest and lands at Dani's feet. I want to tell her she's right. I want to tell her I would never leave her. I want to tell her everything. About me and Nick, and thizz, and how I feel. I take her hand and she bites her lower lip. Blood rushes to places in my body that it shouldn't. I can't betray Nick. As much I as I want to, I can't. There is one thing though. I can tell her why I sent the Myspace message and why I asked her to meet me in the parking lot that day. Not that it makes a difference now, but something inside me wants her to know that I cared. That I wanted her. It won't change anything. She'll probably get a good a laugh out of it. Once the second pill kicks in, anything I say will be a fleeting memory. Nothing is taken seriously when you're high. Words, feelings, kisses.

I'm trying to figure out the best way to start the conversation when a burst of cold air flows through my room. I turn and see Ashley's head peek around the corner. "Oops," Ashely says and disappears.

She is halfway up the stairs when I catch her. Interacting with my little sister while thizzin is a sobering experience. I suddenly feel very guilty about my condition. "Wait, Ash." I pull on her arm. "You want to hang out?" I need something to keep me in check. I don't think I can stand to be alone with Dani another minute. I was about to tell her I wanted to ask her out until Nick swooped in. *What was I thinking?* In no universe would that ever be a good idea. Ashely is the perfect buffer.

"Really?" Ash raises her eyebrow at me. I never invite her to hang out with my friends. "Are you drunk?" She takes two steps towards me with a curious smile.

Damn, she's observant. I'm so glad I didn't take another pill. "Just come back down with me." I usher her through the hallway, back to my room, and close the door.

"Dani, this is Ashley. Ash, this is Nick's girlfriend, Dani." I make the introductions quickly while I slide the box of pills under my bed.

Ashely sits on my bed beside Dani, processing the situation. "Nick's girlfriend? Where's Nick?"

I let Dani answer the question and change the CD to something more upbeat.

"He had to help a friend move," Dani tells her. I laugh at the ridiculous lie, but I have to give her props for originality. She came up with that lie in a split second, and it's believable. She's a good liar.

"So, you came over to hang out with my brother?"

"Yeah, we're friends." Dani smiles at me and my heart smiles back. *Friends*. We are so much more than that. There is no word to describe what she is to me.

"Nick doesn't get jealous?" Ashley asks innocently.

"No," I tell her. He doesn't think I'm competition.

Dani is so cool with Ashley. She asks her questions about her remission, which Ashley can't shut up about. She even teaches her how to put her hair up in some kind of messy ponytail. It doesn't seem like a big deal, but Ash is excited by the lesson. It's fascinating watching them together. I've never seen Dani so content. Ashley has a weird way of putting people at ease.

"I like your pendant. That's turquoise right?" Ashley comments on the necklace Nick bought for Dani.

Fucking show off. He paid two hundred dollars for it at some antique store downtown. Dani stopped to look at it for like two seconds, and he had to buy it for her.

"Yeah, and the old lady we got it from said it has powers." Dani's voice drips in sarcasm. I'm happy to see she isn't impressed with Nick's overpriced show of affection.

Ashley's smile fades when she touches the blue rock. "Turquoise is very powerful, actually. It's supposed to give you clarity and help heal you. I kept a rock under my pillow when I was sick."

"Oh." Dani's smile drops from her face. She's worried her comment offended Ashley.

I grab my sister in a headlock and ruffle her hair. "What are you, a gypsy?" I tease, hoping to lighten the mood.

"No, I'm just saying, it's special." Ashley stops her thought when she hears the next song start. Her eyes light up and she jumps off the bed, pulling Dani with her. "I love this song!" It's a hip-hop tune with an infectious reggae groove. Dani reluctantly stands while Ashley dances around her. Eventually the music overcomes her, too.

For once I can watch Dani without the threat of being noticed. I even forget my sister is in the room until Ashley grabs Dani's hands and tries to twirl her around. Dani looks at me for help as she subconsciously chews her cheek. She's really high. I should get Ashely out of here before she notices the change in Dani.

"Time to go upstairs."

Ashley ignores me until I turn down the stereo. "AHH! Come on, Matt," she complains. "I need to practice for school dances and stuff." The thought of Ashley at Eureka High next semester makes my stomach hurt.

"Go practice in your room." I push her out the door and walk her to the stairs.

"Too bad she's Nick's girlfriend. I really like her," Ashley admits.

"Me too."

Ashley catches the double meaning in my reply and gives me one of her sly grins as she walks up the stairs to the main part of the house. As the door closes, I hear music flowing from my room. I rush back to see Dani spin away from my stereo. She restarted the song. I lean in the doorway and watch her dance. She's graceful in a clumsy sort of way. She sees me and smiles a twisted smile. Then she pulls her hair loose and lets it fall over her face. She's rolling hard and feeling really good right now. A thin layer of sweat forms over my skin when she motions for me to join her. I know her desire to dance with me isn't real—she's just reacting to the second dose of ecstasy. But I've never wanted anything more in my life. She runs her teeth across her bottom lip, turning it a deep shade of red. This is dangerous ground. I can feel it in the way my pulse starts to race when I look at her.

If Nick knew what I was thinking right now, I'd be a dead man.

Good thing Nick isn't here.

I force all rational thoughts from my head and creep towards her, pretending to be lost in the music. She lifts her arms above her head and sways in front of me.

This is really happening.

She spins around as I close the gap between us. Her back is to me, as if she's afraid to look me in the eye at this range. I start to think I've made a mistake when she leans back and brushes her body against mine.

She wants this. She wants me right where I am.

My fingers tremble when I touch her hips. She loses the rhythm for a split second as I slide my hands around her waist. I feel her suck in a breath when my pinky dips into the waist of her jeans. Her stomach retracts at my touch and I pull her to me, burying my face in the crook of her neck. Her hair smells like smoke from the bonfire with traces of her lavender shampoo.

She smells so fucking good.

We move back and forth to the music, pretending to be overtaken by the song and not each other. After a few beats, Dani turns around to face me. She wraps her arms around my neck. I grip her hips and pull her to me. It's amazing how well I've been able to control the monster raging inside of me. It won't hold for much longer if I keep her this close. She looks up with her big dilated eyes and my heart beats against my chest like an angry gorilla. Her bottom lip is pinched between her teeth. I want to pull it free with my mouth. I remember our kiss, how sweet her lips tasted. I want more. I need more. Sweat runs down the side of my face as we stare at each other, neither of us brave enough to make the next move. The music pulsates through us, masking the vibration in my pocket. My phone.

FUCK!

Dani must feel it too, because she drops her arms and spins away from me. I back out of the room and answer it in the hall.

"Matt! Can you hear me?" Nick yells. I hope the music on his end drowns out the beat coming from my room.

"Yeah, what's up?" I can't believe Nick has the audacity to call and ruin what could have been the best moment of my life, even if it was with his girl. *I'm a dick.*

"How's Dani?" he asks as the music on his end fades into the background. "Is she sleeping?"

I move back towards the door to watch her. "No, she's awake." She's standing at the desk with a bottle of water in her hand. Her hips sway slightly to the music as she takes a sip and I bang my head on the doorframe. "She's good." *So good.*

"Where are you?" Nick questions. "What's that music playing?"

Oh shit.

"Oh uh, Ashley came down. She's playing a CD." It isn't really a lie.

"Fuck, does she know where I am?"

"No, I covered for you. I told her you were playing ball with K." As I tell him this, I realize how lame it sounds. Luckily, Nick is too wound up to care.

"Good lookin' out. Tell her I'll be there in an hour."

"I will, dude." I close my phone and I'm hit with a healthy dose of guilt. What am I doing? Dancing with Dani, giving her a second pill. I can't even blame it on thizz. I'm totally fucking sober.

When I step back in the room, Dani is trying to restart the song. I move behind her, and she turns her face towards mine. Feeling her warm breath on my neck makes what I'm about to say very difficult. "Nick's coming." I turn the volume down as the song starts over.

She shrugs and sits on my bed. I snatch the water bottle from her hand even though there are fresh ones on the desk. I want to drink from the same bottle as her. The water tastes like nothing, just water, but any way my lips can touch hers is a win. I can't believe Nick let me kiss her. I wonder if he would have given his permission if it was Arnie. For some reason I get the feeling he was doing it for me, as a favor or something. It sounds fucked up, but why else would he let another dude kiss his girl? I'm a fucking asshole and a shitty friend. Nick trusts me with Dani; I can't abuse that trust.

"I don't want to go home yet." She looks at me with a hopeful expression. "Should I call Nick and tell him I want to stay here?"

"Yeah, I mean, if you want." I try to sound indifferent. Like her staying isn't going to make my day, my year. *Stop it! She's Nick's girl.* He should be here with her, not me. But she's looking at me with a fucked-up thizz smile and the angry gorilla in my chest is screaming *Fuck Nick*.

I dial Nick's number and hand her my phone. I hear the roar of the crowd and the music thumping from across the room. I wonder what she's thinking. He obviously isn't at the beach. She waits until the background noise fades to speak. "Hi, it's Dani," she says quickly. Nick wouldn't be expecting anyone but me to call from my cell. He's going to kill me. "I just wanted to tell you that I'm fine here with Matt."

I don't hear Nick's reply, I just watch Dani's face for his reaction. "Nick? Are you there?" She makes a funny face when he doesn't respond. She's about to close the phone when I hear him say something. She quickly turns away from me. "I love you too," she whispers and hangs up.

Ouch. The gorilla in my chest is now battling a wailing hyena of reason in my head.

What the fuck are you thinking? She loves him.

I don't care. I don't care about tomorrow or Nick or anything. I have Dani with me now. She's high as hell and maybe not thinking clearly. I don't care. I'll let her decide what will and won't happen.

Dani hands my phone back, then leaves to use the bathroom. I put on a new CD. It's a mix of chick songs, Norah Jones and Pink. It seems like a better choice than hip-hop at the moment. I close the blinds to block the morning sun and gulp down a bottle of water. My shirt is damp with sweat. I pull it off and tear through my drawer for a fresh one. I pull out a white t-shirt and my phone buzzes. Not again.

"Where's Dani?" Nick's voice is harsh. I'm sure he's pissed I let her call him. It was a dick thing to do.

"She's in the bathroom." I don't want to be on the phone with

Nick right now. Just hearing his voice makes the hyena shriek—*You fucking loser!*

"Look dude, thanks for doing this. I owe you. I'll be there soon to pick her up, alright?"

I'm an asshole. Nick doesn't yell at me for letting Dani call him or even question why I let her. He thanks me. He says *he* owes me. I don't deserve Nick or his thanks. "No problem, dude." We're about to hang up when I remember Dani is high as fuck. She can't go home, not yet. "Don't rush back, she's cool. Now that Ashely left, she'll probably crash." I try to sound as casual as possible. He can't find out I gave her another pill.

"Well, I'll come over and hang out then. We can go get breakfast."

Hanging out is better than going home. "That's cool," I say, hoping he doesn't detect the disappointment in my voice.

"You're my boy, Matt. Thanks for taking care of my girl."

His girl, I repeat in my head as I close my phone. The pill I took is long gone. I can't do this, I can't play this game with Dani. I grab the extra blanket from the foot of my bed and lay it out on the floor. The gorilla mumbles something about me being a pussy before retreating back into the jungle alone. I need to go to sleep before I do something I'll really regret. No lines have been crossed. I can close my eyes with a clean conscience and still look my best friend in the eye. I don't want to fuck that up.

"What are you doing?" Dani asks from the doorway.

"Sleeping," I snap. Unconsciousness is the only way to keep me from doing, saying, or thinking things I shouldn't. Sleeping is the safest way to pass the time until Nick shows up.

"You don't have to sleep on the floor. There's enough room for both of us."

My sour mood doesn't affect her—nothing will at this point. She picks up the blanket, wraps it around her body, and hops onto my bed like we're having a slumber party. Maybe that's all she sees me as, an innocent friend, no different than Ashley. Someone she can dance with or sleep next to. She doesn't see me as a threat either. I'm a loser for even believing I stood a chance with her.

"Come on, Matty." She pats the space next to her and adjusts the blanket to make a cocoon around her body.

I want to be mad, but the only person I can blame is me for thinking she wanted me. I lie beside her and try to ignore the warmth of her seeping through the blanket. I just want to sleep. I close my eyes, and a few minutes later she says my name.

"Hey Matt."

"Yeah."

"Don't tell Nick about the second pill, ok?"

She doesn't even know Nick's rules, but she's smart enough to realize taking a second pill here, with me, may not have been a good idea. "It's our secret." I hold up my pinky, and she links hers around mine. How can I be pissed about anything with her lying beside me?

"And Matt," she says in almost a whisper. "I know he wasn't at the beach."

My heart races at being caught in a lie. I was hoping thizz would make her forget. I need to explain. I don't want her to think I'm a liar, even if I am. "I'm sorry…" I start to apologize, but Dani stops me.

"It isn't your job to lie to me."

It is my job to lie. I'm a fucking liar. If she ever finds out, she'll hate me.

Dani brushes her hair off her face then places her arm across my chest. "Goodnight, Matt." She looks at the sun shining through the blinds. "I mean, good morning." She laughs a soft, tired laugh. Her body may be exhausted, but I know the pill she took will keep her from sleep. Against my better judgement I lift my arm and wrap it around her. I pull her closer and she nuzzles my neck. I concentrate on her breathing, matching it with my own until I drift off to sleep.

24 Dani

The rhythmic sound of running water is soothing. I run my hand over my arms and feel the tiny bumps that cover every inch of my skin. My body is so screwed up that I'm getting goose bumps even though the water is scalding me. Everything is still a blur. I'm just starting to catch glimpses as I replay the day over in my head.

Sleep and thizz don't really mix. My eyes close, my body relaxes, but my brain keeps working. I can never tell if the images, the conversations, or the feelings are real. Or cruel hallucinations. Even after I wake up, nothing *feels* real. Thizz has ruined my reality, everything is questionable. Did I dance with Matt? Was I fantasizing about him kissing me, or did it really happen? I opened my eyes today and found Nick staring down at me. The warmth and glow of his hazel eyes had vanished. He glared at me cuddled next to Matt with a blank, unflinching expression. I unraveled myself from the blanket and sat up. I asked him what time it was. He didn't answer. He asked Matt where his cell phone was. His jaw was tight, the words controlled like he was trying not to explode. Matt found the phone buried under his pillow. Nick snatched it from his hand. "The ringer is off," he snapped. Matt didn't say a word. He just stared at the ground like a remorseful child. "Next time I call," he paused and looked at me. I pretended to be preoccupied with my shoe laces. "Next time I call, you better fucking answer." He shoved the phone in Matt's chest and walked out the door.

We didn't speak on the ride home. He stopped in front of Lucy's and asked me to be ready in an hour. He said we needed to talk. Nick and I don't talk. We chat, we kiss, we thizz. Talking implies something serious, and we don't do serious. We keep it light and fun. The only thing we're serious about is getting high.

I turn off the shower and reach for a towel, thinking about what I would do if Nick broke up with me. It is possible. He did find me sleeping with Matt. We were literally sleeping, but it still might be considered wrong, and that's only because it felt so right. I'm not in the habit of making excuses for my actions. I've never had to until now. I never did anything worth hiding. All I've done since I moved to Eureka is hide. It's why I came here in the first place. I'm sick of it. The only time I feel normal is when I'm not. Thizz makes it easier to pretend my life isn't totally fucked up. I have to pretend a lot less when I'm with Matt. He knows more about me than anyone because I've given him a glimpse of my old life. Nobody knows both sides of me. Being with Matt would make my life a lot easier. So would the box of pills he has hidden in his closet. No longer being Nick Marino's girl wouldn't be so bad if Matt and I could at least be friends. There is only one thing I need to get through the next eight weeks—thizz. I don't see my future without it. Not being with Nick means no longer worrying about my clothes or hair or plucking my eyebrows.

I open the bathroom door and a cloud of steam escapes into the hall. I walk up the creaky stairs to my room, hugging a towel to my damp body. I really need another few hours of sleep to function, but

I don't have time. Nick will be here soon. The only thing that went right today was Lucy not being home when I got here. She left a note on the kitchen counter saying she was at Johnson's. Beside the note was a cell phone. My new cell phone. Now she can get a hold of me whenever she wants.

My skin erupts in goosebumps as I tear through a pile of clothes on the bed. I'm freezing, but I don't know if it's the air or the thizz still disrupting my body temperature. I finally settle on black low-rise jeans and a shirt Lucy bought me during her last shopping spree. It's a black t-shirt with a big glittery D on the chest that makes me look like a craft store super hero.

I pick up my dirty jeans and take out the pills I stole from Matt. I put the pills in my memory box and finish getting dressed, leaving one on the desk.

Nick's car rumbles to a stop outside. I have to get this over with. I grab my Vans, pulling them on without socks. I lift Nick's hoodie from my desk chair and bury my face in it. I've had it a week, but it still smells like him. More like car exhaust than jasmine at this point, but still one hundred percent Nick. I do have feelings for Nick, they just aren't the feelings I want them to be. Nick is a nice guy, he deserves better than me. I lay the hoodie on my bed and leave. I'll keep it as a souvenir.

When I reach the front door, I take a long deep breath before opening it. I've survived worse things than being dumped by a boy.

Nick reaches over from the driver's side and unlocks the door as I approach. I open it and get in. Before I have the door closed, he speaks.

"Look Dani, I'm sorry for being a jerk. I never should have acted the way I did this morning. I guess I was just jealous. You know, seeing you sleeping next to Matt. I want to be the only guy you sleep with."

He leans his head towards me and offers a sexy smile. "I shouldn't have left you." His eyes are cast down, staring at his hand resting on top of mine.

He's sorry? He's apologizing to me? Nick has to be one of the most trusting, forgiving people I've ever met. I wasn't prepared for this. I was so ready for a break-up that I'm disappointed by the apology. He still wants me as his girl. I suddenly regret not doing my hair and taking that pill. If he isn't going to dump me, then we'll probably hang out all afternoon. If he can tell I'm high, he'll ask who gave me the pill, and I don't want to get Matt into trouble.

Nick squeezes my hand and my thoughts come back to him. He's apologizing to me, hoping I'm not mad at him, and I'm thinking about protecting Matt. It looks like my life is about to get a whole lot more complicated. Nick turns my chin and forces me to face him. I'm scared he'll see the betrayal in my eyes for allowing him to feel bad for leaving me. I'll take Matt's company over some stupid frat party any day.

I don't know what to say. Am I supposed to pretend I'm mad? That I care? I really hope this pill kicks in soon so I don't have to care.

"I'm sorry," he whispers as he brushes his lips against mine. He thinks it's his fault I was cuddled in bed with his best friend. I'm the worst girlfriend in the history of girlfriends. I *should* tell him he's wrong. I *should* tell him how I feel about Matt, but I don't. I can't hurt him like that. The truth is cruel, and it will destroy him. I don't want to be responsible for his happiness, for anyone's happiness. The power is too great for someone to have over another person. I thought Nick held the key to my happiness, but I was wrong. It isn't Nick or Matt, or even me. It's thizz. Now that I have my own stash, I'm in control.

I force a smile and kiss Nick on the cheek. The light in his eyes comes flooding back. The nerves in my fingers, the ones gripping

Nick's hand, start to vibrate. The feelings of dread and regret start to fade as my third pill in twenty-four hours starts to kick in.

Nick is a good guy. I should really appreciate his feelings for me. He pulled me from the ashes of my destroyed life and gave me a reason to wake up in the morning. A reason to shower and put on clean socks. I owe it to him to be the girl he thinks I am. I will be the girlfriend he deserves. "I love you," I tell him, wishing to God it didn't feel like a lie. I have feelings for Nick, I just don't know how real they are since every single word I've ever uttered to him, every feeling I've ever had for him, has been on thizz. Me and Nick don't exist without thizz.

He looks at me like I'm the most precious thing in the world. "I know you do." He's so certain my words are real. Maybe he sees something I don't. If Nick feels loved by me, maybe that's enough.

We walk into the Lost Coast Brewery and get seated immediately. Our waiter, who seems overjoyed to be serving us, doesn't bother carding Nick when he orders a beer. They shake hands like they know each other. I don't know why this still surprises me—everyone knows Nick Marino. He might as well have his face on a dollar bill.

I try to hide any sign that the pill I took is kicking in. I place my tongue in between my teeth to keep from grinding and attempt to limit my fidgeting by sitting on my hands. I smile like my jaw doesn't ache as Nick talks about the party he's throwing for his birthday.

Focus, Dani. He's talking about getting Audiodub to play the party. Oh no, that fell through. He's getting a DJ from one of the radio stations based in San Francisco. "That's awesome." I sit up and lean towards the table like I'm really excited. I am. *I love parties.* Especially parties that involve thizz. And Nick plans on making sure his party is epic. While Nick rambles about DJs, I drink half my soda and get a little rush from the caffeine. Our waiter returns a few minutes later and places a plate of nachos on the table. "Let me know if you need anything else." Nick sends him away and digs into the pile of soggy chips.

We eat without much conversation. Nick continues talking about his birthday. He's working up to something, I can tell. He runs his hand nervously through his hair several times. "When I turn eighteen, I get a small inheritance," he says as our waiter reappears.

"Can I get you another beer?" The waiter asks as he lifts Nick's glass from the table. Nick orders a second beer and I decide to try one. Our eager waiter promises the Raspberry Brown Ale is a favorite of all the ladies and disappears to get our drinks.

"I'm going to use the money to go into business with my uncle." He clears his throat.

His uncle owns a bar in North Beach, a few blocks from where I used to live. "You want to invest in your uncle's bar?"

"Well, sort of. His real business is…" he stops when our waiter returns with our drinks.

He sets the glasses on the table and says they are compliments of the gentlemen at the bar. "They said this round is on them." We turn towards the bar, and two large men in leather vests wave at us from across the restaurant.

"Let's go." Nick pulls out a wad of cash. The bundle has to be at least four inches thick. He pulls out a hundred dollar bill and tosses it on the table. "Keep the change," he says. He stands so quickly his chair falls backwards onto the floor. All the color seems to have drained from Nick's face. He takes my hand and I stumble towards the exit.

"Hey thanks," the waiter yells as we bolt out the door.

I try like hell to keep up with Nick as we weave through the crowded sidewalk. "What's going on?"

"I'll explain later," he yells over his shoulder. "Hurry up." Nick is always so chill, like nothing bothers him. Something about those men scared him. And it's scaring me.

"Nick, where you off to so fast, buddy?"

Nick's back stiffens beside me, but he keeps walking. I turn around and see the two men from the bar following us. I run the last few yards to the car.

"Yeah, we were just about to come over and have a drink with ya," the other one says.

For old fat guys, they sure walk fast. Nick stops at my door and unlocks it with his key. Having an old car without automatic door locks really sucks when you're being chased. The lock pops open and Nick hurries to his side to get in. I push the little button on the silver handle to open the door, and I feel a hand on my back. My entire body freezes.

"Let me get that for you, honey." I step away from the scruffy-faced man as he opens my door. "I just need to talk to your boyfriend for a minute," he says with a twisted smile. I look at Nick. He's standing with his car door open, watching the bikers closely. He nods for me to get in the car. I shake my head no. There is no way I'm getting in the car while these men confront Nick. I'm helpless in there. At least out here I can run for help if I have to. Plus, my adrenaline is pumping so hard I can't keep still. I feel like I'm about to explode.

"Suit yourself," the man says and walks towards Nick's side of the car. His vest has "DEVILS GOLD" written across the back.

The other man has already joined Nick on the other side of the car. He is shorter than his friend, but just as burly.

"Do you know who I am?" he asks Nick.

"Santa Clause," Nick smirks. He doesn't sound worried anymore. A minute ago he was dragging me down the street to get away from these two men, and now he's mouthing off. I'll never understand why men, boys, males in general, have to act the exact opposite of how they feel.

"He's got jokes, Teddy," the shorter one says.

"Yeah, he's a fuckin comedian. Are you a comedian, Nicky?" His face is so close to Nick's, it looks like he's going to kiss his cheek. "Or are you just some punk high school baller?"

Nick flinches when Teddy wraps his arm around his shoulders. "What the fuck do you want?"

I don't think Teddy the biker is used to this kind of disrespect. "Your little after-school job is fucking up my business."

What after-school job? Nick doesn't work.

"Last time I checked, Humboldt County was an open market," Nick challenges. I wish he would keep the attitude to a minimum. Pissing off these two men doesn't look like a good idea.

The small guy shifts and clears Nick's line of sight. When Nick sees the terrified look on my face, he pushes Teddy's arm off his shoulders.

"Do you know who I am?" Nick sticks his chest out and stands a little taller, but he's still several inches shorter than Teddy. The men look stunned at Nick's sudden burst of confidence. Neither of them answers Nick's rhetorical question. Nick spins his keys on his finger and says, "Why don't you ask around, then come back and see me." He pushes past the short guy and opens the door. "Get in." He flashes me a reassuring smile. I jump in the car and slam the door. The sound of the car coming to life forces Teddy and his partner to back up. Like me, the bikers are in shock.

As we pull away from the curb, Nick rolls down his window and yells, "Thanks for the beer!" Then he punches the gas, leaving the men in a cloud of white smoke.

The drive to Lucy's is a blur. Nick barely hits the brakes the entire way. He watches the rear view mirror to make sure we aren't being followed. I don't say a word until we pull into Lucy's driveway.

"Do you want to come in?" I ask him.

"Yeah, we should lie low for a minute." He smiles and opens his door. He's acting like nothing is wrong, but I hear anxiety in his voice. "We need to talk."

I look at the pictures of my parents hanging around the room, and I could care less about Nick asking questions about my family. I sit on the edge of Lucy's couch and brace myself for whatever it is Nick is trying to tell me. He paces from the window to the couch, running his hand through his hair. He finally turns around and says, "I sell thizz."

You know when you watch a movie and a bomb goes off, and special effects shows the impact as a pulse that jolts a room, blowing hair back, shattering glass, and knocking someone on their ass? That's what it felt like when Nick said those three words to me. *Boom!* My mind has officially been blown.

"You sell thizz," I repeat to make sure I heard him right. "You're the drug dealer?" I choke on the words. He nods once; his lips are pressed into a line. He's waiting for me to blow up or freak out. I try to keep my expression calm and even because I honestly don't know what I'm feeling.

As if on cue, his phone rings. Only now, I know why. He shoves his hand in the front pocket of his jeans and pulls out his phone. He checks the number and turns off the ringer. "My uncle Will, the one in San Francisco, got me started." He runs his hand through his hair.

"This is what I wanted to tell you at the restaurant. I want to tell you everything about me."

"So, tell me," I say. I want to know the real Nick. Maybe then I can tell him about the real Dani.

"I never knew my parents. My father died in rehab—he snuck in some drugs or someone gave him something and he overdosed." He sits beside me and takes my hand. I have to fight back tears. "Mariann said my mom was a junkie. That she married my father for his money. That wasn't true. Will said she never did drugs and she loved my father." I bite the inside of my already chewed-up cheek to keep the tears in my eyes from spilling over. "When my father went to rehab, Mariann only agreed to help get my mom back on her feet if she signed away her parental rights. She had to do it. My father needed help, and she had no money to live on." His tone turns bitter when he starts to talk about his family's wealth. "My father blew all of his money on drugs. He left my mother with nothing. She had to give Mariann custody of me, but she never thought she would lose me. It was insurance. To prove she wouldn't take the money and run away with me. She never had a chance. Once she signed her parental rights away, Mariann made sure she never saw me again. My grandmother told me all my mother wanted was money, but that wasn't true. She wanted me, and I didn't know until it was too late. She died of cancer when I was thirteen. That's when I met Will and he told me the truth about everything. My mom and dad, how they met, and what kind of woman Mariann Marino really is."

"I'm sorry," I whisper. I don't know what else to say.

Nick kisses my hand. "I'm sorry I didn't tell you about selling thizz. It's just that you seemed to have your own opinion on drug dealers." I think of our first conversation about the pills in K's bedroom. It all makes sense now. "I want to make my own money, have my own legacy. I want nothing to do with Mariann or her money. She let me grow up thinking my mother didn't love me, didn't want me. I'll never forgive her for that."

I can't reply to anything Nick has just said. I'm speechless. He is from one of the most successful, respected families in the state, and he really believes selling thizz is a career he can be proud of. I don't know what to think about that. I'd be a hypocrite to judge him. I have no problem taking the pills that he sells. Does that mean I condone it?

"Are you doing this by yourself?" I start to wonder about the pills in Matt's room. Maybe he was stashing them for Nick.

"No. Matt and Arnie work for me."

"Matt works for you?" Matt's been lying to me too. Lying about Nick and himself. All this time I thought I knew him. I thought I could trust him. A lump forms in my throat.

"Matt's my boy." He smiles proudly.

Matt is your friend. Not mine.

I suddenly realize what kind of danger we were just in. I knew dating Nick could be dangerous, but I was thinking more like getting my ass kicked by girls like Katie. Not being shot by a biker gang. "Those bikers think you're in their territory?"

"Don't worry. Once they find out who I am, they'll be the ones backing off." His arrogance has a whole new meaning. "I wanted to tell you so many times." He stops and kisses my hand. "I had to make sure my plan worked first." Nick smiles, hoping I will too. I offer a weak grin and pretend I'm not freaking out. "Thizz has been so huge that Will says if we partner up, we'll be major players on the West Coast. We can control the thizz market." Nick kneels on the floor in front of me likes he's begging me to see things his way. "I'm not hurting anyone, Dani. You know that," he says. Is he insinuating that

I know more than most because I love thizz? He's right. I'm not hurt by his product. I can't live without it.

Nick's phone buzzes again; he takes it out and checks the number before declining the call. I've been an accessory to his life this entire time, and I didn't even know it. My father would be so disappointed. Being with Nick is such a betrayal to him, to what he stood for. How can I stay with him now that I know? How do I leave knowing he's the only one I know that has thizz?

"You better go. Lucy will be home soon," I lie.

Nick takes my hand and pulls me into his arms. "Is everything cool?"

"Yeah," I say with way more enthusiasm than needed.

He takes my face in his hands and looks into my eyes. "I love you, Dani. This doesn't change anything." This isn't the first time Nick Marino has told me he loves me. But I do believe it is the first time I've *felt* the meaning in his words. If there is one thing I know for sure, it's that Nick Marino cares about me. His love is a gift, one I should appreciate. "Then I don't care that you sell thizz." The words feel like the truth. Being Nick Marino's girl for a little longer doesn't seem like a bad idea anymore.

Nick stands and I walk him to the door. "So, does this mean I get an unlimited supply?" I'm joking, but Nick doesn't seem to think so.

Nick grabs my shoulder and turns me to face him. "No. We don't get high on our supply. We can party like we've been doing. Once or twice a week is fine, that's it."

His words make me feel two inches tall. "Ok," I say quietly and bite back tears.

"Sorry, I didn't mean to snap. I don't want any of my friends, especially you, taking pills like that. Just like I wouldn't want you drinking every day. It's the same thing. You feel me?" Nick never talks to me like this. I don't like it. I just want him to leave so I can do whatever the hell I want.

"I understand." I fake-smile and kiss him goodbye as the pill I took sends another jolt of pleasure through my body.

Nick leaves, and I go to my room and lie down. Things start to make sense. All the phone calls, the errands. All the lies Matt has told me. I wonder if he really is going to Stanford. I want to call him out, but what's the point. Matt doesn't owe me anything.

25
Matt

I'm sitting in the diner having lunch with Ashley when Nick comes flying around the corner. He would never drive like that through town and risk getting pulled over. Everyone knows his car; it isn't like he can outrun the cops. If they don't catch him on the street, they'll just show up at his house.

Something must be wrong.

I settle our check while Ashely packs our food in a Styrofoam container. She is about to burst when I head back to the table. "Why is Nick driving like someone is chasing him?"

"I don't know. Just hurry up." I usher my sister to the car and listen for sirens. I don't hear anything. That's good news.

I start my mom's Audi and back out of the lot, unsure of where I'm going. I dial Nick's number—no answer. I turn right and drive towards home, toying with the possibility of leaving Ashley while I go find Nick. My parents are at a wedding. They left me strict instructions not to leave Ashely alone, but I have to make sure everything is ok. I need to know Dani is safe. Suddenly a thought crosses my mind. What if Nick isn't outrunning someone, what if he is in a rush to get Dani home? What if he is so upset that he can't wait to get her out of his car? I make a U-turn at the next light and head towards Dani's house. I want to be there for her just in case something has happened between them.

I can't deny something almost happened between us last night. I'm happy I didn't let Dani do something she would've regretted. Not that she wanted to. But it sure as hell seemed that way. I'll try Nick one more time. If he doesn't pick up, I'll drive to Dani's and check on her. Ashley can wait in the car. The angst I'm feeling when I dial the phone causes my legs to shake. Part of me wants Nick to be ok, but another part of me wishes for something else. Ashley sighs when I make another U-turn. I'm driving in circles waiting for Nick to answer his phone. I dial again. It takes me a few seconds to realize he's picked up. "Nick!" I shout. "I saw you blast by the diner, what the fuck is going on?"

"I need to talk to you. Can I come by?"

I tell him to meet me at my place and make another U-turn. He was short, like he wanted to get off the phone, but he didn't sound upset. We get to the house and I tell Ashely to go upstairs while I wait outside. If there is even a remote possibility that Dani broke up with him, he won't be coming over here to talk. Not after the way he looked this morning when he saw me and Dani sleeping in my bed.

As soon as I opened my eyes and saw the look on his face, I knew he was about to blow. I've watched more guys shit their pants over that dead look in Nick's eyes than when he raises his fist towards their face. I've seen dudes beg for mercy, and occasionally even run for their lives when Nick whirls around on them with his clenched jaw and wild eyes. Yeah, I know that look. I've just never seen it directed at me. I would never fight Nick, not over Dani or anything. The question is, would he fight me?

My heart is in my throat when he finally pulls behind my mom's Audi. Nick jumps out of the car with his arms stretched out like he's trying to hug the world. "I told Dani."

I exhale when I see the goofy smile on his face. "You told her what?"

He quiets his voice and steps closer to me. "I told Dani we sell thizz."

I catch the word "we" and feel the burger I just ate move up my throat. "You told her about all of us?"

"Yeah!"

He tells me we don't have to lie anymore or sneak around behind Dani's back, because she's cool with it. I congratulate him and silently curse him under my breath.

"She was surprised at first, especially when I told her you worked for me." Nick smirks and punches me in the arm.

"Really? Why? What did she say?" *She hates me. I know it.*

"She was just surprised. Who wouldn't be? You're sort of a school boy," he teases. When I don't smile, he clutches my shoulders. "Don't worry, everything's cool now." Nick can do no wrong in Dani's eyes, but I'm a different story. I'm her friend and I've been lying to her, covering for him, this whole time.

"You were right; I should've just told her. It would have saved me a lot of aggravation." He mumbles the last part more to himself.

My eagerness to call Dani is gone. I don't even know if I can face her right now. I can barely look Nick in the eye. I can't believe I ever considered breaking Nick's trust.

"Hey Ash." Nick looks past me into the door. "Is she ok?" he whispers.

"Yeah, she was just freaked out when we saw you drive by the diner like you were being chased."

"Oh shit! I was being chased. A couple of those Devil's Gold assholes were trying to punk me."

I feel all the blood drain from my face at the mention of the bikers.

Nick pats my back. "Don't worry, dude. I already called Will. He's going to take care of it."

Will Walker may be powerful in the Bay Area, but up here, the bikers run everything.

Two days later, Nick and I are sitting in Will's bar discussing how to handle the Devil's Gold Crew. This is not how I wanted to spend my spring break. The Devil's Gold are an old-school biker gang that runs most of Northern California. They didn't appreciate Nick's disrespectful attitude during the confrontation at Lost Coast, so Will's having a difficult time forming a truce. Technically, Nick is dealing on the Devil's Gold territory without permission. If Will had gone to them in the beginning of all this and told them he was branching out, they could have come to some sort of agreement. Money would have exchanged hands and we would've been legit. Of course, lines would have been drawn. Nick wouldn't have free range like he does now, but at least we wouldn't be on the verge of a war. The Devil's Gold doesn't even sell ecstasy; they mainly deal with weed, cocaine, and meth, but I guess someone's girlfriend scored pills off of us and brought them to a biker event. When everyone started thizzin and nobody wanted to buy their products, the bikers came looking for us. If Nick wasn't Will Walker's nephew, he'd be buried in a ditch, and whoever happened to be riding in his car would be right alongside him.

"Don't worry, I'll work it out." Will takes a pull on his beer and rolls his neck like a boxer. I think it's a nervous tick. "But you know this means they get a cut."

Nick shakes his head. "That's bullshit. It's a free market. I don't see why we have to pay them a fucking dime."

"See, Nicky. You're still thinking like a legit businessman. There is nothing free about our market. Once you start thinking that way, someone comes in and steals your business. And they take over by taking your life. We have to fight for every inch of pavement we have. There are no laws to protect us. We protect ourselves." Will pats his side, where his gun is hidden by his jacket. "Don't worry about the politics, just keep building your brand. Make sure everyone knows where the good shit is. The last thing we need is competition. I have my supplier on lock; he won't sell to those pricks. But that doesn't mean they won't find another source. I've heard some good things about product coming out of Oregon. They don't press the powder into pills, they're putting it in capsules. It hits harder and it's easier to make. I'm working on some connections up there now. If everything goes right, we'll have the entire West Coast high on our shit." Will holds out his fist and Nick bumps it with his.

"Don't worry, everyone knows where to go for thizz in Humboldt," Nick says arrogantly. He looks at me and I fake a smile. This isn't fun anymore. I want out, but I doubt I even have that option. What's worse, Dani is part of this too.

Will is giving Nick the name and phone number of a contact he has in Lake County when two men walk into the bar. The younger guy is wearing baggy jeans and an oversized San Francisco Giants jacket. He could have been any random hoodlum just stopping in for a beer if it wasn't for the badge dangling from a silver chain around his neck. The other guy has on a dark blue polo shirt and khaki Dockers.

He looks like someone my dad would golf with. Neither man says a word. They just sit down and wait to be noticed.

"What the fuck do they want now?" Will snarls.

"Is everything ok?" I ask as the cops stare at us from the bar.

"Don't piss your pants, kid." Will fills a shot glass and hands it to me. "Wait here." He stands up and walks casually to the bar like he has nothing to hide. "Sandy, get these nice officers a drink." Will says the word officer loud enough for the whole bar to hear. A few customers make a hasty exit, while others turn their faces in the other direction.

Sandy puts her book down and stands in front of the cops with a hand on her hip. "What do you want?"

"Two diet cokes," the older one says, reaching for his wallet.

"It's on me, Ed. I still owe ya." Will pats his back. "Who's your new partner?" Will sits next to the older cop like they're old friends.

"This is Officer Taylor," Ed replies. He glances back at me and Nick.

I put my head down, hoping he can't get a good look at my face in the mirror. Nick does the same and pours both of us another shot. The last thing either of us are worried about is being carded. Nick quickly slides a bag of pills into his pocket.

"So, to what do I owe the pleasure?" Will asks sarcastically, drawing Ed's attention away from our table.

Ed shrugs Will's hand off his shoulder. "I hear you're hanging out with a fancier crowd lately."

"I'd hardly call this crowd fancy," Will smirks.

"I'll give you that," Officer Taylor agrees, taking in the dirty patrons that litter the bar.

"Yeah, well maybe that's because your lawyer buddy ended up

dead." Ed looks back at our table again. I pretend to cough and cover my mouth with my hand in a terrible attempt to hide my face.

"I don't know what you're talking about." Will seems confused by the cop's statement.

"Sure you do. You had a nice chat behind the bar. You were going over a case together. What was it?" Ed pretends to ask his partner, who remains quiet. "Oh yeah, it was Devon Brown's case." Ed suddenly recalls. "What I want to know is why you were discussing Devon's case with his lawyer?"

Will leans on the bar and pops a peanut in his mouth before replying, "I have no idea what you're talking about."

"Sure you do, it was the night Saggy Sam got popped for stabbing the homeless guy on Romolo Street." Ed takes a long sip of the soda Sandy set in front of him.

"I remember the night, but I don't know the guy." Will's patience seems to be wearing thin.

"Batista, Bill Batista was his name. He was a great guy to know in your line of work. He didn't care what kind of scumbag he was defending, as long as he got paid." Officer Taylor shifts on his stool and clears his throat like he's warning his partner, but Ed continues. "Getting Devon off on a third-strike felony must have been a huge payday for him. Every punk in the state would've been knocking on his door."

"I could've used a guy like that." Will smirks and jiggles the change in his pocket.

"Yeah, too bad some piece of shit shot him. Killed his wife, too."

I look at Nick; he meets my wide eyes with a pair of his own. Fuck, this sounds a little too familiar. Dani said her parents were shot in a car-jacking. It's one hellava coincidence. But Dani's last name is DiMarco, not Batista.

Will flicks the peanuts around the bowl with his finger, and then defiantly pops a nut in his mouth. He looks up from the bowl with a sinister grin. "Let me guess, you pinched some crackhead that's trying to make a deal by feeding you some bullshit story about me." He laughs at the officers' frustrated expressions.

Ed sets his glass down with a loud thump. "We have a witness that says you were pretty pissed off at this Batista fellow. He said you were going on and on about paying him to lose the case."

Will glances back at our table to see if we're listening, Nick nods and Will grins, pausing for a second before answering. "You know what I think, Ed?"

"I'd love to know what you think." Ed looks amused, like he's about to get what he came for.

"I think you're desperate." Ed's smile fades as quickly as it appeared. "I think you're still trying to dig your way out of the shit hole you created when you screwed that pretty little redheaded juror at my trial. I think you want me, and you'll do anything to get me." Will gets closer to Ed and lowers his voice. "Tell me, was she worth it?"

Will and Ed stare each other down, neither man acknowledging or denying anything the other is saying. The wannabe lawyer in me is freaking out. I thought conversations like this only happened in the movies.

Taylor stands and places his hand on Ed's shoulder. "We just wanted to stop by and see if you had any information." Ed puts his hand up to stop his partner from speaking.

"I'd lock up my mother if it meant getting you off the street. I didn't know she was a juror on your case. If I had, I wouldn't have touched her. For all I know, she was a con. She conned me into sleeping with her to cause the mistrial. I wouldn't be surprised if she was just some Polk Street whore."

"I bet she was worth every penny." Will grins.

Ed stands up quickly, prompting his partner to jump between the two men. "That's a mistake I'll never live down," Ed hisses. "It's also something I plan on rectifying. You're right; I won't stop until you're put away for life!"

Will snickers at Ed's threat. "Drinks are on me." He flashes a toothy grin as he backs away from the bar. "You can show yourselves out."

Officer Taylor tosses a couple of dollars on the bar while pushing Ed towards the exit. They are halfway out the door when Ed stops. "Wait, I didn't tell you the good news," he shouts. "Their daughter is fine."

Will pauses slightly, but doesn't turn around. His reaction doesn't surprise me, its Ed's partner that looks freaked out. Officer Taylor shakes his head and takes a deep breath, looking towards the sky like a rain of grief is about to be poured on their heads. His reaction to Ed's statement tells me this is information he shouldn't be disclosing.

"Apparently she was lying in the back seat, so the gunman missed her or didn't see her. Either way, she's really anxious to catch the asshole that killed her parents."

Will doesn't flinch. "Like I said, I never heard of the guy. But, I do know another lawyer, Martin Randall; I can call him now if you want to continue this conversation in his presence?" He pulls his cell phone from his pocket.

"We're leaving," Taylor says sternly and pushes Ed out the door.

"Have a nice day, and stay safe," Will's voice drips with sarcasm. When the cops are out the door, he flips them off with both hands. He walks back to our table and sits down. "Fuckin pigs have nothing better to do than fuck with me." Will takes a shot of Patron and curses under his breath.

"What are they talking about?" Nick asks anxiously.

The calm and collected demeanor Will displayed in front of the cops is gone. He takes another shot of tequila and slams the glass on the table.

"Don't worry about it, they're just fishing. If they had a witness, I'd be in cuffs." Will stares at the paint-chipped wall. Something they said got to him. "Fuck it," he finally snaps. "You guys need to get out of here." Will shakes my hand and hugs Nick. Then walks into his office and slams the door so hard it rattles the bottles behind the bar. I'm starting to think I work for a murderer.

26
Dani

I let Arnie have shotgun. I don't feel all that comfortable riding in the front seat anymore. Not since I found out Nick is a drug dealer. I thought long and hard about Nick (and Matt) selling thizz. They aren't forcing pills down anyone's throat. If anything, thizz is making Eureka a better place to live. At least for me, anyway.

Nick has spent every free second and even his unfree ones with me by his side. He let me tag along on a run to a fraternity at Humboldt State this morning. I have to admit, the whole transaction was anticlimactic. We walked into the frat house, dropped a bag on the table, Nick took a stack of cash from the president of the fraternity, and we left. Totally boring.

I thought we'd spend spring break partying every day—that was the plan, until those bikers showed up. Now everyone is freaking out. If it wasn't for the pills I stole from Matt, I don't know if I could've made it through the last two days. Finding out your boyfriend and his friends are the town drug dealers is a lot to digest. Add that to the fact that I still have no letter from CAL—it's a miracle I haven't slit my wrists.

We pull into an underground garage and park next to a convertible S-class Mercedes. Arnie jumps out and greets the driver, Aurora, the newest member of Nick's crew.

"What's up, baby." He kisses her cheek.

She presses her alarm and quickly ducks into Nick's car. She's wearing a black scarf around her head and oversized sunglasses, like she's in a spy movie. When she sees me in the backseat she smirks. "I see why you're late. Picking up chicks at the mall again, Arnie?"

"No, that's just Dani," Arnie informs her as she climbs into the backseat next to me. "You know, Nick's girlfriend."

Her smirk turns to intrigue. "So, this is the girl that stole Nicky's heart?" She places her hand on my knee. "You know how many girls would give their left tit to be with Nick? Whatever you got, I want some," she says in a velvety soft voice.

I'm perplexed by her statement. Is she saying she wants me or Nick?

"Ah, don't I satisfy you, baby?" Arnie sounds wounded as we pull out of the parking lot.

Aurora pulls her sunglasses down. Her blue iridescent contacts glimmer in the sunlight. She places her hand to her glistening red lips and fakes a yawn. "From what I can remember, you were vaguely entertaining." She winks at me and we share a quiet giggle at Arnie's expense.

I'm engrossed in Aurora's retelling of the last time she had her nails done. Apparently, the incompetent salon was out of her favorite shade of polish and thought they could slip one by her. "It definitely had more of a carnation pink than the bubble gum pink I usually get," she recounts. I hide my chewed nails between my thighs. "There is a great day spa in Eureka, I can't remember the name." She looks in the air as if it's dangling there waiting to be pulled from a shelf. Her story is interrupted when Nick turns off the car. I look out the window and realize that we're in Matt's driveway.

"Sorry to break up the princess party, but we're here." Arnie pushes the seat forward so we can get out.

I haven't seen Matt since Saturday. The day Nick found us sleeping together. The day the bikers chased us from Lost Coast. The day Nick told me he sold thizz. It was a trifecta of fucked-up shit. I don't know if he's kept his distance because I found out he's a liar or if he's freaked out about what almost happened between us. I'm not mad that Matt was lying to me. He was keeping Nick's secret the same way I asked him to keep mine from Nick. As for how I acted in his room, I'm blaming that on thizz. The electricity that passed between us when he held my hips, the way my body tingled when I cuddled beside him on his bed—it was all brought on by thizz. I didn't feel anything other than utter humiliation once I was sober. I don't want to ever be alone with him again. I can't be. Ever.

I'm standing in back of the crowd while Arnie jabs at the doorbell likes he's playing one of his video games. *Hopefully, he won't see me back here*. He'll be too busy with their meeting to notice me. Hopefully. Suddenly the door flies open and Matt stands in his doorway—shirtless. His sweatpants hang low on his waist and his hair is disheveled like he just rolled out of bed. Aurora sucks in a breath in front of me. She's wearing sunglasses, but I know exactly where her eyes are focused. I check my chin for drool.

"What the fuck, sleeping beauty?" Nick breaks the silence.

"Hey," Matt runs his hand through his hair as Arnie pushes past him into the house. Matt turns quickly and follows him inside.

Aurora walks in ahead of me and stops in front of Matt to introduce herself. He's standing in front of his bedroom door, guarding it like he has something precious hidden inside.

"I'm Aurora, it's nice to finally meet you," she says then plants a kiss on his cheek. Matt mumbles nice to meet you as Aurora follows Arnie into the living room.

I'm trying to decipher Matt's strange behavior when I notice a faint red streak across his mouth. It isn't from Aurora, her lipstick is flawless. "Are you ok?" I ask as he continues to shield his door.

"Uh, yeah I'm fine." He crosses his arms in front of his bare chest. I sense his embarrassment and divert my eyes from his body. *Which is so naturally perfect in every way.*

"Dude, what the fuck?" The sound of Nick's voice startles me and I step aside. Matt reaches for the handle and stops Nick from turning it. He opens his mouth to object but it's useless—this is Nick. Matt reluctantly moves his hand and his eyes drop to the floor.

"Hey!" A curly-haired girl is sitting in Matt's bed. Another head appears from under the covers. She looks at us then turns over, taking the blanket with her, exposing her friend's breasts.

"Oopsie." The girl laughs as she covers up with a pillow.

I walk down the hall and into the living room in shock. The girl looks familiar. I'm trying to place her when I step on something squishy. Arnie is tossing grapes into the air and catching them in his mouth like a trained seal. Grapes pepper the ground near his chair.

"What's up with Matt? Is he watching porn?" Arnie jokes as he throws another grape in the air and catches it in his mouth.

"Dani, I remembered the name of the spa. It's Lady Luxe, have you heard of it?" Aurora is rambling about getting her roots done while Arnie flips the channels on the TV—both of them oblivious to what is happening a few feet away.

I remember the girl. She was at K's party. The girl with the cups in the kitchen. *What was her name?* Alisa something. Martinez, its Martinez. The other one is her cousin. "Oh. My. God!"

"He was watching porn! That dirty bastard." Arnie hurdles the coffee table in one leap on his way to Matt's room.

"No," I correct him. "He's not watching porn. Well, I guess you could say that if he was just watching, but I'm sure he was participating." Arnie stops his pursuit to listen to my incoherent rambling. "Matt isn't watching porn, he's making porn." I sit on the edge of the sofa and pluck a grape from the bowl on the table. I bite into it, allowing the cool juice to moisten my dry mouth.

"What do you mean?" Now Aurora is intrigued by my evasive remarks.

I swallow the grape and pop another in my mouth. "Matt is in there with the Martinez cousins."

Arnie lets out a loud whooping laugh as he enters the hallway. "That's my BOY!"

Aurora sits beside me on the sofa and takes a grape from the bowl. "You should really get your nails done."

27
Matt

My parents and Ashley went to visit my grandmother in Sacramento for spring break, so I have the house to myself. I really wanted to go. I haven't seen my gram since Christmas, but Nick needs me here. This shit with the Devil's Gold is heating up. It's been three days since our meeting with Will, and he still hasn't made a deal with those assholes. Which is why I think Nick's a fucking idiot for letting Dani ride with him on a run this morning. His number-one priority shouldn't be locking down territory, it should be her safety. It was just a drop at a fraternity, but you never know what could happen.

I walk outside to check the mail. If I don't get into Stanford, joining Nick's crew was for nothing. I have to get in, and when I do, the money I've earned will help me survive. Because that's what this is all about—survival. Surviving high school, surviving Nick, hell, even surviving Dani. I can't shake her no matter how hard I try. I haven't seen her all week, but it doesn't stop me from dreaming about her every night. Her hair, her eyes, her lips, and the way she smells like burnt coffee and lavender. I caught myself sniffing my mom's coffee cup the other day just to get a whiff of something that reminded me of Dani. Which is exactly why I have to stay away.

I walk to the end of the driveway and open the mailbox. I pull out three envelopes, none of them from Stanford. As I'm walking back to the house, a white car pulls up behind me. I pick up the pace. I don't think the Devil's Gold knows anything about me or where I live, but you never know. I hop onto the porch and push open the door. I'm about to close it when someone calls my name. It's not the voice of a biker or a hit man. It's a chick. I open the door and find Alisa Martinez's curly head hanging out the passenger window. We hooked up at K's party, after Dani and Nick left. I haven't seen her since. She goes to St. Bernard's, so I knew I wouldn't have to worry about her following me around at school. I never even got her number. That was kind of a dick move, but she didn't seem to mind.

"I thought that was you!" She tells her cousin Amy to pull over, then gets out and skips to the front door.

I'm so fucking happy she isn't some asshole trying to shoot me, I overlook the fact that she was probably stalking me and invite them in. Alisa looks like one of those hot chicks in a rap video, and her cousin is just as built. After a few shots of rum and a joint, I'm feeling pretty nice. I don't need the thizz, but I give the girls one when they ask. Half an hour after the pills kick in, the three of us are tangled up on my bed. A few hours later I wake to the sound of bells and Alisa shaking me with her foot. "Get the door," she mumbles from somewhere under the covers.

I climb over the girls and slide on my sweats. The ringing is non-stop now. There's only one person who rings my bell like that. I fling open the front door ready to sock Arnie in the chest.

I don't see Arnie.

I don't see anyone but Dani.

A few minutes later, she sees Alisa and Amy in my bed, and I go to the bathroom and puke. I send the girls home, and Nick starts our meeting. Aurora isn't the only new addition. Alex, the guy Will hooked us up with, is here too. He's a thirty-two-year-old stoner from Lake County who looks like he hasn't showered in a month.

"Alex, you'll be working Lake County. Aurora will be heading up the Humboldt State operation and a few surrounding areas. Arnie, you keep doing what you're doing, and Matt, you'll be with me." Nick hands out new cell phones and reminds everyone they need to watch their minutes. "I know I've said this before, but it needs to be said again. Thizz is our business, it's a product we sell to make money. We don't get high on our own supply. When we party, we do it in a controlled environment. We don't act a fool, we have to stay in control." Nick looks at Arnie when he says the last bit. He's been on a few binges lately. His father has been on him to join the army. We've been hearing about this since freshman year, but now he's serious. Arnie will be eighteen this summer, and with no plans to go to college, it doesn't look like his old man is going to let up. Arnie nods in agreement. It's cool that Nick didn't bust him out in front of Aurora and Alex. Then again, Nick is cool like that.

Nick ends the meeting and takes Alex into my room to count out the pills he is taking back to Clearlake, and the rest of us fall into pockets of conversation. Dani won't look at me. I don't even want to look at myself. I pull my beanie down until it's just above my eyebrows. My head is pounding. I want to crawl back in bed and sleep until spring break is over.

I hear Aurora brag to Dani about her new car and her plans to travel to Europe after she graduates from college and I look up. Why is she even here? I pull Arnie aside to complain. "She drives an eighty-thousand-dollar Mercedes, what does she need to sell thizz for?" Aurora looks up like she heard me. I don't care. "She's just a bored rich girl that wants to play badass."

"Dude, listen to what you just said. You could be talking about Nick." Arnie's right. Nick doesn't need this lifestyle either. He doesn't sell drugs out of necessity, and that's what worries me. I always believed he would stop once we graduated. We had plans to go to Stanford together, and he didn't even apply. Even if Nick leaves Eureka, it won't be for school. It will be for the two most important things in his life. Thizz and Dani.

Nick finishes up in my room and walks Alex out. When he comes back, he motions for me to join him in the kitchen. As soon as the door swings closed he says, "We might have a problem."

I pull an oatmeal cookie from the bag on the table and pop it in my mouth. Ashely must have left them down here for me. "What kind of problem?"

"The Devil's Gold is putting up some resistance. They don't like me very much." Nick smiles like it's something to be proud of. I choke on the dry crumbs. Nick pulls a bottle of water from the fridge and tosses it to me. "Don't worry, Will's working on it, but I wanted to give you a heads-up."

I nod as I gulp down the entire bottle of water. I crumple the bottle and toss it in the sink. "Are they coming after you, us?"

"No, hell no. They don't have the balls. You know who I am?" He puffs his chest out and flexes.

He's pretending it's no big deal, but he wouldn't be telling me this if there wasn't something to worry about. "Can you be serious?"

"Will told the Devil's Gold president that he'd put Eureka on pause while they're negotiating, out of good faith. That's why I have Alex and Aurora running shit from out of town. Arnie is using some guy he knows in Arcata to sell his shit. This way we can lie low."

I take a deep breath and tell him I have no problem lying low. The lower the better.

"There's one more thing." Nick leans on the sink and runs his hand through his hair. This must be the real bad news. "Will's worried that Devon, his old partner, will find out about our beef with the bikers and make them a counter offer. If the bikers back Devon, they'll give him Eureka and all of Humboldt County. If that happens, Devon will try to move in on Will's action in the city, and Will won't stand a chance. With all the heat he's getting about that dead lawyer, the last thing he needs is a war."

"I thought they were fishing?" I feel a burning sensation in my throat.

"Yeah well, they caught something. Will found out the witness is real. He's got his guys looking for her now." Nick opens the fridge again and rummages around for something to eat while I'm fighting the urge to puke.

"You think Will shot those people?"

"I don't know, probably." Nick shrugs as he pulls another bottle of water from the shelf and tosses it to me. "My uncle is old-school. He has his ways of dealing with shit. Good and bad."

I crack it open and take a huge drink. I let out a loud burp and fan the air in front of me. "Fuckin rum." It isn't just the regurgitated alcohol making me sick. "What's he going to do with the witness if he finds her?"

Nick looks at me like I'm an idiot. "What do you think he's going to do?"

A cold chill runs up my back at the thought of some innocent girl being hunted by Will Walker. What makes it worse is the fact that I'm not doing anything to stop him. *What can I do?* For all I know, Will is just paranoid. The cops have no evidence it was him; if they did, he'd be in jail.

"None of this bothers you?" I look at my best friend, the guy that cried when we were six because he nailed a squirrel with a baseball, who is acting like murdering innocent people is no big deal.

"Yeah, I know." He runs his hand through his hair. "It's fucked up, but what can we do? It isn't like I can tell Will how to run his life. I respect my uncle. If that means turning a cheek when some bad shit goes down, then I will. But I don't plan on following in his footsteps."

"Well, that's a fucking relief." It is, it really is. Nick isn't a killer or even a gangster. He's just a fucked up kid with a really fucked up role model. Unfortunately, Will can do no wrong in Nick's eyes.

"Sorry to interrupt." Dani pokes her head into the room. "Aurora needs to go. She has an appointment."

Nick rolls his eyes and I give him an I-told-you-so look. "Give us a minute, babe." Nick winks at Dani, and she disappears without looking at me. "I gotta get this girl back before she drives me crazy. I just wanted to let you know what's up. I got your back." Nick gives me a bro hug and says it's best not to tell anyone about Devon or the cops. By anyone, he means Dani. I agree. She's in enough danger as it is with the bikers on our ass.

"Why don't you call those chicks back to keep you company," Nick jokes as we walk to the door. "It's a shame you have the house to yourself and you'll be all alone."

Dani brushes past me without saying goodbye.

"Nah, I'm just going to crash."

"Alright then, later dude." He waves as he gets in the car.

I watch Nick drive away, hoping he isn't stupid enough to get into another confrontation with the bikers, not with Dani in the car. Who knows what will happen next time. Nick's first priority should be Dani's safety. I hope for her sake he does everything he can to make sure nobody ever hurts her. I also hope the daughter of the people Will shot is somewhere safe, someplace he will never find her.

28 Dani

I pull my memory box off the shelf and open it. The box was a gift from my parents on my twelfth birthday. I don't have jewelry, so I crammed it with birthday cards and old photos. It's the only memento I let Lucy bring me from home. I didn't want anything else. I would have driven out of the city with the clothes on my back if it weren't for Lucy. She spent all night driving to San Francisco to pick me up from the police station the night of the shooting, and I wouldn't even let her rest a few hours before heading back to Eureka. I couldn't wait to leave the city, leave everything that happened behind.

I don't know who called the police. They showed up within minutes of the gunshots. My ears were still ringing when the swirling red lights came from three directions and surrounded my father's Denali. They yelled for me to put my hands up, they asked if I had a weapon. After they figured out I wasn't involved and realized I had just lost both of my parents, they left me alone. I sat in a room used to interrogate criminals for six hours waiting for Lucy. I thought about the last movie we saw, the last meal we shared. I wondered how long it had been since my mother kissed me goodnight or held my father's hand when we walked down the street. I couldn't even remember the last time I told them I loved them that wasn't written in a card. The night I told Nick I loved him was the first time I uttered those words to another person since I was ten years old.

The first few weeks I pretended they were on some exotic vacation without me. It was easier to hate them than miss them. Only I could never hate them. They were the most loveable, likeable people on the planet. They were perfect, and I never lived up to their expectations. My grades, my hobbies, my hair, nothing was ever good enough. Not that they told me I was a disappointment as a daughter. I just was. I hated my mother's charity events; they were boring and lasted forever. I usually had to dress in some dipshit-looking dress that fit too tight around the waist, especially after I attacked the snack table. Even though my father believed his clientele were good people at heart, I was still afraid when they came to his home office. I would always lock the door to the main house and hide in my room until they left. I'm not one of those people that see the good in others. My parents met at CAL and they were saints. I imagined walking onto the CAL campus and being magically transformed into a socially and environmentally conscience liberal out to save the world from injustice and the use of plastic water bottles. That was my goal. Is my goal. Only now I don't see a future without Nick or thizz. They sort of go hand in hand. I don't think of one without the other. How can I?

In the bottom of my memory box is a pack of my father's favorite gum—Big Red. I pull out the gum and dump the pills I swiped from Matt into my hand. I place one in my mouth and swallow with a swig from an old water bottle next to my bed. I didn't plan on popping alone, but Nick had to go out of town with Arnie to make a drop, and the meeting at Matt's house was just a meeting. A very eye-opening one at that. Seeing those girls in Matt's bed made me realize I was right all along. Matt doesn't want me. He never did. I really thought, maybe, Matt had feelings for me. *What do I know?* I didn't even notice my boyfriend and his friends were drug dealers. My perception of the world is seriously warped. I should blame thizz, but I don't. Thizz is the only thing that makes sense to me. It puts a smile on my face. A happy thought in my head. Thizz is my best friend.

I feel the pill kicking in when my fingers start to tingle. The rush isn't like it was a week ago. Every time is less powerful than the last. I need something to help stimulate the feelings. Music. I turn on the radio and Fergie's "London Bridges" is on. It reminds me of Heather. I have to admit, she's been less of a bitch since the night we thizzed. And now I know that Nick wasn't at the beach with her, so I let myself keep an open mind to this new and improved version of Heather King. I pull a slip of paper from my desk drawer and go downstairs to use the phone in the hall. She answers on the third ring. "Hi Heather, its Dani."

"Uh, hi." She sounds very surprised to hear my voice.

"I was just wondering if you wanted to come over, for like, a girls' night." I contemplate telling her I have pills. *Would that be weird?*

"I can't, I'm grounded," Heather whispers into the phone. "My mom found my journal and flipped out." She tells me she mentioned getting high and my heart stops. "She is threatening to send me away to some reform school our church has in Mexico."

My heart is beating out of my chest, and not in a good way. "Does she know who you were with? What you took?"

"No, I'm not that stupid. It wasn't like I was broadcasting it on Myspace. Don't worry, I didn't mention your name. I don't think she even knows when I wrote it. I already told Arnie; he knows I would never rat him out."

"What is up with you and Arnie?" She said Arnie wouldn't let her take thizz, so he must care about her. They never did more than grope each other the night we took thizz, but it was more of a friendly groping.

"Our fathers grew up together, so we've been friends our whole lives. He's like a big brother to me. We have this stupid pact that we'll marry each other when we turn thirty." She laughs, but I can tell it's something that means a lot to her. To both of them probably.

"That's so sweet!" I gush. *Oh shit, the thizz is really kicking in.*

"Yeah, he really is a nice guy, once you get to know him."

I really hope I get to see that side of him one day.

"I'm sorry I can't hang out. I'll try to stop by the café this week to say hi." I hear a knock on a door and Heather says she has to go. "Check your Myspace, it's the only way I can communicate without my parents snooping."

I tell her I will and we hang up. Heather really has everyone at school fooled into thinking she's this socialite, sneaking into clubs and partying. She went out one night and her parents are ready to ship her off to Mexico. I was wrong about Heather. She's just as fucked-up as the rest of us.

I lie across my bed and pull out a piece of my father's favorite gum. I fold it into my mouth with a sigh. My boyfriend ditched me to meet his uncle, my best friend is having a threesome with the town sluts, and the girl that's made my life a living hell since the day we met has turned out to be sort of nice. Can things be more fucked up?

I rummage through my desk and pull Nick's Audiodub CD from its case. I borrowed it from him and never gave it back. My CD, along with my CD player, was never retrieved from my father's SUV. I place the disc in my computer and crank the speakers as loud as they will go. "The Story that Never Ends" fills the room. The familiarity of the rhythm is like a hug from an old friend. Halfway through the second chorus, the phone rings. I storm down the steps to the hall and answer it.

"Dani, thank God you're home! Can you close tonight?" Mary's voice sounds twenty times worse on the phone. "I just got invited to a party and my parents are actually letting me go," she squeals. "I'll owe you, please!"

I want to say no, I want to tell her to piss off, but that isn't what comes out. "Sure! I'll be right there!" Empathy—a side effect of ecstasy.

The twenty minute walk takes ten minutes. I run all the way. I open the door to the café and steady myself to act normal in front of Mary. Three girls are fixing their makeup in the mirror on the wall.

Mary comes out of the storage room looking like she's headed for a red carpet event. She throws her arms around me and I hug her back. Her gratefulness makes me happy. I feel like I've done something right. The praise induces another surge of serotonin.

I let her go and step back to admire her dress. "You look amazing."

"Thanks." She steps away, remembering who I am, who she is, and the mutual disgust we usually display for each other.

I think maybe I should insult her so she doesn't think I'm acting weird, but I can't think of anything clever to say. So I grab the bar rag from the counter and begin wiping things. The social aspect of thizz has me longing to join Mary and her friends in their inane conversations about hairspray and eyeliner. "Where is the party at tonight?" I ask nobody in particular.

"You wouldn't know her," a snotty girl answers. A few of the others sneer in my direction then turn back to the mirror with lip gloss in hand.

"I was just making conversation." I turn from the counter and ferociously wipe down the train. Mary never bothers to clean the dried milk from the steamer or wipe coffee grounds from the counter. I don't care where those bitches are going anyway. I'm sure wherever it is, it's going to be lame.

"It's a girl that goes to our school," Mary says ruefully as she places three empty mugs in the sink. She hands me a fresh towel and offers an apologetic smile. "She comes in sometimes. Her name is Alisa."

My head whips around at the sound of her name. "Alisa Martinez," I hiss. Alisa has been in the café? I guess I never really pay attention to the people plucking coffee cups from the counter.

"You know her?" one of the girls in the group asks, as if my knowing Alisa was the most ridiculous thing she's ever heard.

"Actually I do," I sneer back. *I saw her boobs today!*

"Yeah right," the snotty girl rolls her eyes and whispers something to the group that makes them giggle.

My out-of-whack brain starts to process the situation. Mary is going to a party at Alisa's. I wonder if Matt's going to be there. I want to call and ask him. I might have yesterday, but now it seems wrong. It's none of my business what he does with Alisa or any girl.

After Mary leaves, I sit on the counter and watch headlights come and go.

I wonder if we would be going to the party if Nick didn't have to meet his uncle.

I wonder where I would be if my parents were still alive.

I wonder how the side of the espresso machine got so dirty.

I grab a bottle of comet and a sponge from under the sink and start to scrub. I clean every cup, plate, and crevice in the café.

"Dani, you did this all last night?" Patty runs her finger along the edge of the counter.

"I was bored." I hope I didn't overdo it.

"Well, thank you. And thank you for covering for Mary. She really appreciated it." She puts her arm around me and squeezes my shoulders. The fact that Patty is thanking me for covering for Mary tells me she went home last night, so chances are she didn't get high.

Patty is gushing over the cleanliness of the floor when Matt walks in. I try to smile, but my teeth grind together. *Shit.* After I left the café last night, I went home and took another pill. If Matt suspects I got high alone, or that I'm still a little bit buzzed, I don't know if he will rat me out. During Nick's meeting yesterday, he went on and on about not getting high on their supply. I know he wouldn't be cool with me taking pills alone and running all over town at night.

"What are you doing here?" I pretend to be preoccupied with wiping down the counter and avoid eye contact. I take a sip from my ice coffee and realize the overdose of caffeine I've consumed this afternoon has enhanced the residual thizz coursing through my veins.

A couple of middle school girls swoon when Matt walks up to the counter. They bat their eyelashes at him as they take their drinks from the bar. He doesn't even throw a look their way. His crystal-clear blue eyes are on me as he yanks the rag from my hand. I slip my tongue between my teeth to stop my jaw from grinding and pick up my ice coffee. I hate not being in control of my emotions right now. I hate that the smell of Matt's body spray turns me on in some sick and twisted way.

He leans over the counter and whispers, "I don't want there to be weirdness between us."

I take a sip of my coffee and try not to chew the straw. "Why would there be weirdness?"

"Please don't make me say it." He smiles and I bite the straw even harder.

I wonder if he's referring to the fact that I saw two naked, closely related girls in his bed. Or it could be the fact that I acted like a total slut the last time we were alone together. Or maybe because he's been lying to me pretty much every single day that we've known each other. He's worried about weirdness? We are way past weird.

"No, no weirdness at all." I snatch the rag from him and hide it behind my back. I recall Alisa's naked body under the covers where I'd slept a few days before and my face turns hot. "What are you doing here, getting coffee for another family threesome?" I wish my tone was a little less harsh, but I don't really have control at the moment.

"Geez, Dani, lighten up. You really have no right to be mad." I try to turn away, but Matt grabs my arm. "You should be happy for me." His eyes search my face for some sign of his friend.

I know I'm being unreasonable, but what I'm feeling isn't even close to happy. "Why would I be happy for you?" I yank free.

One of the regular gossipers places her empty mug on the counter between us with a curious smile. Nosy old crow. I reach for the mug, but Matt gets to it first. He picks it up and walks around the counter. What is he doing? I follow him to the sink.

He spins around when he's out of earshot from the rest of the café. "For the same reason I'm happy for you and Nick." He's whispering, but I hear the desperation in his tone. He hands me the empty mug. "Because I'm your friend and I want you to be happy."

Blood races through my veins and my body tingles all over as I focus on Matt's eyes. I fight the urge to say what I really want to say, what I really feel. That it's easier to tell yourself you're happy, because it hurts less than being jealous. Is that what Matt is trying to tell me? I feel my jaw tighten and release. Matt sees it, too. He searches my face and raises a curious eyebrow.

"I'm happy for you," I tell him. I walk into the storeroom.

He follows me in and closes the door. "I never wanted to hurt you, Dani."

I can't look at him. I don't want to touch him. I definitely shouldn't be alone with him.

"Come here." He spins me around and holds his arms open. I'm weak, I can't fight it. I lean into him and he wraps his arms around me. He feels so good. "If it makes you feel any better, I'd rather be sleeping next to you."

My entire body erupts in joy. I want to blame this on thizz, but I won't. I can't. Thizz has nothing to do with the pleasure I feel in Matt's arms. I wasn't on thizz during our computer class four months ago when I first saw him and my heart suddenly started to pump back to life. I wasn't on thizz when I got his message and fantasized for an hour that he was in love with me. My feels for Matt were never thizz induced.

He shifts his weight and lets me go. "At least you don't snore." He laughs. He's acting like what he said was a joke, but it doesn't feel like one. Or maybe it is and I'm wishing for things that aren't real again.

Matt doesn't want me. He wants Alisa and her cousin, and he's had them. Multiple times probably. Matt is nothing more than a good friend, he said it himself. He's happy for me because he's my friend. Just a friend. That's good enough for me. It has to be.

I step away and whip Matt with the towel in my hand. "Get out of my way. I have to get back to work." And just like that, the mask is back on.

Matt stays with me all afternoon, helping me remember orders and laughing at me when I spill things. When Nick calls to tell me he's running late, I tell him Matt is here, that he can walk me home. Nick is so protective, yet he has no problem leaving me alone with Matt. If that isn't reason enough to believe Matt doesn't have feelings for me, I don't know what is.

My feet tingle as we walk down the street, and I can't wipe the smile from my face. I guess I wasn't as sober as I thought. "Do you believe in destiny?" I ask as we cross West Harris.

"Sure." Matt pulls my arm and holds me back as a car makes a right turn in front of us. He doesn't comment on the fact that I was almost taken out by a Honda.

"Do you think it was my destiny to come here?" This is something I thought about last night. "I feel like I was meant to be right here, right now. But that would mean my parents were destined to die."

Matt slides his hand down my arm and presses his palm to mine. He's holding my hand the way a parent would hold a child's as we cross the street. It looks innocent, but my heart is racing.

"Not destiny, it's more like fate. Fate can go either way, good or bad."

I see what he's saying, but it doesn't make me feel any better. "If I had a choice to go back to my old life with my parents or stay here, I don't know what I would choose. Does that make me a bad person?"

Matt stops walking and turns me to face him. "Something horrible happened and you ended up here. You had no control over that. Your parents would want you to be happy. They would want you to feel the way you feel right now." *I doubt that.* They wouldn't want me to be high. Just happy. And I am happy right now, right here, with Matt.

I choke back tears and throw myself into Matt's arms. "I'm so glad I met you." My heart feels heavy in my chest. Like it's weighted down with too much emotion. Emotions I can't act on or even acknowledge. There are things I can never say to Matt, to anyone. What I want to say is a betrayal to Nick. So, I choose my words carefully. "You're my best friend, Matt." I kiss his cheek just a few millimeters away from his mouth. A kiss on the cheek is nothing. We've kissed for real, even if it was a game.

"You're not mad about, you know, the lying?" He looks at his feet. "I never would have lied to you, but Nick said…"

"I know." I squeeze his hand. He doesn't have to apologize. I know it was Nick. Matt would never betray me. It's the one thing I know I can count on. "I understand."

When we get to Lucy's, I have no problem asking Matt if he wants to come inside. It isn't like I have anything to hide from him. He hesitates at the door as if he's not allowed to be alone with me. "Are you sure?" He looks around to make sure nobody is lurking in the bushes, ready to jump out and catch him doing something he shouldn't.

"Why not? We're friends, Matt, we hang out all the time. What's the difference if we do it at your house or mine?" Something that feels like guilt surfaces as I try to convince Matt to stay with me. Maybe being alone at my house is crossing a line. I don't even let Nick come inside when he drops me off.

Matt reluctantly steps inside the foyer and asks to use the bathroom. I point him in the direction of the guest bathroom and go upstairs to change out of my coffee-stained shirt. I'm looking for something to wear when I hear Lucy's car pull into the driveway. I don't know if I'm happy she's here or totally disappointed. I grab a white tank top and pull it on as I hurry back downstairs in time to see Lucy introduce herself to Matt.

"Are you Nick?" Lucy extends her free hand with a smile.

"No, I'm Matt, Nick's friend—Dani's friend." Matt shakes Lucy's hand.

"Do you want to stay for dinner? We have more than enough." She sets a bag on the dining room table and removes several cartons of Chinese food.

"Thanks, but I can't. I was just leaving." Matt sees me standing on the step and waves. "I'll see you later, Dani."

"I'll walk you out." I take Matt by the forearm and walk him onto the porch. "Thanks for the walk and talk and everything." I lift my arms to give him a hug, and I feel his hand slide into the back pocket of my jeans. I step back and put my hand on my right butt cheek.

"Anytime." Matt smiles and walks down the stairs. "Have a nice night." There is a bit of sarcasm in his voice.

"Very cute." Lucy appears beside me. I don't deny it or agree with her.

I slide my hand in my pocket and feel a tiny bag full of pills. I knew I could trust him.

After dinner I tell Lucy I'm tired and go to my room. I pull my memory box from its shelf and place it on the bed. The smell of cinnamon overcomes me as I pull the last three sticks from the pack. I empty the little packet of pills into the bottom of the package and replace the gum, leaving one pill on the bed. I put everything back in the box and place it on the nightstand. I swallow the pill then wait for the thizz to take over, but I can't keep still. I dump the contents of my memory box on the bed. I eat another piece of gum even though I'll regret it later, and I start to look through the pictures. When I come across the last one in the stack, I feel a knot in my throat. It was taken on my seventeenth birthday, the last birthday we celebrated together. I stare at the eyes of the girl in the picture. Her round, chubby face, her frumpy clothes—they belong to someone that doesn't exist anymore. She died that night with them. That girl has never felt the rush of thizz. She never kissed a boy as perfect as Nick. She has never been in love. She's also never felt the pain and loss of losing her parents. She never watched someone perform CPR on her mother or pull a sheet over her father's lifeless body. The girl trapped in this photo, in this moment, I wish I was her.

The picture was taken at my favorite Italian restaurant in North Beach. I remember the waiter singing "Happy Birthday" as he carried out a tray of tiramisu with seventeen candles stuck in it. That's when I noticed my father was missing. I looked at the strangers that gathered around our table, but his face wasn't among the crowd. Then I saw him. He was on the sidewalk having an animated conversation with a man I'd never seen before. He wore baggy jeans and an oversized puffy jacket like the public school kids I used to see on the bus. Their heated exchange was evident by the way people watched them as they walked by. When he finally came back in, I asked him if everything was ok. He waved his hand in the air and shrugged it off like it was no big deal. He looked frazzled, and that wasn't like my father. He was an expert at hiding his feelings. I asked him if the man was a client, and he told me he wanted him to take his case, but he couldn't because his calendar was full. That would explain why the man was upset. Landing my father as your lawyer was like winning the lottery.

My mother called for us to smile and snapped the picture just as I blew out the candles. My mother's picture caught the man's reflection in one of the many mirrors that surrounded the restaurant. It's funny that I remember the guy on the street, but I can't recall what I wished for.

29
Dani

Tonight is Nick's eighteenth birthday. We're celebrating at one of his family's beach houses. The house is decorated in typical beach cottage décor. Lots of large ships and big vases filled with sea glass. The walls are a soft blue that plays well off the dark hardwood floors. The wall facing the ocean is solid glass. It looks like one of those moving paintings they sell at the mall. I watch the silent waves roll in as the sun sets on the horizon. The house, the beach, it's perfect for what I have planned. We head up the stairs to the second floor and Nick shows me two bedrooms.

"This one is bigger, but the one across the hall has a better bathroom." He steps back into the hall. "Or we can check out the third floor…"

"This one." I pull him back into the room and he closes the door.

Nick and I haven't gone past second base. I think. I don't really know the bases. Heather says we've only gone to second, and I trust her. It's weird, trusting Heather. I wish she was going to be here tonight. Her parents still have her on lockdown. Thankfully, we've been communicating through Myspace. I typed her a five-thousand word message the other night when I was high. Her message back was just as long. While I was stuck in my room with a gum package full of pills, she was at home with her parents and their pastor praying for her soul. When she told me she was grounded for spring break, I assumed it would only be a week. I had no idea Eureka's spring break was two weeks long.

I pull a bow out of my backpack and place it on top of my head. The bow was also Heather's idea. "Happy Birthday."

Nick laughs at the silly gesture, then realizes what I'm offering him. He pulls me into his arms and kisses me. "Are you sure?"

I pull him towards the king-size bed in the middle of the room. "Positive." This is the next step in our relationship. I'm ready.

"Right now?" He hesitates.

If I stop now I might chicken out. "Yes, now." I kiss the spot on his neck below his ear that always makes him moan. Nick grabs my waist and lifts me into his arms. He's about to lay me on the bed when his phone rings. "Are you serious?" I yell to the ceiling.

Nick gives me one of his apologetic smiles and pulls his phone out. The party tonight is going to be huge; he has to answer it. "S'up, Matt?"

Of all people, it's Matt.

"I'm upstairs." Nick winks. I can tell from his responses that Matt is asking if I'm with him. He's trying to be coy, but I know he's dying to tell Matt that we're about to have sex for the first time.

I didn't think anyone was going to be here for another few hours. I thought we'd have the house to ourselves so I could give Nick his gift. So I could prove how much I love him. That's a horrible thing to say. Of course I love him. I wouldn't be with him if I didn't. I don't need to prove anything to anyone. I take the bow off my head and walk towards the door.

He takes his phone from his ear and holds it against his body. "Dani, wait…"

"You can unwrap your gift later." I give him the flirty, sexy smile I practiced in the mirror yesterday when I was high.

He exhales slowly and says, "I can't wait."

I close the door and stand in the empty hall. I can't do this. Not like this. Not sober. At least I tried.

30

Matt

I'm pretty sure I just cock-blocked my best friend on this birthday. How was I supposed to know they would be here hours before the party? Ok, so maybe I did know that they might be here and told Arnie we had to pick up the keg an hour earlier than scheduled. I'm an asshole. A cock-blocking asshole.

Arnie comes crashing through the back door. "Give me a hand." He's dragging a keg behind him. I help Arnie pull the keg into the kitchen and set it up in the corner. He asks me where Nick is, and I tell him he's upstairs with Dani.

"Oh yeah! It's about time she gives it up." Arnie says as he puts two bottles of vodka in the freezer. When he closes the door, Dani is standing behind it. He jumps when he sees her. "Fuck, D. You scared the shit out of me."

She pushes past him and grabs a bottle of water from the counter. "Well, you shouldn't be talking shit." She cracks open the bottle and takes a drink.

I watch her watching Arnie. His back is to her, so he doesn't see the pill she pops in her mouth. I can't believe she's doing that with him in the room. She's crazy.

"Hey Arn, you check out the bedrooms yet?" If there is one thing to get him out of here, it's the idea of getting laid.

Arnie raises an eyebrow at me. "Good lookin' out, bro." He points at Dani and says, "We're all getting laid tonight!" I give him a thumbs-up. *Yeah, sure.*

After he leaves, I turn to Dani. "What the fuck was that?"

She shrugs and sits on the counter. "It's a party, right?"

"Nick isn't stupid, Dani. He can tell when you're high."

"No, he can't." She smiles and takes another drink from the water bottle. "Neither can you."

She's out of control. Maybe I should pull back on the pills I've been giving her. I thought she could handle it. I gave her six on Tuesday and she was already out yesterday morning. She texted me and asked if I had any more gifts I could spare. I slipped another four in her pocket when Nick and I picked her up from work yesterday. I don't know what I was smoking when I thought giving Dani pills was a good idea. It's just that she looks so happy. She's high, yes. But it isn't like when we get high. We're bouncing out of our skin. Dani looks content, like she can finally unravel the cord around her neck and breathe. Maybe I'm wrong for giving her pills, but I'll do whatever little I can to be the one that makes her smile.

"Come here." She reaches for my hand and places a pill in my palm. Then she hands me her bottle of water.

"Let's be crazy together." She pulls her bottom lip with her teeth and smiles. My smile.

I'm wrong. She isn't out of control. She's insane.

And I don't give a fuck.

31
Dani

We're standing on the beach behind the house toasting Nick's birthday. It's me, Matt, Alex, Arnie, and Aurora. It's almost eight and I've already taken two pills. I'm nervous about tonight. About having sex with Nick. I've already made up my mind that tonight is the night. I want to get this over with. I want to give Nick the most precious gift a girl can give a guy. I owe him. He gave me thizz; it's the least I can do.

Alex is passing around a joint. When it gets to me I take a hit then pass it back. It burns far worse than I ever thought it would. Nobody seems to notice me choking to death as Nick gives his no freebies and no fights speech. I stop listening because my throat is on fire, but the rush feels amazing. I start to dance to the music already pouring out of the house. The DJ must have finished setting up. I can't wait to go inside and dance. That's how fucked up I am.

When Alex offers me the joint again, Nick intercepts. "Nah dude, she doesn't smoke."

I'm a little peeved that Nick cut me off. *He's not the boss of me.* Before I can mount an argument, Matt appears before me with a gift—two hits of thizz. I take the pills and smile. A big goofy smile.

Arnie yells, "Two to the face!" and shoves a bottle of tequila in my hand.

I wash the pills down with a swig from the bottle since my throat is still burning from the weed. I don't even gag, that's how high I am.

We head in the house and disperse among the crowd. I dance and laugh and drink until I'm dizzy, but not really spinning. Just seeing things in fast motion. Too fast. I need to lie down or drink a bottle of water or maybe take another hit off that joint. I stumble into the hall, feeling like I just ran a marathon. A door opens and I fall inside. I slide to the ground and curl up on the rug. I lie there for an hour, a minute, I don't know. Time doesn't exist on the floor.

The next thing I know, I'm being helped outside. "I don't wanna leave," I slur as Nick and Matt talk over me.

"Dude, she is fucked up. How many did she take?" Nick sounds like he's freaking out.

They set me on a chair. I remember this secluded area from my tour with Nick earlier. We're in the side yard with the fire pit and chairs set up to watch the sunset. There are large plastic shields blocking out the wind.

"Two, I only gave her two." Matt's voice drips in guilt.

"Shit, you don't think she took anything else, do you?"

"Like what? Plus, who would give it to her?" *Matt is such a bad liar.*

"What should we do?" I look up and see Nick pacing and running his hand over his head. The constant movement starts to make me sick, so I close my eyes.

"I'll stay with her, you go back inside." Matt suggests.

"No, I won't leave her again." Nick kneels down next to me and strokes my face. His cool hand feels nice against my skin, almost as nice as the tingly feelings rushing through my body. I reach for his hand and guide it lower. He pulls away quickly and smiles at my naughty behavior.

I'm feeling brave. I want to go back upstairs right now.

"Dude, we have to sell the rest of this shit tonight," Matt interrupts. "This is our payday. You want to leave it all up to Arnie?"

I wonder if Matt really cares about selling their stash or if he's just trying to get me alone. I hope it's about sales, because I don't think I will be able to hold back my feelings in my current mental state.

"I know, dude." I can tell from the pitch in Nick's voice that he is really high right now. "Dani, I'll be inside. I'm not leaving you," he insists. He kisses me on the lips and whispers I love you in my ear.

"I love you," I whisper back. At least I think I did. I can't tell if I'm speaking aloud.

"Dani, how many did you take today?" Matt's tone is harsh, scared.

Matt cares about me in his own way. I knew it. He always looks out for me. He keeps me happy. Makes sure I have pills. He's my best friend.

"Dani," the shrill of Matt's voice brings me back to earth. "How many pills did you take?" He's practically on top of me, trying to coax a response.

How many? How many what? Oh yeah. I hold up my hand and count out one, two, three, four fingers and show them to Matt.

Matt stares at my fingers. Once he finishes counting, his eyes pop out of his head. "Fuck! Fuck!" Now he's pacing around my chair. "Dani, what the fuck!"

Oh no, wrong answer. He's mad at me. "Sorry, Matty." My mouth is so dry it's hard to form words. I take a mouthful of water from the bottle in my hand, swishing it around before I swallow. I feel the chilly water slide through my chest before it hits my empty stomach.

"I'm fucked if Nick finds out I've been giving you pills!" Matt reappears in my line of sight. "Do you hear me? Are you even listening to what I'm saying?"

I shake my head. "Sorry, Matt."

"That's it, I'm cutting you off. You only take what Nick gives you. No more on the side."

He's talking crazy. I don't know why he's so mad. I wish I knew what to say to make him feel better.

"This is my fault. I shouldn't have…I was being selfish. I'm sorry."

"Why?" I smile. "I'm not sorry. I'm happy." I attempt to sit up, but my hand slides through the plastic lines of the lawn chair and I fall over.

"You are so wasted." Matt laughs and helps me up. "You're lucky you're with us, otherwise half the guys here would be trying to take advantage of you."

"You're the only one here in a position to take advantage of me." A warm tingly feeling flows through me at the thought.

"I know," he says quietly. He squeezes my hand tighter.

"Thank you for restraining yourself."

"Believe me, it's hard." He smiles mischievously.

"Is it really that difficult?"

"No, I mean it's really hard."

I laugh at his crude joke and feel him relax beside me. He's fucked up, too.

The last time we were this high together was the night nothing happened. Not because I didn't want it to. Matt made sure I didn't do anything I would regret. "Well, I'm never worried, you know why?" I point my finger at Matt. "Because I know you watch out for me." My breathing becomes erratic when the tip of my finger comes in contact with his chest. "You always look out for me, because you love me." I said that out loud. I can tell by the way Matt is looking at me.

I thought I knew all of Matt's faces, but this one is brand new. "Yes, you crazy girl." Matt strokes my face then checks the back door. "I love you."

His words vibrate in my ear. I feel everything he is saying. I close my eyes and let my senses take over as Matt's emotions emanate from his body into mine. I feel his hand on my cheek and his breath on my face. When I open my eyes, his mouth is inches from mine.

"I love you too," I breathe into the space between us. He smiles and holds me another few seconds before breaking away. I feel like he's just dropped me from a cliff. I reach for his hand, and he slowly pulls it away.

He sits on the edge of the lawn chair with his back to me and runs his hand over his face. He moans in desperation or frustration, maybe a little of both.

A few minutes pass and I start to realize what I've just said to Matt. What he just admitted to me. I want to say something, change the subject, but the reggae song we danced to in his room echoes into the yard. All gloves are off. Thizz takes over.

"Remember that night?" I slide my hand down Matt's bare arm.

He nods, but refuses to look at me. He's still trying to be strong.

"You know I wouldn't have said no." My heart beats at a fast, steady rhythm.

Matt's head snaps in my direction. His eyes are full of emotion. "I wanted to kiss you." He stares into my eyes, daring me to look away.

I accept his dare and look directly into his blue eyes. "Do you want to kiss me now?"

"I've wanted to kiss you every day since the day I met you."

I'm not sure if my heart is racing at the thought of his lips on mine or for the utter betrayal I feel for wanting him to do it. The moment is getting way too intense. I bite my lip and look away, unsure of what I want to happen next. What I want and what is right are not the same thing. I can't let Matt betray his best friend. Especially on his birthday. I'm a shitty girlfriend, we've established that. Matt is a good friend, the best. I can't drag him down to my level. I need to stop this now.

"You're a good dancer," I blurt out.

Matt laughs at my lame compliment and pulls back. "You're a horrible dancer."

"What!" I pretend to be offended. "Help me up!"

Matt watches me struggle to stand then offers his hand and yanks me to my feet. I'm not ready for the sudden burst of movement, and I fly into his chest, knocking him back a few steps. His arms wrap around me for support. Suddenly the backdoor opens and sounds from the party fly out into the sanctuary Matt and I have created. Matt tosses me back onto the chair. I put my hand out to stop my fall, but it slips through the plastic and my head hits the chair's metal base.

"Oh shit, sorry Dani." Matt helps me up. "Are you ok?"

Instead of offering my stock answer of yes, I shrug my shoulders and tilt my hand back and forth. Matt isn't ready for the honesty. "Are you hurt, or is it—" He stops himself from continuing.

My mouth is suddenly filled with the salty taste of tears. There is something about Matt that allows me to be honest about my feelings. It's something I can't do with Nick. I feel emotionally safe with Matt. With Nick, I feel safe because I won't have to show emotion. I feel him pull back slightly when the back door opens then relax again when it closes.

"Nick's going to come out here and wonder why you're crying."

"I'll tell him you hit me."

"Yeah right. Seriously, we should get out of here. We can sneak out the side gate and go for a walk."

I can't tell if Matt is serious or not. I know he would gladly take me anywhere I asked, but we both know leaving isn't an option. At least leaving the backyard is out of the question, but eventually we'll both leave Eureka.

"I want to go to Berkeley."

"Can we limit it within walking distance?"

"NO! I mean I want to go to UC Berkeley in the fall." I declare it officially for him and for me as I wipe tears from my cheeks.

"I know. And I'll be at Stanford. We'll be rivals," Matt says with false enthusiasm.

I settle back into my chair and a sense of relief washes over me. This is the first time I've admitted I want to leave Eureka, leave this all behind. A Mac Dre song comes on, and the house erupts in cheers. "Where do you think Nick will be next year?"

Matt exhales loudly and moves to the chair next to me. "I have no idea."

32
Matt

"Let's go find Nick." I stand and offer Dani my hand. If I stay out here any longer, I'm not sure I can stop myself from doing or saying something I can't take back. I've already said too much.

Dani takes my hand and doesn't let go, even after we walk into the house. If she doesn't care, neither do I. The crowd looks like it doubled in size. We squeeze through the kitchen, into the living room. I spot Nick in the corner, surrounded by chicks. Luckily, Dani's too short to see over the crowd. I don't think seeing Nick in a circle of sluts would make her very happy right now. I stop to see if we can make it back to the kitchen just as the thizz national anthem pumps into the room. The house explodes and everyone starts dancing. Including us. I turn Dani so her back is towards Nick. I don't want to ruin this moment, her mood. I spot Arnie over Dani's head. He's got some chick bent over in front of him. *Fucking Arnie*. K and a couple of cheerleaders are dancing next him. K yells my name and points at me. I point back and Dani turns around to see who I'm looking at. Suddenly, she stops dancing.

I follow her line of sight to Nick, who is smiling at an Angelina Jolie lookalike. She slides her arms around his neck, and he lets her. He doesn't realize his girlfriend is watching some hot girl rub up on him. I have to save him. I yell his name as loud as I can. K sees me shouting and looks at Nick. He cups his hand halfway around his mouth and yells. Nick doesn't look up. I feel Dani move away, towards him. I yell one more time and catch Arnie's attention. I point down at Dani and then to Nick. He tosses his chick to the side and slides through the crowd. I can't read his lips or hear what he's saying, but Nick slips out of the girl's arms. He dances through the crowd, giving high fives as he goes. He finally reaches us and lifts his hands above his head in a double high five to me. He gives me a small look of appreciation and then turns all his attention to Dani.

Where it belongs.

I take a long pull from my joint and put it out on the wall. I don't know why I volunteered to wait for the pizza guy. Everyone is still too fucked up to eat. Nick and Arnie have been pushing sales hard tonight.

"You want some company?" Dani closes the front door and wraps her arms around herself. "It's cold out here."

I pull off my Stanford sweatshirt and offer it to her. She takes it and pulls it over her head. "You look good in my colors."

She smiles and rests her head on my shoulder. "You're sweet."

This is the reason I started giving her the pills. Moments like this, when it's just us. When Nick and Arnie are making sales and we're stuck in a side yard or in the car together. A hug, a smile, a look from Dani is all I ever wanted. I put my arm around her, pretending to keep her warm. I'll use any excuse to hold her. "You don't have to wait with me." I pull her tighter. I don't want her to go, but it's the right thing to say. "Go back inside and hang out with your friends."

"You're my only friend."

I want to say something more, tell her I love her again. I know I can't. But I really fucking want to. I let her go and shove my hands in my pockets.

She wraps her arms around my left arm and snuggles me. "This time next year we'll be in college."

I can't tell if she's being thoughtful or implying something.

"Stanford isn't that far from CAL." She lifts her head and looks at me. "Just a train ride away."

What is she saying?

"We can still see each other on the weekends and stuff."

"Yeah, of course." I don't want to think that far ahead. I have to remember who she is now. I have to assume Nick will be in the picture. It's the right thing to do. He's still my best friend, she's still his girl. If they break up, it won't be because of me. If she breaks up with him, I can't date her, ever. It will have to be Nick's decision if they decide to end things. The only way I can be with Dani is if I know Nick doesn't want her. Since that is highly unlikely, then I'm pretty much dreaming. "We can all get together and hang out. It'll be cool."

"Oh." She lets my arm go. "Yeah, of course, all of us." She leans against the wall away from me and wraps her arms around herself and looks towards the street.

I want to punch myself in the face. I let her believe I don't want to see her. That I don't want her. I had to. It's the right thing to do. "It's freezing out here." Weather seems to be a safe topic.

"Yeah." She puts her hands inside the sleeves of my sweater and blows on them. In some sick way, it turns me on. "Does it ever snow here?"

"No. It doesn't get that cold. Last New Year's Eve was the closest we ever got to snow. It hailed pretty hard but it never snowed."

Dani rests her head against my arm again and says, "I know. I was here."

"You were in Eureka?"

She nods.

"That's crazy. Nick and I were at a house party that isn't too far from Lucy's." I remember the chick Nick hooked up with that night. She was a senior when we were freshmen. She was like the holy grail of hot chicks in our school. And Nick got her. He gets all the girls.

"My parents died last year on New Year's Day." Dani clears her throat.

Holy shit. I'm standing here thinking about Nick getting laid and Dani's thinking about her parents. I'm an asshole.

"We were supposed to go home the day after Christmas, but Lucy begged my mom to stay for her birthday. Lucy was born on New Year's Eve. I always think, if we left earlier or a day later…" she trails off.

I've wondered about Dani's parents ever since she told me they were killed. I never ask her any questions, because, well, the death of your parents doesn't make for good conversation.

"It happened right under the Bay Bridge." She's shaking, and I wonder how much of it is from the cold. "It was foggy that night. I remember looking up at the sky and only seeing gray. No stars. No moon. I don't want to die on a foggy day."

"You're not going to fucking die." I pull her into my arms and hear her sniffle. "You're safe here. Nobody is going to hurt you." I kiss the top of her head and squeeze her tighter.

"I know, but I'm scared. I'm scared to leave. I'm scared to stay. I'm not the same person I was last year. I don't know who I am." She isn't crying, but I hear the threat of it in her voice.

"I know who you are. You're Dani DiMarco. I won't let you forget that." It's moments like this that I hate Nick. I hate him for not being the one to comfort her. I hate him for not knowing who she is. He's never here for the bad; he only gets the good. The smiles, the kisses, maybe even more.

She pulls away and looks at me. Her hands tap my chest and she smiles. "That isn't my name."

33
Dani

The street is quiet except for the music echoing from inside the house.

"DiMarco is Lucy's last name." It feels like a huge weight has been lifted from my chest.

"But your parents did die in a carjacking, right?" Matt looks like he's trying to figure out a puzzle in his head.

Just tell him. Tell him everything. You can trust him.

"The police consider the shooting a failed carjacking, but there's more. My father may have been the target." I think about some of the people my father defended. "He had a lot of shady clients. They think one of them may have been angry with the outcome of his case or something. Since I was in the backseat when they were shot, I'm technically a witness. Only I didn't see anything. I had on headphones and my music was turned up pretty loud. I heard the shots, but by the time I realized what happened and sat up, the gunman was gone. They have one witness. A waiter in the restaurant across the street saw a man run from our SUV. That's their only lead."

Matt's face looks white, like he's about to pass out.

"Are you ok?"

"So, the witness is a waiter," he confirms. "You didn't see anything?"

"Yeah, don't worry. The name change was really just to give me a chance to start over. A clean slate. I was never in danger."

Matt finally exhales. "You scared me for a second. I thought...I don't know what I thought. I was confusing you with another story I heard."

Other than the muffled sounds coming from inside the house, the block is quiet. The roar of the motorcycles is faint at first. By the time I realize it's getting louder, they're here. We watch eleven bikes park in front of the house before Matt pushes me inside the door and yells for me to get Nick.

"Dani, go!" Matt closes the door and I run to find Nick.

The crowd has thinned. I see pockets of people talking, dancing, rubbing lotion on each other. No Nick. No hot girl Nick was dancing with.

My pulse races.

I look for Nick in the kitchen. I knock on the bathroom door. I run to the deck out back, the courtyard. No Nick. No girl.

Upstairs. I don't want to go upstairs.

"Dani!"

I turn and see Nick with K by his side. They're coming through the door that leads to the garage.

"Matt." I can only get his name out.

"I know." He grabs my hand and pulls me into the living room. "Stay here," he demands.

Nick and K run out the front door along with half the party. I stay behind and watch the garage door. Before I know it. I'm at the door. I open it.

Two girls are sharing a cigarette. One girl nods in my direction and her friend turns around. She shrugs and turns her back to me again. They laugh at something. At me.

I want to murder her.

"Dani." Aurora moves me aside and looks in the garage then closes the door. "They're desperate. And they aren't worth your time. We have bigger problems."

She drags me to the second floor, turns off the lights in the room, and stands next to the window. "Come here," she whispers.

I join her at the window just as Arnie comes out of the house. "We got a problem here?" He lifts his arms at a funny angle as he walks towards the bikers.

Teddy, the biker that chased us from the Lost Coast, smirks and says something about everyone being strapped. He tells Nick he's just here to talk.

"Talk then." Nick stands next to Arnie. K is with them too. I don't see Matt. I'm glad. I don't want him anywhere near those bikers.

Teddy takes off his helmet, sets it on his seat, and leans against his bike. "I heard it's your birthday, Nicky." He crosses his arms over his massive belly.

I'd like to think Nick could beat him in a fist fight. Nick is twenty years younger and faster, but Teddy's tree stump arms look like they can do some damage.

"Who told you that?" Nick doesn't sound at all worried. Just like the day we ran into them at Lost Coast. His confidence astounds me.

"A little birdie." Teddy snickers and his followers laugh with him.

"This is a private party." Arnie sounds anxious. It must be pretty hard to be serious when you're high on thizz. "Unless you've brought some strippers for the birthday boy, I suggest you leave."

"We aren't here to break up your sweet sixteen. I just want to talk to Nick. Man to man."

Nick steps in front of Arnie. "You could've just called. I'm sure some of your boys have my number." He nods to some of the younger-looking guys. I can't tell if Nick is bullshitting, and from the look on Teddy's face, neither can he.

Teddy takes a step towards Nick and K moves forward. I'm not sure if K would actually hit Teddy. K has a lot to lose, like a scholarship to play football at UCLA. He shouldn't even be here.

"Look, you cocky little fucker." Teddy points at Nick. "You tell your uncle we've got a better offer on the table. Turns out he wasn't the only city scum trying to move into Humboldt."

Teddy's news stuns Nick. He doesn't say a word as Teddy rallies his guys to leave. The bikes start up with a loud roar, and they pull away one by one. Teddy starts up last. Just before he backs away, he pulls his bandana down and yells to Nick.

"You're eighteen now. That's big time. You do real time." He pulls his skull bandana over his hairy jaw and rides away.

"What the hell was that?" I step away from the window and look at Arora's frightened face.

She sits on the bed and pulls out a cigarette. She fiddles with her lighter and finally gets it lit. Smoke circles her head as the red tip of her cigarette pulses. She sucks in a lungful of smoke, then exhales. "I think we just got shut down."

34
Matt

I search the house and find Dani and Aurora in the bedroom upstairs. Aurora looks like she's going to puke.

"Dude, I'm fucking out." Aurora snuffs her cigarette on the bottom of her shoe then tosses it in her cup. "I can't have those biker assholes after me. I'm graduating next month. I don't need this shit."

"Chill the fuck out." I lie on the bed and close my eyes. I feel good. Real good. The pill I just took has kicked in. I needed something to calm me down. It seems to for Dani. "Nick's got this."

"Yeah, that's what you think," she says in a loud whisper. "You don't know them like I do. My uncle was in their crew, now he's doing thirty-eight years for murder." She lights another cigarette. "You tell Nick I'm done."

I sit up just as she slams the door. Dani is pacing the room. She moves from the window to the door and back. She's scared. "Hey, it's gonna be ok. Come here." I sit up and pat the space beside me. "Aurora is just freaking out."

"I know." She bites her thumbnail and continues to pace.

I want to say something to make her feel better. But words don't come. I don't know if it's because there is nothing I can say to make her feel safe, or if it has anything to do with the fact that I'm high as fuck.

"Here." I pull out my stash and take out a pill. She takes the pill and puts it in her mouth. She looks around for a drink and I point her to the bathroom.

Once that pill kicks in, she'll relax. We can hang out a little longer, maybe watch the sunrise. Nick is busy working shit out with Will. He's been on the phone since the Devil's Gold crew left.

I get to have her to myself a little longer. Maybe we can finish our conversation from the yard earlier.

Dani opens the bathroom door at the same time the bedroom door opens.

"Hey, I was looking for you guys." Nick steps inside and closes the door. He doesn't have an ounce of worry about anything that's going on. He trusts me. Right now, he shouldn't.

"Is everything ok?" Dani rushes into his arms.

Nick caresses her back and kisses her head. "It's all good, baby. You know I got this."

It kills me that he's the one that gets to comfort her.

"Matt, I'm going to take Dani home."

Dani pulls out of his arms. "No, why?"

I don't want her to go. But I don't say anything. I can't without sounding desperate.

"I don't want you here in case those assholes come back."

I see the worry on his face now. He's right, she should leave. We all should.

"I don't want to be alone." Dani looks at me quickly, then back at Nick.

I'm about to suggest we go to my place. Nick may even leave her and come back here to close up. That would be perfect. That would make my night. And Dani's, I think. If anything she said in the yard was true, then we have a lot to talk about. What am I saying? We had this conversation already. Who cares, have it again, maybe this time with a better outcome? One I will benefit from. Thizz is so smart. I don't know what I'd do with it.

"You won't be alone. I'm staying with you." Nick raises an eyebrow, and Dani's face turns red.

I suddenly regret giving her that last pill. Giving her any pills. I hate pills. I hate thizz.

35

Dani

The house is almost empty. The bikers scared everyone away. Even the DJ left.

Arnie comes out of the kitchen with the two girls from the garage trailing behind him. "Are you guys out?" He takes Nick's hand and they bump chests.

"Yeah, I'm taking Dani home. You guys can hang out. Just make sure you call me if any shit goes down." Any apprehension I had about Nick staying with me disappears when I see the girls from the garage. The last thing I want is Nick alone with them.

Arnie pulls Nick to the side, away from the girls. "Dude, everyone's fading and nobody's got any funds. Can I hook these two up?"

Nick looks at the girls and smiles. They smile back. I want to scratch their eyes out.

"Yeah, go ahead."

Arnie holds up his hand for a high five.

"But Matt's in charge," Nick adds. Matt looks up with a bewildered expression. He's really high.

"Hell yeah! I told you we're all getting laid tonight," Arnie says to me.

I look at Nick and scowl; he shrugs like he didn't say anything. "Let's go." *Before I change my mind.*

"Later, D." Arnie gives me a hug. "Take care of my boy."

"Dude, shut the fuck up," Nick scolds him as they shake hands.

Arnie pretends to be sorry, but we all know he isn't.

Nick offers his hand to Matt and they do their ritual handshake. Matt's eyes never leave mine. He's sorry. Sorry I'm leaving. Part of me is too.

I don't remember the drive home or how I even got in the house. One minute I'm standing in the living room of the beach house saying goodbye to Matt. The next thing I know I'm in my room undressing while Nick watches from the doorway. He's grinning as I struggle to pull off my boots. He laughs when I fall onto the bed. The pill Matt gave me kicked in. I'm totally wired. Totally not myself. Totally happy Lucy isn't home. I get my foot untangled from my pants and toss them on floor in front of Nick. He stops laughing. His eyes follow my hands as I unhook the buttons on my shirt. When I reach the bottom button, he steps inside and closes the door. I don't think I'm much to look at, but Nick doesn't seem disappointed.

Nick takes his shirt off and I realize I've never seen him shirtless. His body is nothing like Matt's. Matt's chest and abs have more of a natural curve. They suit his build. Nick's body is bulky. He has a deep V separating his abs and hips.

I reach for his hand and pull him onto the bed. He pauses slightly to kick his shoes off. Each one falls to the ground with a thump, and he arranges himself beside me. Until this moment I felt as if I were putting on a show. That I was just going through the motions, not really committing to what we are about to do. All of that changes once I'm wrapped in his arms. This is the most intimate we've ever been, and not because we're lying half naked in bed. I've never felt as close to him as I do right now. My jaw tightens and my teeth chatter. I take a deep breath to try and gain some control. It's really difficult given the amount of drugs I've taken tonight.

Nick runs his hand down the side of my face then lowers his lips to mine. I'm lost in the movement of his mouth when he kisses me and the way he pulls me closer with every breath he takes. Just as I fully succumb to the rush of emotions flowing through my body, he pulls back.

"Is something wrong?" I ask nervously. Then I realize we've forgotten something. "Don't worry. There's, um, protection in the bathroom." Lucy has kept the bottom drawer stocked with condoms ever since she found out we were dating.

"It's not that." He kisses the tip of my nose. "I actually brought something." He blushes, then slides a misplaced hair from my face. "I just wanted to look at you." The utter devotion I feel is indescribable. If I ever had any doubt about my feelings for Nick, they are washed away in this moment.

"I love you, Dani." The vulnerability in his voice makes my chest ache. I don't know how to respond. Words are just words. Saying I love you isn't enough. I need to show him.

I want to believe the millions of tingles rushing through me have nothing to do with thizz. That the chills, the pleasure, the euphoria I'm experiencing is without a doubt, one hundred percent caused by Nick.

Only that would be a lie.

36
Matt

I slide into the booth next to Nick and watch the parking lot of the diner. Nick and I felt pretty confident after the party when Will said he had everything under control. That was a week ago. Sitting in the diner across from Will Walker today, I'm not feeling as bullet proof.

"Shit isn't looking too good, kiddo." Steam from the scalding hot coffee rises around Will's face, making the situation even creepier. "Devon made a deal with those DGC assholes. They're giving him Humboldt."

Nick swears under his breath. This is a guy who gets everything he wants. He isn't going to give up without a fight. "So, we're out. Just like that?"

"It's politics, Nicky. Shit that goes way beyond a bunch of kids slinging dope." Will leans back and rests his arm across the back of his bench seat.

Nick makes a grunting noise at Will's comment. Politics or not, Nick is offended.

Will realizes he's just insulted his nephew and starts to backpedal. "I didn't mean it like that." He reaches over and messes Nick's hair. "I've got bigger problems to deal with. They're trying to pin me with a double homicide. I can't make any moves until this blows over. I gotta find this witness. I have my guys on the street using some fancy online shit. It's all fucking high tech now."

I choke on my spit and start to cough as I think about Dani. The story she told me about her parents, the shooting. I have to make sure it's just a coincidence. "Do you know who you're looking for?" I clear my throat. The cop said it was the daughter of the people that were killed. So, it can't be Dani. She said she didn't see anything. She said it was a waiter.

Will's eyes shoot in my direction like he just realized I was sitting here. "Don't worry about what I know. My intel is solid. It's a witness, that's all you need to know."

I relax when he doesn't say it's the daughter. Even if it isn't Dani, the thought that any girl is being hunted by Will makes me sick. He wouldn't care about the witness if he was innocent.

We're sitting at a table having coffee with a murderer. I continue choking. Nick slides me his iced tea and asks Will if he can help.

Will laughs and leans in towards Nick. "Look at you, ready to put in work for me." He rustles Nick's hair again. It's so demeaning, yet Nick looks like a happy puppy. He's so desperate for Will's approval, he'd do anything for him; even help him hunt an innocent girl.

"I want to help. I'll do whatever I have to. I can't lose Humboldt. We're building something huge here. We have guys in Arcata and Chico..."

Will cuts Nick off. "Forget Humboldt. You're out of here in a few months anyway." Will's phone buzzes, and he walks outside to answer it.

Nick looks at me, confused.

"I think he means college." I clear my throat.

Nick lets out a long sigh. He doesn't want to have this conversation with his uncle, and I really don't want to be here for it. Nick throws some money on the table and we head outside. Will is standing by his truck. He's got a Ford F150. It's covered in mud, like he's been off-roading.

"Come here." He grabs Nick around the shoulders. "I'm proud of you. You know that, right? I mean, what you've done here is pretty impressive. You're gonna be the next Tony Montana if you play your cards right."

"That's what I'm saying. We have all the contacts up here. Maybe we can work something out with Devon."

I hate watching Nick plead with his uncle. Losing Humboldt is the best thing that could happen to Nick, to all of us. This was never supposed to be a career.

"Look, I get it, you're pissed. You gotta let it go. Devon's got Humboldt now. You need to focus on school."

Nick kicks at a rock and shoves his hands in his pocket like a sulky kid.

Will opens the door to his truck and leans against the seat. He pulls out a joint and lights it up. "Where did you apply?"

Nick runs his hand through his hair. "I was thinking I'd move to the city for a little while. Maybe work with you and learn more about the business, then next year…" Nick stops talking when he sees the look on his uncle's face.

Will closes his eyes and flicks the joint across the parking lot. Some kid is going to score big when they find that. Will slams the door to his truck and stands in front of Nick. He towers him by two or three inches. "Please tell me you applied to school?"

I don't know why Will is so worried about Nick getting a college degree. What does he have to gain from it?

Nick looks at Will like a defiant son. "Fuck college. I'm not going."

Will sucks in a long breath and exhales slowly to calm himself down. "What did I tell you about going to school?"

"I know what you said but—"

"But nothing!" Will raises his voice, causing some unwanted attention.

I take a few steps away and pull my hood over my head.

"How many times have I told you that you need to graduate from college? How many times, Nick?"

"A lot," Nick says quietly.

"So, what the fuck is this shit about not going?" He throws his hands in the air and shakes his head like Nick is the biggest disappoint of his life. "Did you apply to *any* schools?" Will stares Nick down.

Nick shrugs and shakes his head. I don't think he's ever felt as bad about anything as he does right now. Will kicks at the ground, then opens his truck door and slams it shut. He throws the biggest bitch fit I've ever seen. I doubt Nick's ever taken this type of abuse. Unlike Arnie. We've all seen Arnie getting yelled at by his old man. He's a high-strung ex-military guy. When you go to Arnie's place, you expect to see some sort of confrontation. Arnie's father would pace back and forth in their small house screaming orders to Arnie like he was a private in boot camp. To make matters worse, Arnie always, and I mean always, talked back, which drove his old man even more insane. I've seen Arnie tossed out the front door, thrown against a wall, and verbally abused by his father more times than I can remember, but I've never felt as bad for Arnie as I do for Nick right now. I'm waiting for Nick to come to his own defense, to tell Will to fuck off or something. But he just stands there and takes it.

"Do you realize what this means?" Nick's eyes stay transfixed on the ground. "It will take that much longer to get the money!" He screams at Nick like he's nothing—a nobody.

I finally get it. Will is referring to Nick's inheritance. The Marino's have this rule. You can't get your inheritance unless you graduate from college with a degree. I'm just wondering why Will cares so much. Why is he's so invested? Unless he is. Does Nick plan on going into business with Will?

"I'll make it right," Nick promises.

"God damn right you will. We didn't work all these years to lose it in the home stretch. Don't do what your old man did. Don't fuck this up." Will grabs Nick around the neck and kisses the top of his head.

That was a low blow. Everyone knows Nick hates being compared to his father.

"I won't. I guess I thought I could get a jump-start on the business now with the money I got for my eighteenth. With the way things were going, I could have tripled it in a year," Nick starts to explain, but Will cuts him off again.

"Patience, nephew." He nods his head in my direction like I'm not supposed to know what they are up to. I don't want to fucking know.

"So, how was your party?" Will walks back to the door of his truck with his arm around Nick's neck. I've never seen anyone play with Nick's emotions like Will Walker. He goes from an abusive thug to a loving uncle in the blink of an eye. "I hope you at least got laid!" Will looks at me. "I hope you had some fine girls lined up for our boy."

I sort of laugh in a shut-the-fuck up kind of way.

"It wasn't like that. I have a girlfriend," Nick reminds him. "I really want you to meet her."

"Yeah, sure." Will opens his door and gets inside. "I'll call you next week. You better have a plan to get into some kind of fucking school. Have granny pull some strings."

"I'll take care of it," Nick assures him. I guess this is a good thing. At least now Nick is motivated to go to college, even if it's just to please his asshole uncle.

Will points at Nick and smiles. "I have faith in you, kid."

Nick beams at his uncle's approval. I feel sick.

"And you." Will points at me. "Take care of our boy!"

I keep my hands in the pockets of my jacket and give him a nod. "Yeah, of course." What a prick.

I hate the way Will just had Nick groveling for his approval. I can't believe Nick doesn't see it. He's blind when it comes to Will. What's worse is that I can't say shit about it. Will is the closest thing Nick has ever had to a father. He can do no wrong.

We get in Nick's car and head to the café. There is only one thing that may change Nick's mind about school, and that's Dani. She deserves better than a drug dealer for a boyfriend. We're at the light waiting to turn into the parking lot of the strip mall when Nick pulls an envelope from under his seat and hands it to me.

"What's this?"

"It's for Stanford."

I open it and look inside. There is at least a year's worth of tuition in my hand. I look at Nick; he's staring straight ahead with a smile on his face. I didn't earn this. Saying I'm in Nick's crew and putting in work are two different things. Arnie is the one out there selling and risking his life, not me.

"I don't know if I can take this," I force myself to say.

"It isn't a gift. This is your cut." My cut should be somewhere around nine or ten grand. This looks like five times that. I want to mount some sort of argument, but I don't know how to refuse the money without insulting him.

"Really? Business is this good?" I ask just to hear him say yes. Just so my weak ass can keep the money. "Are you sure you can afford to pay me after what Will said about closing shop?"

Nick scoffs at the question. Nick can afford to pay all four years of my tuition plus housing. He doesn't need drugs to make money. All he has to do is go to the bank.

"You earned it for having my back."

"I'll always have your back, dude." He doesn't need to pay for my friendship.

We navigate through the parking lot and my eyes go directly to the café out of habit, not because I'm desperate to see her. I've stayed away from her all week. I said too much at Nick's party. Things got way too intense, but that's over now. I'm not giving her anymore pills, and I'm going to keep my distance. I tell myself it's the right thing to do—for her. But I'm really doing it for me. It's too hard to be around her now. She told me she loved me. She was whacked out of her mind, but I know she meant it. Then she went home with Nick. I can't play this game with her emotions or mine.

Dani walks out the door and I look at Nick. He sees her too. His tunnel vision almost causes him to hit a shopping cart.

"Whoa!" I yell just as Nick swerves out of the way.

"Damn, Matty!" Nick points to the floor. The money from the envelope is scattered at my feet.

"Oh shit." I reach down and start scooping bills as Nick parks the car.

Nick leans over to help. He names each bill as he goes. "This is English, this one is math, and this bad boy is art history."

"Art history?"

"Yeah, you need some place to meet girls."

"Very funny." I snatch the money from his hand and put it back in the envelope. "What about you? Why is Will so interested in you going to college anyway?" I try to sound clueless.

"Because it's a sweet deal—a college degree to be set up for life." I don't know how much Nick will inherit, but it's a lot.

"I thought you wanted to make your own money? You've been preaching that for years," I remind him. I always thought he was full of shit. I want to hear him say it.

"In the back of mind I always knew I would take the money. I was going to apply to barber college or something just to fuck with Mariann." Nick opens his door and gets out. "I just wanted to do it my way, you know?"

"Sounds like it's Will's way," I say sarcastically and regret it immediately.

"Hey, Will's just looking out for me. And he's right, I'm being the asshole. I don't want to be like my father. He was three credits away from graduating and quit. I'd be just like him to walk away and get nothing. There is no shame in taking the money. Not when it's that much money. I can buy myself some pride later," Nick jokes, but I know it kills him to take anything from Mariann. Nick is prideful to a fault.

"I thought your dad graduated." That's what I heard anyway.

"Nah, he never finished. After football was over, he started getting high; that's around the time he met my mom. He wanted to go into business with Will, but he fucked up. He couldn't stop using. And well, you know."

"Yeah." I nod. The rumor is he went on a binge right after Nick was born. Maria finally reached out to Mariann for help. Mariann agreed to take them in, but only if he went to rehab. He died a few weeks later. I really hope Nick isn't trying to finish what his father started. "Do you plan on going into business with Will?" I ask as we walk towards the café.

"I don't know. I might branch out on my own."

He can't do that. I won't let him do it. Not to himself and not to Dani. "What does Dani think about all this?" I look in the café and see her wiping down the counter.

Nick stops walking and pulls my arm. "Hey, dude. You can't say anything. She doesn't know how deep I'm in. She thinks this is a part-time thing."

So did I. Nick needs to know he can't stay with Dani and keep his business. "Has Dani ever told you about her father?"

"What do you mean?"

I know I shouldn't tell him about Dani's father being a lawyer, but he needs to know where her head is. I tell him about her dad's practice and his views on drug dealing that seemed to be passed to Dani. "I know she gets it, she gets you. But Dani sees dealing as a last resort in life, not a career choice. She thinks you're out come graduation. If you plan on staying in business, you need to let her know now."

Nick runs his hand through his hair. "I just can't walk away, Matt. I tell myself every day that I need to stop. That I'm going to get myself killed or locked up, but I can't stop. It's a rush better than thizz."

It hurts to hear my best friend tell me dealing drugs makes him happy. "Well, if you want to be with her, you have to choose. She deserves better." Nick knows I'm not trying to put him down. He knows Dani deserves better than the life he would give her if he stays in this game. She'll always be looking over her shoulder, waiting for someone to use her to get to Nick.

"I know I have to let her go." Nick looks into the café like it's a million miles away. "I know."

I almost can't believe what Nick is saying. He would rather break up with Dani than quit his business. I want to punch him in the face, tell him he's a fool. I should. But I don't. If he's willing to let her go, then he doesn't deserve her.

"So, what else did she tell you about her parents?" Nick sounds a little hurt that I know something about Dani that he doesn't. I do, I know a lot. I know her last name isn't DiMarco…I realize she never told me what her real last name is. The bikers came, then she went home with Nick, and I guess I forgot about it. Thizz is turning my brain to Swiss cheese.

"Uh, just that they were killed in a carjacking." I can't think about that without thinking about Will's witness, even though I've decided it can't be Dani. Those cops wouldn't lie and put someone in danger like that unless she was in protective custody.

"Oh man. That's fucked up." Nick runs his hand through his hair.

"Don't tell her I told you." I grab his arm, suddenly aware that I just broke her trust.

"Of course, dude." He doesn't ask when she told me, and I'm grateful.

I check my pocket to make sure the envelope is still inside. I've never held this much money in my life. "You sure you can afford to give me this? If you're branching out on your own…"

"Shut the fuck up." He grabs me in a headlock, then let's go and pulls me in for a bro hug. "Hell, you're the best investment I'll ever make. You know I'll need a good lawyer someday."

We both laugh, but in the back of my mind, I hope it isn't true.

37

Dani

The café is packed; a low rumble of voices fills the room. The clientele has changed a lot in the last month. It looks like the yard at lunch in here. Heather stopped by earlier. Her mother was attached to her side so we really couldn't talk. She told me she got into the University of San Francisco. The news sent my heart into spasms. I still haven't heard from CAL.

Nick and the guys are sitting in the corner talking, and even from behind the counter I can catch bits and pieces of their conversation. Nick is trying to sell Arnie on the idea of moving to Chico. I want to tell them to keep it down. Patty is in the back. The last thing I need is for her to catch the guys planning their next drug deal in her café.

"Imagine the possibilities. College girls, dude. They'll fucking love you. I'll set you up in a house off campus. All you have to do is party."

"I'll think about it." Arnie bows his head. I can tell he hates disappointing Nick.

"You'll think about it? What the fuck does that mean. I need you in Chico." Nick's been edgy ever since his party. We all have. Nick's almost out of pills, so we haven't partied at all. And Matt cut me off.

He said it's because they're low, and Nick's watching his stash, but I think it has to do with something else. He knows we slept together. It isn't like Nick broadcast the information. Matt actually showed up at Lucy's in the morning with some lame excuse about dropping off the keys to the beach house. He's been standoffish with me ever since. I don't know why. Arnie gave us a nice play by play of their night with the sluts, which involved whipped cream and a bottle of caramel.

The bell above the door jingles, and Alex coughs MILF into his hand. I look up and see Lucy strut through the door, dressed in her scrubs. Alex and I don't really speak. He doesn't speak to anyone. He just watches, and that creeps me out. He creeps me out.

"Hey, that's Dani's aunt. Show some respect," Arnie scolds him. He raises an eyebrow in Lucy's direction.

Lucy's here, Nick's here. This is the perfect opportunity for them to meet. I wave him over before I notice the worried look on Lucy's face. I see little sweat marks already forming under her arms when she lifts her backpack onto the counter.

"You want the usual?" I ask. I see Nick taking off his hat and running his hand through his hair. *He's so damn cute.*

Lucy twists her face and wrinkles her nose as if she's just tasted a lemon. "Yes. No. Make it a decaf," she says and spits out a piece of gum.

"What's wrong?" She never chews gum and never ever drinks decaf, especially before a night shift. She hastily removes another foiled-covered stick from her pocket and fidgets with the wrapper, ignoring my question.

Nick walks up beside her. "Um, Lucy, this is Nick."

She turns to face him with a huge smile. "It's about time!" She pulls him in for a hug, and they both seem to relax. Nick is charming as ever. He makes small talk with Lucy while I take another order. When I return, I find out she's invited him to dinner next weekend.

"Great," I say dryly and fake a smile. Nick sees through my false enthusiasm and laughs.

"See, that wasn't so bad, was it?" Lucy says, as if their meeting was equivalent to eating broccoli for the first time.

"Whatever, here's your coffee." I turn to Nick and ask if he needs a refill.

"No, I'm good." He turns to Lucy. "It was nice to meet you." He shakes her hand and heads back to his table.

Lucy smiles at me as if she just won a bet and spins away from the counter.

I haven't told Nick about my parents yet. There is no way I can get through a dinner with Lucy and not have it brought up. I have to tell him this week. I think it's safe to say I can trust him now that he's seen me naked. I just wish I hadn't taken my last pill. If I had known Matt was really going to cut me off, I would have conserved a a little better. It's been four days since I had a pill, and I'm starting to unravel.

"Whose coffee is this?" Patty points to the cup on the counter.

Lucy forgot her coffee. From the window I see her at a table outside flipping through her calendar. I thumb towards the window.

"What wrong with her?" Patty asks as Lucy folds another stick of gum into her mouth.

I shrug and hand her the cup. "Decaf."

Patty rolls her eyes as she takes the cup and heads outside. Maybe Lucy's getting the stomach flu that's going around. I hope note, I was looking forward to spending some alone time with Nick. Since we've been put on pause, as Aurora calls it, we can't go to any parties, which means no thizz for me. I've been trying to carve out some alone time with Nick, hoping he might want to pop a pill alone. Thizz and sex is like peanut butter and jelly. They are ok on their own, but together they are orgasmic.

"Can I talk to you for a sec?" Arnie leans on the counter. "I was wondering if you could help me." He glances over his shoulder at Nick's table. "I need to take the SAT."

I guess Nick finally got to him. "I didn't think you were going that route."

"My old man wants me to join the army, but fuck that. I'm not trying to get killed. I figured if I got into college, he'll get off my back."

"That usually is the case," I assure him.

"I'll take college girls over getting my ass shot any day."

He says the next testing date is in a week, so I invite him to the house for a study session.

Arnie arrives a little after five. Lucy shows up an hour later saying she isn't feeling well and blows my plan to have Nick over later tonight. I text Nick and tell him Lucy is home. He sends back a sad face and tells me he'll see me tomorrow. I'm beyond disappointed.

Arnie is reading the sentences I wrote for him. His lips move, even though he's reading in his head. It's annoying. Everything annoys me these days. I text Matt a short note: *Hey you.* I can't think of anything else to say. I hit send.

Arnie finishes and looks up with a smile. "She has big tits. Big would be the adjective."

"Yes, exactly." I found that turning the lesson into something he could relate to helped him grasp the concepts.

"This isn't as hard as I thought."

"You're not as dumb as you think you are." I check my phone to see if Matt replied. Nothing.

Arnie smirks at my back-handed compliment. "Once I make up my mind to do something, I do it. You know what I mean?"

"What made you decide to go to Chico?" I ask, even though I know it's what Nick wants him to do. Nick told me he wants to go into business with his uncle. I'm just glad he isn't trying to pull Matt in with him.

"Nah, I want to go to Humboldt State," Arnie confesses. "I spoke to a coach there about playing ball. He thinks I'm good enough to make the team. I just need to get my shit together."

I never pictured Arnie as anything more than a lackey for Nick. Watching him talk about a possible future playing college basketball is enlightening.

"My father was in the army, he was a ranger. I respect him and all because he's my dad, but I'm not him. I don't want to kill people. I'm a lover, not a fighter." Arnie smiles, and I recognize the smile. It's his thizz smile.

I'd kill to feel that rush again. I wonder if Arnie has any pills.

"Dani, sweetie, can you go get the mail?" Lucy calls from the kitchen. "Is your friend staying for dinner?"

"No, we're done." I start clearing the table. I need to get him out of here before I do something stupid like ask him for drugs. "Take these." I shove a stack of study guides in Arnie's backpack.

"Hey, can you do me a favor?" Arnie asks as I walk him out. "Can you not tell Nick about this? I mean about Humboldt. I don't want you to lie or anything. But in case this doesn't work out, I don't want to mess things up for nothing." I don't think Nick would object to Arnie going to Humboldt, but I get it. Nobody wants to defy Nick.

Arnie starts his moped and speeds off down the street. When he's gone, I pull the mail from the box. I see the CAL logo peeking out from underneath Lucy's phone bill. My heart is in my throat. This envelope holds my entire future. Getting in means I can fulfill my parents' dream. Not getting in means I failed them. I fold the envelope and shove it in my back pocket. I'm not ready to find out my future yet. Not today. Not sober.

38
Matt

Dani's walking a few feet in front of me and I don't even call her name. She's wearing her old khaki cargo pants, a Eureka Coffee t-shirt, and beat-up old Vans. She looks like her old self. The girl she was before Nick. The Dani I knew when nobody else did. See, thoughts like that are the reason I can't be around her. What do you do when you're in love with your best friend's girl? You don't give her pills so you can sneak a hug or a grateful smile. You stay away. I've done just that for the last week. I'm only going to class today because Mr. Davis cornered me in the hall this morning and threatened to fail me if I kept ditching.

Mr. Davis closes the door and stands in front of the room. "I'd like to congratulate you all on your websites. You did a great job. The sites are live, so you can share them with your friends and family…"

Dani leans over in the middle of his speech and asks me if I want to see her page. "It's not great, but I did it all on my own." There's no sarcasm in her statement, but I feel bad for not helping her.

"Sure." I scoot my chair over and watch the page load. I try not to think about the smell of her hair or the pink in her cheeks. She looks good. Healthy. Her website pops up and the first thing I see is a picture of her parents. Dani looks just like her mother.

"If this computer had speakers, you'd hear the song I loaded." She points to the widget on the bottom of the screen. It reads *Eagle's Greatest Hits – Hotel California*. "It's my dad's favorite song." She blushes slightly and bites her lower lip. I offer her a smile. I want to give her more, a hug, or even just squeeze her hand. But I can't. Touching her, caring for her, is a betrayal to Nick. Her photos are set up in slide-show format. They flip from pictures of her in elementary school, to her parents at their college graduation. "I know it isn't really fancy, but I like it." She's fishing for some praise, and I'm ready to tell her she's done a good job when a picture pops up on the screen.

He's standing outside a window, watching Dani and her father. My heart stops.

Mr. Davis is still talking. "The sites will only be up until the end of the school year. If you want to keep your site, you'll have to purchase a web address. I can help you transfer it to a new server..."

"That was my seventeenth birthday." Dani points to the picture. "We're at this restaurant in North Beach that has the best tiramisu..."

"What is your last name?" My voice cracks as I brace for what she's about to say.

"I thought told you. It's Batista."

"You have to take this site down!" I push Dani out of the way. Her chair slides to the side and hits the wall.

She's pulling at my arm, trying to stop me, trying to ask me what's wrong. She doesn't know the man standing in the window. I don't want to be the one to tell her. I don't want to be the one to ruin her life, again.

"Matt, what is going on?" She grabs my hand and yanks the mouse from me. It disconnects from the computer.

"Fuck!" I drop to the floor and battle nine months' worth of dust to plug the mouse back in. I climb from under the desk and sit in my chair. She's glaring at me like I'm a crazy person. *She doesn't know.* I point to her slide show. The picture is frozen on the screen. I notice my finger is trembling and pull it away quickly. "Have you ever met Will Walker?"

39

Dani

"You're telling me that man is Nick's uncle Will?" I point at the screen. At the man staring into the restaurant. The man my father argued with on the street.

"Yes. We have to take the site down right now."

"Do you think he..." I can't bring myself to say it. I can't even think it. "How does he know my dad?"

"I don't know anything for sure, but we were sitting in Will's bar a couple of weeks ago and two cops came in. Will said they were harassing him about a case, a murder case." Matt looks around to make sure nobody else is listening. "It was a lawyer and his wife."

I don't believe him. Matt is a known liar after all. "He was being questioned about a case, so what. That doesn't mean he was involved." I don't believe anything I'm saying, but I don't want to jump to any conclusions. "Did he tell you something?"

"He just said he was getting heat...there was a wit—" Matt cuts himself off. "He thinks there's a witness that can identify him." Matt's voice cracks, and all the color drains from his face.

He's not lying. Nobody can fake that kind of fear.

"The cop said the lawyer had a daughter that witnessed the whole thing. He knows who you are and now you just published *where* you are." He points to the computer screen, to the Eureka High logo in the bottom right corner.

My hands start shaking. This can't be happening. "I didn't see anything. Maybe it's a different—"

"No, it's you. The guy's name was Batista." Matt clicks the mouse around the screen. "I knew your stories sounded similar. I should've figured it out, but I got high instead. I guess I just hoped it wasn't you. You said you didn't see anything. You said the witness was a waiter."

"It is, I didn't see anything."

"Well, that's not what the cops said." Matt finally finds what he was looking for and starts to click through folders to find my student file.

"Why are you doing this?" I gesture to the screen. "He can't find me from one picture I posted on a school intranet."

"I don't want to take any chances. He said he's got some technology to find people online." Matt reaches for my hand and I pull away.

I stand up and reach for my backpack. My pocket starts to vibrate. I pull out my cell phone and check the caller ID. "It's Nick. Does he know?" I shove the phone back in my pocket without answering it.

"Yes," Matt says and spins around to look at me.

I sit down and put my head in my hands. I don't know if I'm going to cry or scream. "I don't understand. Nick's uncle is looking for me because he thinks I saw him shoot my parents. Which I didn't. And you guys just do nothing?"

Matt grabs my chair. "It made me sick to think he killed those people." I see him swallow hard. His Adam's apple bobs up and down. Matt is just as scared as I am. I can see it in his eyes, hear it in his voice. "What was I supposed to do? It isn't like I had any evidence. Shit, the cops don't even have anything to tie him to the shootings. If they did, he'd be in jail. There was nothing I could do."

Matt's right. Will Walker doesn't know who I am. Nobody does. "If we take down the site, chances are he didn't see it. I'm still ok." It sounds reasonable. "It's only been up one day."

"He has resources that can find you. If one of them got a hit on this website, then they know where you are."

"This is a school intranet. You have to know what you're looking for to find it. The odds are in our favor."

"Odds? You want to talk odds?" Matt spits through gritted teeth. "You are dating the nephew of the man that shot your parents!" Matt whispers not so quietly. The girl in front of me turns in her seat slightly.

I tell him to keep it down and let him go back to hacking the Eureka high server. There has to be an explanation for all of this. Something I can do. I didn't see anything that night, I was asleep in the back. The cops know I didn't see the person who shot my parents. Why would they tell Will Walker I was a witness if it wasn't true?

"I can talk to Nick, he can explain that I didn't see anything. He can tell him the cops lied." I don't know if what I'm saying will work. I want to believe it will. "We should call Nick."

"No!" Matt grabs my hand. "Nick is loyal to his uncle."

Matt has lost his mind if he thinks Nick would do anything to hurt me. To put me in danger. "Nick is loyal to me." I push Matt's hand away and take out my phone.

I have a voicemail.

"Hey babe, it's me. Something came up with my uncle. I'll call you later. I love you."

I relay the message to Matt, and his head explodes.

"Did he say what's going on? Is Will coming here? We have to go to the police." Matt puts his face in his hands. "We're so fucked. I'm so fucked." He's mumbling to himself. He's scared. I'm not. Nick will protect me. This is all just a misunderstanding. Will might be freaking out because he thinks they are trying to pin a murder on him. He's desperate, and desperate people do stupid things. Those are my father's words. Someone like Will, someone on the opposite side of the law who feels like they will never get justice, will go to great lengths to protect themselves. Even commit another crime.

"Nick can explain the situation, tell him I didn't see the shooter."

Matt looks at me like I just kicked him in the stomach. "What are you saying?"

The bell rings and we both jump. The room starts to empty, but Matt and I stay in our seats.

"The cops are assuming it's him. He didn't actually confess to killing anyone, did he?" I try to state the facts. Matt and I both understand the law. He knows I'm right. If the cops had evidence, Will would be in jail, so chances are they are just trying to scare him. It's a tactic they use to get people to rat on their friends. "Maybe Will is innocent, and he's just scared. Or maybe he's lying to you and he isn't looking for anyone. Did you ever think about that?"

Matt looks me in the eyes and just stares at me. "You're in shock. That's why you're saying all these ridiculous things."

Mr. Davis clears his throat near the door. He looks at me and Matt huddled behind my monitor with a curious expression.

"Let's go, I can't leave you here alone." He snatches my backpack and heads out the door.

We walk three blocks without speaking. Matt's too busy scanning the street. He actually thinks someone might be following us.

"If Will Walker is such a bad guy, why do you work for him?" I finally ask.

Matt stops walking. "I don't work for him. I work for Nick." He says Nick's name like it's a disease. "You have no right to judge me. I didn't see you caring about Nick or his uncle when you were getting free pills!" He grabs my arm and drags me the last block to Lucy's house. I don't struggle to get away because I don't want to cause a scene, and honestly, Matt's concern is comforting to me. Maybe I am in shock, or maybe he's just overreacting.

I take out my key and open the door. I try to slam it in Matt's face, but he blocks it with his foot.

"Are you going to call the police?"

"Not until I figure this out. Not until I know for sure." I try to close the door, but Matt holds it open.

"Will Walker wants to kill you," he says, and hands me my backpack. "And Nick was ready to help." He storms down my stairs and jogs away.

"Nick doesn't even know who I am!" I yell.

"Exactly," Matt yells back without stopping.

I slam the door shut and lock it.

I scream until my throat burns.

40

Dani

I tear through my room looking for the one thing that will make everything better. I dump my memory box on the bed, and pictures scatter across the comforter. I pluck the Big Red package from the pile and pull out the gum.

It's empty. Of course it's empty. Matt stopped giving me pills once he realized he wasn't benefiting from me getting high. Some friend he is. I pick up my phone and type a text to Arnie then delete it. I can't ask Arnie for a pill, he'll tell Nick. Arnie is loyal to Nick, more than Matt. Matt is a liar. He lied to me for weeks about why Nick was going off to run errands all the time. He lied to me about his feelings. And now this. For all I know, he's making up this story to turn me against Nick.

I fall onto the bed and cry. My tears run black as my makeup smears all over the pillow case. I don't care. I don't care about anything. I need thizz. I need it more than I need answers about Will Walker. I need it more than I need Nick, Lucy, coffee, or air. I pick up my phone, scroll through the contacts, and click on his name.

"What up, D?" The music in his car quiets while he waits for me to speak. I contemplate hanging up. No. I need this. I can do this. "D, you there?"

"Yeah, can you come by my house, right now?"

I'm sitting on my bed when he rings the doorbell. I send a text telling him the door is unlocked, and to meet me on the third floor. My heart pounds with every step he takes closer to my room.

"Dani," he calls out when he's on the stairs to the attic.

My head is spinning.

Oh my God. What am I doing?

A long, low-pitched creak echoes into the room as Alex pushes open the door.

I remember Nick standing in that same spot watching me undress. Alex has the same stunned look when he sees me in yoga shorts and a tank top.

"What's going on?" His voice is a mix of optimism and fear.

I exhale and try to force a smile, but it's more difficult than I anticipated. I don't have it in me to put on the same show I gave Nick.

Just do it! All the pain will be gone as soon as you have a pill.

I stand up and hold my hand out to Alex.

He hesitates at my gesture, and his guard goes up. "Where's Nick? Is this some kind of joke?" He steps back like he's going to leave, and I panic.

"Wait! No!" I reach for him. "Nick isn't here. I promise."

My plea stops Alex's retreat. He leans against my desk and crosses his arms. I suddenly feel very self-conscience about the way I'm dressed. *What the hell were you thinking?* I pull a jacket from the pile on the floor. I put it on and zip it up as I fight back tears. "Um, I just had a really bad day, and I was hoping you could hook me up."

The skepticism in Alex's face is quickly replaced with pleasure. He drops his arms and reaches into his jacket pocket, pulling out a small baggy with about a dozen pills inside. "Is this what you want?" He shakes the bag in my face and grins.

"Yes." I step forward and reach for the bag, but Alex moves it quickly and grabs my hand, pulling me to him in one quick motion.

I try to yank free, but he's too strong. "Alex, wait!"

"What? Isn't this why you brought me up here?" His breath smells like cigarettes. Every time he exhales, I suck in a mouthful of second-hand smoke. "Wasn't this for me?" He opens my jacket and runs the back of his hand over my bra-less chest. I look into his eyes and realize this is the price I have to pay to get high.

The pain will be gone as soon as I take a pill. *You don't have to hurt anymore. You don't have to care. Thizz makes it all better.* If I do this, my relationship with Nick is over, forever. *Isn't it over already?*

I inhale another mouthful of Alex's nicotine-laced breathe. "I was, I can…pay you." I look at the bag then back at his yellow-stained teeth. "How much do I owe you?" Alex lets me go and I pretend to look for my wallet.

"So what, you got tired of giving it up to Matt and thought you'd call me?" Alex sneers.

"What are you talking about?" I don't want Alex to know he's even partially right about Matt giving me pills. Not that I should care about what happens to Matt.

"Matt's stash always came up short. Then I saw you two on Nick's birthday, all over each other in the yard. You're lucky Nick's a fucking jerk-off and thinks none of his boys would have the balls to do him dirty." I step away from him, towards the door. "But I ain't his boy.

I'm just here to watch him for Will. Since that's over now, I don't owe him shit."

"What's over?" I ignore all his other comments, focusing only on what he said about Will.

"Will partnered with an old buddy; he's letting him run Humboldt for him."

Will isn't closing shop here, and the Devil's Gold isn't shutting Nick down. Will is giving Humboldt to someone else. Alex's phone buzzes before I can ask him who this partner is. "Speak of the devil," he snorts. "Here's Walker now." Alex reads the text and closes his phone. "I gotta go, sunshine." Alex puts his phone away and straightens his belt. "Sorry we couldn't get to know each other better." He steps towards the door, and I back away. "No need to be that way. I didn't force my way in here. You invited me, remember?" He's right, he didn't do anything wrong. He isn't the bad guy. I am.

Alex pauses at the door and places the bag of pills on my desk. "A goodbye gift."

I hold my breath until I hear his car pull away, then I run downstairs and lock the door.

A few minutes later, Lucy pulls into the driveway.

I hide the pills and scramble to put my regular clothes back on, avoiding my reflection in the mirror. The shame of what I was about to do crushes me, and it takes every ounce of control I have not to cry. My bed is still covered in pictures and trinkets from my memory box. I shove the contents of my former life back into the box and close it.

"Hey Dani, you home?" Lucy calls from downstairs.

"Yeah, up here." I listen to her clogs gallop up the stairs and try to gain my composure.

"Are you sitting down?" She peeks her head in, then bursts into the room. "I'm pregnant!"

I literally choke on the tears hidden in my throat. Lucy, pregnant? No way. "And this is a good thing?"

Her smile fades slightly as if my reaction wasn't what she expected. But after years of hearing her swear she would never have children, I think my response is accurate.

"Yes, of course it is," she says confidently. "I mean, I was shocked at first and in denial, but I mean, overall I'm thrilled. Johnson is beyond thrilled!"

"Then I am too. Congratulations." My anti-climactic response perturbs her even more.

"Are you ok?" She looks around the room. "Is everything ok?"

I bite my lip. This lie will make or break me. If she doesn't fall for it, I have to tell her the truth. Tell her about Will. I don't want to tell anyone until I talk to Nick. I have to give him a chance to explain. I need him to tell me he will make it better. I need him to tell me Matt was wrong.

"I'm fine, really." My voice raises an octave higher than normal. The forced grin hurts so bad I have to fight back tears. "I'm so happy for you, for both of you. You guys are going to be awesome parents." I hold the smile for a second longer, then pretend to scratch my back. I make a dramatic effort and reach around my back, dropping my smile like a ton of bricks.

She pulls me into her arms. It takes everything I have not to cry. "Your parents loved you so much, Dani." She pulls a small square photo from under my leg and hands it to me. "You know it's ok to miss them. You don't have to hide it."

I must have missed the picture in my mad dash to clean up. It was taken when I was around three years old. I'm standing on a table with my parents on each side of me, kissing my cheeks. I can't tell where it was taken and I don't remember the day, but I look like the happiest kid in the world. I look into their eyes, the eyes of a family I had forgotten. I know what I have to do.

41

Dani

I stand on the porch, gasping for air as I ring the bell. I look at the black Audi parked in the driveway and pray his mother doesn't answer the door. I'm about to ring again when a brand new black Mustang rumbles to a stop next to the Audi.

"Dani!" I hear Ashley's voice from inside the car.

The passenger door opens, and a man in a black suit steps out. Matt's father is tall and slender, with short dark hair and blue eyes. He's very handsome for his age. He holds the seat forward, and Ashely and her mother get out of the car behind him. Ashely runs over to say hi.

"Hi Ashley, how are you?" Her skin is pale, and a thin veil of sweat dots her forehead.

"Been better." She smiles her infectious smile. "What do you think of Matt's new car?"

I look towards the driveway and notice Matt is still sitting in the driver's seat.

"Nice."

Matt's parents are standing behind Ashley, waiting to be

introduced, and I wonder if they find it odd that Matt isn't getting out to make the introductions.

"This is Matt's friend, Dani," Ashley says with a sly smile like there's more to it than that. I wonder what she knows. What has Matt told her?

"Nice to meet you." Matt's mother pats my shoulder as she walks past me into the house.

Mr. Augustine stands on the porch with me, and we stare back at the car, waiting to see what Matt is going to do. At least I know he hasn't called the police, or even Nick. He hasn't had time. He must have come home and found the car waiting for him. The only thing that could have distracted him from our discovery today is a brand new muscle car.

"Nice car," I finally say.

"Yeah, it's an early graduation present. Matt has some good news." Mr. Augustine stops speaking when Matt honks the horn. "I'll let him tell you." He winks at me and takes Ashely in the house.

I get in Matt's new car and he pulls out of the driveway. Neither of us speak until we're two blocks away.

"What are you going to do?" he says impatiently.

"I'm going to the police, but I need to talk to Nick first." I can't go to the cops behind his back. I owe him more than that. I also owe my parents. They deserve justice, and if there is even a remote chance Will Walker had something to do with their murder, then I have to make sure he pays. To do that I need Nick on my side.

Matt says he will tell the police everything Will told him. Which is hearsay, but everything helps I guess. If they think Walker had something to do with the shooting, then they must have some evidence, just not enough to arrest or convict him. I'm sure Nick knows more than Matt. I hope I can convince him to help us.

"Do you know where Nick is?"

"I texted him right after I left you. He's at home."

He's home? His message said he had something to do with his uncle. I don't have time to care. "Take me there," I tell Matt. "Take me to Nick's house."

"Are you sure?" Matt gets in the left lane to make a U-turn. "Nick is very loyal to Will."

Matt's feelings for me jade his perception of Nick. "He would never hurt me." If anything, I'm about to hurt him.

We drive along the winding private road until it leads us to a large metal gate adorned with the Marino family crest. This is the closet I've ever been to Nick's real life, and I feel like an intruder.

Matt pulls to a stop in front of a gray box and presses the button. When the screen pops on, a man in a gray uniform recognizes him immediately.

"What's up, Matt. Does Nick know you're coming? He didn't call it in." He looks down and I hear papers rustling.

"No, I want to surprise him. I got a new car, man." We watch the camera swivel around.

"Oh shit! You're going to give that boy a run for his money." The security guard laughs. "Pull around back. He's in the cottage."

The driveway leads us through a tree-lined courtyard, past a water fountain that looks like it belongs in a piazza in Italy. Water trickles from a stone olive oil barrel held by a beautiful goddess. The fountain is so beautiful, I almost miss the house. To call it a house would be an insult to architecture. This is a modern-day castle, with wide columns and towers. The white exterior and brown accents give it the look of an old California mission.

Matt drives around the side of the house and parks in an even larger courtyard. Nick's car is parked in between two silver Mercedes.

A man in a white oxford shirt is hosing down the SUV on the right. I realize this is why Nick's car always looks like it just rolled off the showroom floor.

Matt honks to get the man's attention. When he turns around, I recognize his face, although I know we have never met. The man looks like an older version of K.

"What up, T." Matt parks sideways, blocking the three cars. He jumps out and shakes hands with the oversized K. "You think I'll take Nick's trailer queen over there?"

"Ah man, I don't know. What you got?" He walks around the car. "GT, hell yeah!"

"V8, 305 horsepower. I think I have a chance," Matt brags. We're here to crush Nick, and he's bragging about his engine size.

"Dude, I don't know, but I want to be there when you guys go." T slaps Matt's hand the way guys do that is part high five and part handshake. "Ah man, sorry for being rude." He rushes over to me and takes my hand in both of his. "I'm T, nice to meet you."

I force a smile. "Hi, I'm Dani."

Matt sort of skips over to us to clear the air. "Uh, T, this is Nick's girl," he clarifies.

T's demeanor changes instantly. The casual introduction becomes something formal and uncomfortable. "Oh sorry. It is very nice to meet you," he says, shaking my hand again.

"You look so familiar."

"He's K's cousin," Matt says.

"You know my little cousin?"

There is nothing little about K, but compared to T, I get it. "He's a great guy, makes me laugh." I smile at the thought of K and his big toothy grin.

"Yeah, he's a character." He smiles a big K smile and excuses himself.

"If you aren't too busy, you can do mine too," Matt teases.

"HAH!" T scoffs and disappears into the garage.

The smile drops from Matt's face as soon as we're alone. "This way."

He leads me onto a dark tree-covered path. There is little sunlight on this side of the house because of the giant redwoods that fill the yard. The pungent smell of wet soil and pine fill the air. I stay close as we pass an enormous Roman pool surrounded by a beautiful garden. When we approach a green fenced area that I assume are tennis courts, he stops.

"Are you sure you want to do this? Maybe we should call someone first."

"Who am I going to call?"

"I don't know, the cops?" he suggests, as if it's the most obvious thing in the world.

"I have to talk to him first. I owe him at least that." Nick will make all of this right. He will straighten out his uncle and clear the air. I know he will. He loves me no matter what.

Nick's cottage is hidden deep in the back of the property. The moss-covered building looks like it belongs in the Amazon jungle. Bamboo shoots line the sides and the heavy overgrowth of foliage offers ample privacy. Even though we are surrounded by fragrant trees and flowers, the smell of marijuana overpowers them all.

Matt walks up the two short steps to the door and knocks, something I'm sure he has never done before.

"S'up, Matty?" Nick doesn't see me on the landing. "What are you doing here?" He opens the screen and moves back inside.

"Dude, wait." Matt holds the screen door open and I step around him.

I wouldn't say Nick is disappointed to see me, but his reaction is definitely not something I've seen before.

"Dani?" He looks at Matt then holds his hand out to me. "Come in."

Nick's cottage is a mess. There are hats and t-shirts strewn all over the main room. The marijuana smell barely masks the stench of old food and dirty clothes.

The cottage has an open-floor plan. The main room flows into the kitchen, and there is a small breakfast nook in the corner. The main room and kitchen are separated by a granite counter. I stand in the center of the main room while Nick places dirty dishes in the sink.

"Can I get you a drink?" He opens his fridge, and I look at Matt. He leans against the wall near the door, waiting for me to say something. Nick closes the refrigerator and catches us staring at each other. "You guys are making me nervous." Nick looks at Matt. Matt looks at me. I look at the picture in my hand. I forgot I was even holding it.

"What's going on?" He moves from the kitchen to the middle of the room. He's equal distance from me and Matt.

This is it. I have to tell him everything. He will protect me, I know he will. "Matt and I were in computer class today and I showed him my family page. You know the one I've been working on." Nick nods his head. "There was this picture from my birthday. Matt said the man in the picture is your uncle Will." I pause for a second before delivering Matt's theory, but Nick doesn't give me a chance to finish.

"No way." Nick looks at Matt. "No." Matt nods one time and looks at the floor.

The look on Nick's face confirms everything Matt told me, and I realize why he was so scared to come here. He knows more than he let on. He knows for a fact that Will Walker killed my parents.

"FUCK!" Nick screams and throws the bottle of water in his hand. It bursts against the wall beside me. "No fucking way!"

I stumble back and fall onto the couch. Nick paces the room, and Matt rushes to my side.

"Dude, calm down. We don't know anything for sure." Matt motions for me to stand up.

Nick keeps pacing.

Matt grips my hand as we move towards the door. Nick stops and leans on the counter that separates the kitchen from the living room. He puts his head in his hands. "I thought your parents were carjacked?"

I want to go to him, to comfort him, but Matt won't let me.

Nick looks up. He looks at me and my heart snaps in half.

He hates me.

"Not exactly," Matt starts to answer for me. I pull his hand to stop him.

I want to be the one to tell him. "My father's name was Bill Batista. My name is Danielle Batista. My parents were shot and killed in our SUV while I slept in the backseat." I start to cry. "I didn't see anything. I didn't see who shot them. I woke up after…" Matt takes me in his arms and rubs my back. I'm sobbing into his chest, wondering why it isn't Nick that's comforting me. I wipe the tears from my eyes and turn around.

Nick swears under his breath and pounds his fist on the counter. I wait for him to calm down. I wait for him to come to me. To tell me everything is ok. He doesn't say any of those things. After a long silence, Nick finally looks at me. "I want to see the picture." He spits the words at me, like I'm a liar. Like I'm a killer.

Tears stream down my cheeks. Matt puts his arm around me and pulls me towards the door. Matt. My friend. My best friend. He is the only one here who cares about me.

"I'll take Dani home to get it then I'll be back, alright?"

I don't want to go. I want to give Nick another chance. He's in shock. He isn't thinking straight.

Nick's eyes drop from my face to my hand in Matt's. Matt notices it too and grips it even harder. Matt takes another step towards the door. I don't move.

I fling the picture on the floor. "Here," I cry. "Here's your proof!"

Matt scrambles to pick it up and lets me go in the process. He picks up the crumpled photo and places it on the counter in front of Nick. Nick barely looks at it. He doesn't need to. He knows Will killed my parents and wants to kill me. He knows some part of him wants me dead, too.

He looks at me like I'm the enemy, like I'm the one ruining his life. I charge towards him. "Don't you care that your uncle is a murderer!" I scream in his face. "Don't you care about how I feel? Don't you care about me?" My body is heavy with grief as Matt pulls me away.

Nick doesn't reach for me to stay.

He doesn't say he'll protect me or make it right.

He doesn't tell me he loves me.

He lets Matt take me out of his cottage.

He lets Matt walk me back to the car.

Nick lets me go.

Matt drives me home and insists he wait with me to tell Lucy. I convince him that it's best for me to talk to her alone. He doesn't know she's spending the weekend at Johnson's to celebrate their impending parenthood. This is the happiest day of her life. I won't ruin it.

I lock the doors, pull the bag of pills from my desk drawer, and swallow two.

An hour later I take two more. I follow this pattern until the bag is empty.

Nick

I don't know what I was thinking.

I wasn't thinking. I just let her go.

I need to get to the city. I need to talk to Will.

I fly down the road, away from my house, and skid across the intersection.

I close my eyes at the light and see her face. She fucking hates me. I hate me.

Why didn't I go to her? I should go see her now. I want to, but I don't know what to say.

What can I say? I'm sorry I wanted to kill you. Sorry I didn't give a shit that my uncle shot your parents?

Matt is right, I don't deserve her.

I never did.

I need to talk to Will. I need to make this right. I can't call him. I need to see him face to face. I want to tell him how much she means to me, even if she hates me. I want to tell him not to hurt her.

I'm stuck at the light on Myrtle when I see Arnie fly by on his scooter. I make a crazy U-turn and follow him into the parking lot of the café.

"Dude! Check this out." Arnie waves a piece of paper in his hand.

"Get in!" I don't have time to dick around or the patience to listen to one of his stories.

"Wait, I need to go see Dani." He revs his scooter and moves around my car.

"She's not there," I yell out the window. I wonder where she is, if she's with Matt.

She belongs with Matt. She always did.

Arnie pulls into an empty space in front of the café to park his scooter. Mary walks out to wipe down a table. Our table. It's not our table anymore. I fucked up. I let her go.

"Come on!" I yell. I don't know what Mary knows. If Dani told her about the picture. I need to get to Will. I don't trust anyone.

Arnie runs to Mary and hands her an envelope. I can't hear their conversation, but he's got a huge, goofy grin on his face.

I should just go. I don't need Arnie right now. I just don't want to be alone.

Arnie jogs to the car and gets in. "What's up, dude?"

I don't answer him. I peel away from the curb and head towards the highway.

"Where we going?" Arnie asks as we pass under the sign that reads *San Francisco 375 Miles*.

"I have to see Will." I stab the gas pedal to the floor and turn on the radio.

All I can think about is Will. What his next move will be after I tell him. I wonder if he has people in Eureka he can call if I can't reason with him? Alex was supposed to head back to Lake County today. I'm not worried about him. Matt will kick his ass if he tries anything. Matt will protect Dani. He'll make the right choice, he'll put her first.

I didn't. I didn't think of her. I only thought about Will and what this meant for me. For my business. What a fucking joke I am.

I wanted to go into business with Will. I wanted to be something more than just a Marino. No matter how hard I worked in school or how successful I became, it would never be impressive. My success is expected. I thought going into business with Will was my chance at something beyond my expectation. It's not the most respectful business, but it meant power, money, and making a name for myself in a market that doesn't give a shit about my family's wealth. The people Will deals with aren't impressed by my last name. It's about your name in the street. That's the one place the Marino name hasn't conquered. That was going to be my legacy. My mark on the world.

All of that changed when I saw the picture. When I saw the look on Will's face, the way he looked at Dani as she blew out her birthday candles. Knowing he hurt her in a way that nobody should ever feel. People don't get it. Losing your parents is like losing a part of yourself. Something you can never get back. You will always have this hole, this emptiness. You don't know what it's like to grow up never being able to celebrate Father's Day. I've never bought a card on Mother's Day. I don't have any family pictures. I don't care how much money my grandmother threw at me. She couldn't buy me that kind of love. I've never felt truly loved, until I met Dani. I never knew I could love someone the way I love her.

I should have taken her in my arms. I should have told her everything was going to be alright. I didn't. Because I'm a piece of shit. I'm no better than Will. I might as well have pulled the trigger on her parents. I was ready to pull it on her. Not her, a faceless witness. Someone I didn't know. That doesn't make it right. Even if the witness wasn't my Dani, it would've been someone else's version of Dani. Someone who was loved and didn't deserve to have her life taken.

Arnie tries to talk to me; he has some big news. He may have even told me, but I tuned him out. Eventually he falls asleep, and I somehow make it to the city without killing us.

It's dark when I get off the bridge. I fly up and over hills, dodging buses and taxis as I make my way to North Beach. I'm banking on Will being at the bar since I don't know where he lives. I know it's somewhere in the Sunset District, but he's never invited me to his house. We always meet at the bar.

Arnie wakes up when I turn onto Columbus. As usual there's no parking, so I double park in front of the Lucky Charm and jump out.

"DUDE!" Arnie yells and shuts off the car.

"Wait here," I tell him. "I'll be right back."

I burst in the bar and call Will's name.

"Whoa kid, slow down." Stacy, the doorman, pushes his hand into my chest.

"Get your fucking hands off me!" My hand balls into a fist. A natural reaction when I'm being challenged. Hit first, ask questions later. "Where is he?"

Stacy stands up from his stool and pushes me back with his enormous chest. When standing, he's about six inches taller than me. "Back the fuck up," he warns.

I don't stand a chance against him, but I don't give a shit. I want to hit someone. The rage that built up over the long drive is finally boiling over. "Fuck you." I push against his chest.

Stacy's body stiffens and I brace myself for what's coming next.

"Hey! What the fuck, Nick!" Will grabs me by my hood and shoves me out the door.

I stumble onto the sidewalk. Arnie sits up when he sees me. I put my hand up, signaling him to stay in the car.

"What the fuck are you doing here, Nicky?" Will looks at my car sitting in the street. "Is everything alright?"

I don't want to beat around the bush. "Who's Bill Batista?"

A flash of uncertainty crosses his face. He pats my back with one hand while he jingles the change in his pocket with the other. "He's the fucking lawyer, the dead one."

My stomach does a somersault. I can't believe Dani is the witness Will has been looking for. The same witness I wanted dead because she was ruining my business. I wish Stacy would have hit me. That pain is nothing compared to what I feel in my chest right now. I don't know what I can say to stop Will from wanting to kill Dani. There was nothing he could say to me at the diner when I was ready to do it. Not that I would have. I could never hurt someone like that. But I wouldn't have stopped Will, not if it meant I got to keep Humboldt.

I look at Arnie sitting in the driver's seat of my car. I feel bad for dragging him all the way down here. I don't even know why I brought him. It wasn't like I wanted company. He's another victim in my fucked-up life. He nods his head and I follow his eyes to a group of girls walking down the street. Fucking Arnie. He's always trying to get laid. Nothing ever brings him down. I'm glad he's here with me. He's always good for a laugh. I look back at the car and see Arnie smiling. Then we hear them. Motorcycles screaming up the street.

Will pulls me to the ground and I hear the *pop pop pop* from a gun, followed by screaming. Before I realize what is happening, it's over. I look up from under Will's arm in time to see two bikes speed across Columbus Avenue and disappear into the Broadway tunnel.

Then I hear someone scream, "He's been shot!" I look at Will. He gives me a thumbs-up. I stand up and dust my hands off. That's when I see the shattered windshield.

"ARNIE!" I open the door and his head falls out. "NO! FUCK! Somebody help him!" My eyes are blurry with tears. I scream for someone to call 9-1-1. I scream for Arnie to wake up. I scream because my friend is dying in my arms.

Suddenly, Will is at my side trying to pull me away, but I won't let Arnie go. *I'm sorry, Arnie. I'm so fucking sorry. Please don't die. Please keep breathing. I love you, bro. I love you.*

Will is speaking to me, but I can't hear him. The world goes silent. I hold Arnie's head in my arms until the ambulance arrives. They jump out and run over to me. There is nobody to save here. Arnie is dead.

"Nick." Will's voice finally breaks through the silence. "Remember what I told you. You were just stopping by to say hi. Nick? Are you listening?"

Cops come and go. Arnie is dead. They take his body away. They ask me questions. Arnie is dead. I give them Arnie's phone. His burner. The one he used to sell my drugs. Arnie is dead and it's my fault.

I lean against the wall outside the bar. Arnie shouldn't have been here. I shouldn't be here. I should be with Dani. Will comes out and offers me a bottle of water.

"Dani's last name is Batista." I slap the bottle out of his hand.

Will looks at me like I lost my mind. "Who's Dani?"

"My girlfriend," I say, then I wonder if that's still true. After what happened today I doubt she'll ever speak to me again. "She has a picture of you. She saw you with her dad."

I start to walk down the street towards the Bay, I think. I don't know the city very well, not like Dani does. She could have lived around the corner for all I know. Matt probably knows. He knew about her parents. *Why don't I know? Why didn't I ever ask? Why didn't I go to her? Why didn't I know I love her more than I love Will?*

"Hey, where did she see me?" Will spins me around. "What picture?"

"On her birthday. You were outside a restaurant." I can tell by the look on his face that he knows what I'm talking about. "She's my girlfriend."

"Yeah, well, you're young. You'll get over it." Will turns to go back in the bar, leaving me alone on the street.

"Hey!" A few of the cops that are still hanging around taking pictures to document the scene turn when I yell. "I LOVE HER!" I don't care who hears me.

Will grabs the front of my shirt and throws me against the wall. "I get it, you love her, but you know what has to happen. Grow some balls and deal with it."

I feel like spitting in his face and running to the cop with the camera and confessing everything I know. But I can't do that. I can't bust myself, because that would mean busting Matt and Aurora. I don't have to worry about Arnie. Arnie got something far worse out of all this. I won't hurt anyone else.

Will isn't going to let this go. He's going to find her. He has to get rid of her because he thinks she can identify him. He thinks she can, but the cops don't know that. Will was right. If they had evidence, they would have arrested him. So, Dani really didn't see anything.

Will drags me into the oversized closet that doubles as his office. I sit down and try to gain some composure. Will reaches into the bottom drawer of his desk, and for the first time in my life, I get nervous around my uncle. He pulls out a bottle of Patron and pours me a shot. "You need to chill." He slides the glass across the desk to me, then takes out a bud and some rolling papers.

I drink the shot. It burns going down. The pain feels good. I reach for the bottle, but Will hands me a joint instead.

"You just lost your friend, I know what it's like. I've lost a lot of good men. But you gotta man up. You dodged a bullet today. Be grateful."

I light the joint and pretend to pay attention. The only thing on my mind is getting out of here alive and protecting Dani. I owe her so much more than an apology.

"As for your girl." He pauses when I look up.

Don't say her name. You don't deserve to say her name.

"What does she know?"

He doesn't know about our fight, he doesn't know she probably called the cops by now. If I can convince him that I can control her, that I'm watching his back, then maybe I can stop him from going after Dani himself. "Nothing. She doesn't know anything. I saw the picture, I figured it out on my own." I won't tell him Matt knows. I take a long drag and let the smoke overtake my lungs. The weed makes it a little easier to lie. "I asked her how her folks died, she said it was a carjacking. She was sleeping in the backseat and didn't see anything. The cops are full of shit. You're right, if they had proof, you'd be in cuffs. They're fishing to see if you take the bait. If you go after her now, it's like admitting you did it."

Will reaches for the joint and I pass it to him. He takes a long drag.

"Alright, you watch her. Don't let the cops get to her. And whatever you do, don't tell her nothing about me. Sometimes witnesses' get their memories back and want to testify to shit they didn't see. If she doesn't know I was involved, don't give her any reason to. You got me?"

It's too late for all that. She knows everything thanks to me and Matt. She's probably calling the police right now. "I got you." I hold out my fist and Will bumps it.

He hands me the joint, and there's a knock on the door.

"Excuse me, Will." Suzy comes in, followed by two cops.

"Mr. Walker, we just wanted to let you know we caught the shooters."

I drop the joint to the floor and jump up.

"Who was it?" Will sits back in his chair like they're telling him the score of the Giants' game.

"One of the men was identified as Devon Brown."

They tell us Devon and the other shooter sped through the Broadway tunnel and out onto Van Ness Avenue, where they are repaving the streets. Devon lost control when the bike hit uneven pavement and swerved in front of a Muni bus. He was killed on impact. The other guy is in critical condition.

After the cops leave, Will's mood changes. "It looks like we just got Humboldt back."

Like I give a fuck. My best friend is dead and the girl I love is on my uncle's hit list. All I care about right now is making it right. I can't let him know that. I play along. "Does that mean we're back in business?" I lean back in the chair and balance on the hind legs.

"Let me make some calls first, but it should only be a couple days before I can get a new supply up to you.

I crack a smile and stand up. "Let's make some paper." Will stands and takes my hand, then pulls me in for a hug. My back straightens and I feel like head butting him. Instead, I pound his back twice and let go. I'll let him believe its business as usual until I come up with a plan.

"You know I love you, kid." Will looks me in the eye; he's looking for the loyalty I've always shown him. "We're going to do great things together."

I smile and tell him I love him. He believes the lie. He thinks I have his back. I don't. I'll die before I let him get away with what he's done to Dani.

I'm actually relieved when Mariann shows up. She doesn't go inside the bar. She sends T in to get me. I've known T as long as I can remember. He went to school with my father. They were best friends. He's always been like an uncle to me. He gives Will a dirty look, then gives me a bear hug and tells me she's waiting outside in the SUV.

I open the back door and see my grandmother wiping tears. I look out the window and see the tow truck loading my car onto a flat bed. I don't want the car, they can keep it. Burn it.

"Are you ok?" She reaches for me, then pulls back.

I tell her I'm fine.

"I called Arnie's parents. I told them I'd help with the funeral."

It's so typical. Money solves all her problems. "Is that your answer to everything? Money? Some things can't be bought. People can't be bought!" She bought me from my mother, but she couldn't buy my love, my loyalty, or my respect. Instead I gave it to Will. I thought he deserved it more than her. I was wrong. They were wrong. I have to make this right.

She wipes her eyes with a handkerchief and stares out the window. "I don't know how to help you. You won't let me in. I've tried everything. I don't know what else I can do."

I feel bad when I hear her crying. *Did she try? Was she there for me?* I've warped the truth so much I don't know anymore.

"I want to help you, Nick. Just tell me what you need me to do."

I need a way to get out of this without sending me and Matt and Aurora to jail. I need to find a way for the cops to get the evidence they need to bust Will for murdering Dani's parents. I need to make this right.

"Do you know anyone in the San Francisco Police Department?"

42
Dani

I wonder what it must feel like to lose a child. I wonder if it hurts more than a child losing a parent. Loss is loss, I guess. Lucy didn't even know Arnie and she's taking it hard. Maybe because she keeps thinking it could've been me. She's been watching me like a hawk since the morning she woke me with the news.

I was dripped in sweat and barely sleeping. You don't really sleep when you're on that much thizz. Your body conforms to the element you place yourself in. The way some people will sit for hours with a bottle of lotion, while others dance and dance and dance. I like to kick back and just feel the moments. Feel the tingles and the good vibes. I laid on my bed Friday night, turned on the radio, closed my eyes, and stayed like that for nearly twelve hours. My body looked relaxed, but my brain stayed on. I thought about Nick, the way he looked at me in his cottage. I actually saw the moment he started to hate me. I thought about Lucy and Johnson and their baby. As long as I'm here, they aren't safe. I thought about leaving, the places I'd go. The people I'd meet. Imaginary friends I'd make. Ones that would never know the real me. The real Dani is dead. I killed her.

I remember opening my eyes and seeing Lucy and Johnson standing over my bed. I thought it was a dream. Until Lucy yanked me into her arms and started to cry. She heard about Arnie while on her shift at the hospital. A friend of a friend or something. I don't know. It doesn't matter. I just kept thinking, thank God it wasn't Nick. Feeling happy Nick was alive feels like a betrayal to my parents. I shouldn't care, I don't want to care, but I do.

Thizz and grief and fear are a bad mix. I hid in my room for two days waiting it out. Waiting for the drugs to leave my body. Waiting for Will to come and find me. Lucy figured I was in shock. She left me alone. Matt called every other hour to check on me. I never heard from Nick. My heart aches when I think about him. He must be devastated. I am, and I didn't even like Arnie. Matt is wondering if he'll show up today. I can tell he wants to see him too. He misses him too.

Matt picks me up in his new Mustang and we drive to the funeral together. Lucy and Johnson are taking his truck. They said they'd meet me at the church. Matt and I pull into the parking lot of St. Bernard's just as Arnie's family is arriving in a black stretch limo. I watch in the side mirror as Arnie's mother is helped out by an older man dressed in formal military attire. I wonder how they found the strength to get out of bed this morning. Arnie's mother is greeted by friends of Arnie's I recognize from school.

"I'm going to say hi," Matt says and opens his door.

"I can't…"

Matt takes my hand and kisses it. "It's ok, I'll meet you inside."

I get out of the car and walk up the steps of the church. I watch as Matt works his way through the crowd and finally reaches Arnie's mother. He taps her shoulder and she turns around. Her eyes light up when she sees him. She takes his face in her hands and kisses his cheeks. Matt collapses onto her shoulder and sobs. It seems unfair that she has to console him. She's the one that lost a son. She's the one that needs comfort. This is why I didn't go to my parents' funeral. It wasn't for me. It was for them. Their grief is limited to one day, a few hours, then it's over. For us, it's a daily struggle. We have to live, breathe, eat, and sleep with it for the rest of our lives. That's what I did, until I discovered thizz. Thizz took all of that pain away. I don't know if I would have survived Eureka without it. That's a lie. I didn't need thizz to deal with the boredom or loneliness. I needed it to be with Nick. Living in his world was unbearable without it. Being with Nick was impossible without thizz. One didn't exist without the other. Now that I have neither, I'm starting to see things clearer.

"Dani." Mary's baby-soft voice surprises me. She's standing at the top of the stairs in her school uniform.

"What are you doing here?" I'm happy to see her. I don't want to be alone.

She gestures to the building behind the church. Her school. I forgot.

We watch Arnie's teammates from the basketball team assemble behind the hearse. They all have on white gloves and black suits. Nick isn't among them. Matt is still standing beside Arnie's mother, watching as they pull the casket from the car. I wonder who carried my parents' coffins. I wish I knew. I should know. Tears roll down my cheek.

"I have something," Mary whispers as the boys start up the steps. "It's from Arnie."

I pull her to the side and ask her what she's talking about.

"He came to the café looking for you that day." She hands me an envelope.

I already know what it is. I open the envelope and read the words on the paper. "He did it."

Mary says she has to get back to class and leaves me standing alone as Arnie's casket is carried into the church. I watch the crowd follow him, wiping tears from under their sunglasses. Then I feel someone behind me. I'm afraid to turn around. A hand touches my shoulder and I close my eyes.

"Dani," Heather says quietly. "Are you ok?" I throw my arms around her and start to cry. I didn't think I would make it through the day without tears. I just didn't expect to feel this level of sadness.

"How are you?" I straighten up. I know how close Heather and Arnie were.

"I'm keeping it together." Heather tries to smile. "I'm glad you're here."

It's strange to hear Heather King say those words to me. She hated me before thizz. I loathed her. Now, we're standing here hugging. I guess I can thank thizz for that.

By the time Matt comes to find me, we're so overtaken by grief, neither of us try to speak. Heather joins us, and we walk into the church together. She stops to dip her fingers in a pot of water at the door then crosses herself. We find a row towards the middle and slide in. Arnie's casket is a large shiny black box with gold trim. It's closed. Someone placed a framed picture of him on top. A basketball sits beside it. It looks like it's been signed by the entire team.

"Have you seen him?" Matt whispers as the priest says a prayer.

I can only assume he means Nick. I shake my head.

Matt makes a disgusted face and looks straight ahead as the first speaker takes the podium. There is a steady stream of friends, family members, and even teachers speaking on Arnie's behalf. I wonder who spoke at my parents' funeral. I bite the inside of my cheek. It's still sore from the other day. I bite until I taste blood, but tears keep coming. Heather places a box of tissues in my lap. I look down and see the letter crumpled in my hand.

The next thing I know, I'm standing. I step out into the aisle. Matt calls my name, but I keep walking. The priest spots me and waves me up. I don't know what to say. I don't know why I'm up here, staring at these people who don't know me. They don't know this is my fault. If I didn't move here. If I didn't fall in love with Nick. Arnie would still be alive. They're waiting for me to tell them a story about Arnie. I don't have one, not one I can share. All of my Arnie stories are drug-induced antics. The same drug that got him killed. I look at the paper in my hand. The paper that is useless to him now. I look at the picture on top of his casket. He has that crooked smile, the one he always had when he was thinking something dirty. That's Arnie. He's the fool. The stories people told about him were full of crazy pranks, like the time he dyed the school's pool for St. Patrick's Day. Suddenly it comes to me, the reason I'm standing up here.

Arnie's family is watching me from the first row. I focus on them as I start to speak. "There's nothing I can add to this service that will tell you what kind of person Arnie was." I look at Arnie's little brother, he looks just like him. "But I think I know the man he wanted to be. Arnie was very passionate about playing college basketball." I see Arnie's father react to what I've said. He sort of shrugs and shakes his head. His mother places her hand on his. I can't tell if she's comforting him or scolding him. Arnie told me his father wanted him to join the army.

"I was helping Arnie study for the SAT, and he said once he sets his mind to do something, he does it." Arnie's father looks up at me. "I just wanted you all to know, that he did it." A tear runs down my face. "Arnie met with a coach at Humboldt State. He said he needed to score at least one thousand on his SAT to get a scholarship. I found out today, he got a 1050."

The church is silent except for the sound of Arnie's mother's uncontrollable sobbing.

Oh no. Why did I think this was good news? I'm rubbing it in their face. Telling them their son will never go to college. I'm an idiot. I step around the podium and try to make it past Arnie's family without looking.

Mrs. Monroe reaches out to me and I instinctively hand her the test results. "We had no idea he was planning on going to college." She looks at her husband. "We didn't think he gave much thought to his future. He never seemed very ambitious." She looks away, embarrassed or ashamed maybe for not giving Arnie credit. "Thank you so much for helping our son." She takes my hand. "Thank you for confirming what I always knew in my heart."

I don't think I've ever felt as proud of myself as I do right now. It's a high like no other.

"And thank you for helping him achieve his dream." Mr. Monroe stands and gives me a hug.

I start back to my seat and see Matt and Heather smiling at me. Then I see Lucy and Johnson a few rows behind them. Lucy waves, and I see him. Nick is standing at the back door. He isn't dressed for the ceremony. He doesn't look like he's changed his clothes in days. He sees me watching him and leaves. Fear, adrenaline, love. I don't know what is keeping me from running out of the church after him. I want to see him. I need to talk to him. I need to know where we stand. I need to know if I'm safe.

43

Matt

"At least he showed." I pull out of the parking lot and drive towards the marina.

"I guess." Dani is fidgeting. She looks like a junkie that's contemplating her next fix. Only the drug she's craving isn't a drug. It's Nick.

With everything that's happened in the last three days, we haven't even talked about Will Walker. I don't even know if Nick had a chance to tell him about Dani before the shooting. I hope not.

I was able to take her website down. Hopefully nobody saw it.

"Have you told Lucy yet?"

"No. I don't want to worry her for nothing."

"This isn't nothing, Dani. Just your life." I hit the brakes harder than I need to and we jerk to a stop. There is a line of cars waiting to turn left into the Wharfinger building. The Monroes are having a celebration of life, that's what they're calling this. I don't want to go. I don't feel like celebrating. From the look on Dani's face, she doesn't want to either. I have to go. Arnie was my friend, and if it were me, he'd be there.

We finally make it onto the service road that leads to the parking lot, and I realize the lot is full. I drop Dani off and head down Waterfront to the supplemental parking lot. I find a space with minimal chance of door dings and head back to the Wharfinger building. Yeah, I know it's a douche thing to do, but it's a new car. Arnie would understand.

I scan the room and spot Dani at a table with Lucy and Johnson. Nobody is getting to her with Johnson around. I better find my mom and Ashley. I saw her car in the lot, and I want to at least say hi. My mom grew up in Eureka; she's known Arnie's parents since they were kids. She's been pretty wrecked. Probably because she thinks that it could have been me.

"Hey Matt."

I turn around and see a couple of guys from school waiting to talk to me—Sam and Brian. They played basketball with Arnie. We've all hung out a few times. They're cool. A group of older women push past us towards the buffet, so we step into the corner to talk.

"What's up?" I shake both their hands. We look out at the group that's gathered here in honor of our friend. "This is fucking crazy."

"I know, man. Have you seen Nick? He must be fucked up," Brian says.

"No." I don't tell him that he was at the church. I don't tell him about the last time I saw him. I don't tell him we're not friends anymore.

Sam steps closer to me and forms a little circle with his back to the room. "So, are you guys still in business?"

Is this fucker really asking me for a hook-up at Arnie's funeral? Is that the only reason they're here? They just want drugs? Is this what I've turned my friends into? Fiends that don't give a shit about anything except getting high. Our friend is dead. My friend is dead. My other friend is...I don't even know. He's dead to me.

I push him before I realize I'm pushing him. "Get the fuck out of here." I don't stop when he tries to apologize. I don't stop when my mom waves at me from the corner. I don't stop until I reach Dani.

"Let's get out here." I hold out my hand, and she takes it.

Lucy and Johnson watch as she gets up and leaves with me.

They don't try to stop us.

44
Dani

If Matt didn't suggest we leave, I would have. My speech at the church drew a lot of unwanted attention. I met all of Arnie's family, cousins, aunts, uncles. They thanked me. Thanked me for spending one afternoon with Arnie.

Matt starts to drive towards Lucy's house when his phone rings. We both jump. We both hope and dread it being Nick. I want to see him and I don't. I think Matt feels the same.

We hate him, we love him.

"It's my mom," Matt says.

I find myself looking out the window. I'm looking for him. For his car. Only he doesn't have it anymore. His car is gone, just like Arnie.

"Shit. My mom's Audi has a flat. I have to go back and help her."

Matt pulls over and waits for the road to clear so he can make a U-turn.

"I don't want to go back there. Can you take me to the café or something?"

"Are you sure? It won't take that long for me to change the tire."

"Patty's there, I'll be fine." I force a smile. "I'll text Heather to come keep me company."

Matt doesn't really have a choice. He drives to the café and stops in front. "Wait for me here. I don't want you to walk home alone," he says as I get out of the car.

He sounds like Nick.

"Yes, sir." I give him a fake salute and close the door.

I watch Matt until his car is lost among the traffic. The café is packed. Some of the overflow from the funeral must be inside. I don't want to go in. I start walking towards West Harris. Lucy and Johnson might even be home soon. I doubt they'll stay long without me being there. I should call Matt or Lucy. I should, but I don't. I want to call Nick. I look at my phone. I flip it open and look at his name in my contact list and I hear our song. *Am I hallucinating?* It's faint, but there is no mistaking the whining guitar riffs.

I can face a mountain, but I could never climb alone......

You're the reason the sun shines down....

Only you that I hold when I'm young, only you as we grow old....

I turn around and see a black SUV pull up behind me. The passenger window slides down, and I see Nick in the driver's seat. I wonder if running into me was really a coincidence. Nick leans over and tries to smile. I don't know what there is to smile about. We buried his best friend today. The friend that died because of him, because of his uncle. I'm suddenly overwhelmed with anger. Anger at Nick.

"We need to talk," he says.

"Do we?" I can't even look at him. I keep walking towards Lucy's.

Nick rolls beside me. "Dani, please. Give me a chance. Please get in, I'll explain everything."

He's begging. Nick Marino is begging me for a chance. I look at his humbled face and feel empowered. For once I have the upper hand.

Nick stops, and I walk around the front of the SUV and get in.

"Explain."

45
Matt

A tow truck is already at the car when I get there.

"Can you please take Ashley home?" my mom says. "She's tired."

I look at Ash. She looks a little pale. I thought it was the stress of today, but when I think about it, she's been pale for weeks now.

"Ok, let's go."

We get in the car, and Ashley tries to tell me she feels fine. "Mom is overreacting." She looks out the window. "She's suffocating me."

She's right, but we all do it. It's not because we think she's weak. She's the strongest person I know. We do it for ourselves. We protect Ashely because we can't handle her being sick. It's a fucked up, selfish way of looking at things, but it's true.

"She's just worried. Plus, she probably wants to help Mrs. Monroe with food and stuff. You'll just be sitting around bored." I mess her hair, and she rolls her eyes at me.

"Yeah, whatever."

I turn onto West Harris and see an SUV pull away from the curb. That looks a lot like the Marinos' Mercedes. There aren't many in town. It's Nick, it's got to be. Why is he parked down here?

I make a quick left and turn into the parking lot of the café. I jump out and leave Ashely in the car. The bells jingle as I burst through the door. Patty looks at me like I'm a terrorist.

"Dani!" I yell. Everyone is staring at me. Twenty pairs of eyes, none of them hers.

I run back to the car and peel out of the parking lot.

"Matt, what the hell!"

I stab the gas and drive to Dani's. The SUV isn't there. Lucy's car isn't in the driveway. I remember seeing it back at the marina.

She's with him.

46

Dani

I sit next to Nick like he's a stranger on the bus and not my first love. There are so many things I thought I wanted to say, but none of them come to mind. We drive through Pine Hill, past the golf course, and I know where we're headed. Nick doesn't drive through the front gate, he drives past the entrance to his house onto a service road. He gets out and unlocks a gate with a key and waves for me to drive through. I don't drive, but I climb into the driver's seat and ease the gas until I'm past the gate. I put the car in park and climb back into the passenger seat. The SUV reminds me a lot of my father's Denali. The same car they were shot in. The car Will shot them in.

Nick locks the gate and returns to the truck. "That was pretty good."

I ignore the compliment. "What are we doing here?"

"I just wanted to be alone with you. I need you to know what's going on and that…"

Nick's cell phone buzzes in the ashtray. He picks it up, looks at the caller ID, and sighs.

"Aren't you going to answer that?" My sarcasm catches his attention.

"Dani, I know you hate me right now. Just give me a chance to explain."

I cross my arms across my chest. There is nothing he can say to make things right. He's protecting the man that killed my parents.

"Let's go inside."

I open the door and jump out of the SUV. I don't want to go inside, but sitting in the car brings back too many memories of my parents.

We walk through the winding path of the Marino estate, and I recognize things from the first time I was here. The gnome next to the rose bushes, a row of blue hydrangeas that line the green fence surrounding the tennis courts. I make notes in case I need to find my way out.

We reach the cottage and Nick stops. "Everything's going to be ok." He kisses me quickly on the mouth before I can protest and opens the door.

It smells like weed and some kind of incense. A man in a San Francisco Forty-Niner jersey is standing at the counter pouring himself a glass of orange juice. He frowns when he sees me. "What are you doing, nephew? I thought this was handled." He's got dark hair, almost black. His eyes look a shade darker than Nick's, but he has the same smoldering smile.

"Yeah, it wasn't." Nick runs his hand through his hair.

I look back at Nick, the first boy I've ever loved and the last one I'll ever trust.

He walks around the counter and pats Nick on the back. He stops in front of me with his hands in his pockets. "Do you know who I am?" Will Walker is tall and muscular, with a swagger you only see in movies. Some people might think he's good looking. All I see is a murderer.

I nod my head.

"Of course you do," he says arrogantly.

"Hey Will, she doesn't..." Nick starts to tell him something, but Will cuts him off.

"Don't worry, Nicky. I'm not going to hurt her. I just want to see what she knows."

Will moves his arm around my shoulders and I shrug it off.

"Don't fucking touch me." I step back and look at Nick. He doesn't look at me. His eyes never leave Will. "Is this why you brought me here?" My voice cracks. *Don't cry. Don't cry.*

Nick closes his eyes and looks at the ground. "I'm sorry." I hear his apology, I feel his regret. He's a fucking liar too.

Will grabs my arm and tosses me onto the couch. Nick flinches and steps towards me.

"What?" Will dares him. Nick stops. He clenches his fist and backs away. His obedience makes me sick. He is supposed to protect me. To love me.

Will runs his clammy fingers down the side of my face and I knock his hand away. I try to get up, but he pulls me back and holds me so I can't move my arms.

Don't cry.

Will feels around my coat and pulls my phone out of my pocket. "Hey Paulo," he calls and another man joins us. He must have been in Nick's bedroom. I've never even been in Nick's bedroom. "Make sure nobody can trace this."

Paulo takes my phone to the kitchen. I hear drawers opening then pounding. He holds up what's left of my cell phone, and Will nods in approval.

"She's a hottie, we could make some money with her." Will smiles and looks at Nick. Nick doesn't react at all. He's watching Paulo in the kitchen and then turns back to Will.

I'm trying desperately to prevent Will's hands from exploring my body any further. When he starts to feel up my dress, I elbow him in the stomach and try to stand.

"You little bitch!" Will grabs my arm before I can escape and yanks me back onto the couch. The back of my head hits his chin. "What the fuck is your problem."

A surge of adrenaline pulses through me. "You are my problem, you piece of shit!"

Will smiles at my outburst. He's laughing at me as I struggle against him. The harder I fight, the tighter he holds me. He's got me and he isn't letting go. He will never let me go. Nick knew that, and he brought me here anyway.

Nick moves closer. I see tears in his eyes. For me. He knows Will is going to kill me. He knows and does nothing. Just like when he found out Will killed my parents and did nothing.

"Will, she didn't see anything…" Nick finally says. It's too late for explanations. Even I know that. It doesn't matter that I didn't see him. It never did. He knows he did it and he knows he was sloppy. He missed me the first time. He won't make that mistake again.

"Shut up, Nick!" I scream. "Don't act like you're not just as bad as he is." Nick's jaw clenches and he looks away. *I hate him. I hate them both.*

"See Nicky, you got nothing to feel bad about. No regrets. No looking back. We're gonna run Cali, together." Will boasts. "Once she's gone, I got nothing and nobody stopping me."

"You think killing innocent people makes you a badass? You're nothing but a coward!" I cry. I'm crying.

"Innocent? I don't think so," Will scoffs. "Your daddy took a job and he didn't come through. Simple as that."

Will's words shock me. "My father wouldn't have anything to do with scum like you." I think of the picture from my birthday. "He told me you wanted him to take your case, and he refused."

"I paid your daddy to lose the Devon Brown case, and the lucky bastard won." His words knock the fight out of me.

The Devon Brown case was huge. He was proud of that win. He saved Brown from a third strike and life in prison. My father would never jeopardize his integrity for money.

"You're lying!" I swing my fist around and hit him in the ear. He grabs my hand before I can land another blow but let's my body go. I jump up, and Nick grabs me around the waist. He pulls me out of Will's reach.

Will stands up with fire in his eyes and slaps me across the face. "This bitch is done." He reaches around his back and pulls out a gun.

"Whoa!" Nick steps in front of me. I move back towards the door. Paulo jumps up and stops me.

I'm trapped. Nick is my only hope.

"What are you going to do, pop her in here? Cops will be all over this. Let's go to the beach house. You have the entire ocean as a dumping ground."

Wait. What. Nick is helping him. Vomit burns the back of my throat.

"Nick," I cry. "Nick, no."

He doesn't turn around. He won't look at me. He won't save me.

"You're right, nephew. You pack up the money and the boat. Let's get out of here. I fuckin hate Eureka." Will walks to the counter and picks up his juice. He drains the entire glass.

This is really happening. Nick moves to the table with a duffle bag and starts to shove things inside. I feel my legs go weak. I stop resisting Paulo. I close my eyes and think of my parents. I think about the day Matt walked me home. He said fate could go either way. Good or bad. My fate was to die at the hands of Will Walker, one way or another.

I let go. I let go of any hope I will survive. I let go of the idea that Nick Marino will save me. He isn't my champion, he's my executioner. I feel Paulo's grip tighten as I start to fall unconscious. Then there is a knock on the door. Not really a knock. It's pounding, banging. Yelling.

"Where is she!" It's Matt. *No, not Matt.*

Paulo motions for Nick to toss him the gun on the table. All the blood has drained from Nick's face as he hands over the gun. He can betray me, he can let Will do awful things to me, but he can't hurt Matt.

"No." Nick stops Paulo. "I'll get rid of him."

Will pulls me from Paulo's arms and wraps his left arm around my neck, clamping his hand over my mouth. Paulo stands behind the door with the gun in his hand.

Nick opens the door. "Get the fuck out of here!" He may not love me, but I know he loves Matt.

"I saw you on West Harris near the café," Matt yells into the door. "I know she's here."

I scream into Will's hand when Paulo opens the door and pulls Matt inside.

47

Dani

Nick is pleading with Will as Paulo holds a gun to Matt's head. "Will come on, he's with us."

"I'm not with you," Matt yells again.

"It doesn't look like it, nephew." Will picks up the duffel bag. "Looks like we're cleaning house today."

Nick runs both his hands through his hair. For the first time today, he looks defeated.

Will tosses the bag to Nick and opens the door. "Come on, kiddies. We're going for a ride."

We walk around the back of the property, down the path, past the gnome, to the black SUV. Nick leads the way. Paulo and Matt are next, then Will and me. I can't let them hurt Matt. He's an innocent bystander.

"Nick, why are you doing this? I know you love me. I still love you." I choke on the words. I don't know if I'm actually lying. Nick keeps walking. "I love you." I say again, and I see him pause.

"Shut up!" Will yanks my arm and I scream in pain. "Keep walking, Nick. You don't need this bitch. You're going to be rolling in pussy once we get set up."

His comment makes me sick. I wish I could puke all over him right now. We reach the back gate and Will yells for Nick to get the lock.

"You don't deserve her," Matt hisses as we watch Nick kneel down to unlock the gate. "You never did."

"And you do?" Nick spits back.

"Yeah, I do. She deserves better than some wannabe drug dealer like you!"

Nick stands up and looks at Matt with pure hate in his eyes.

"Nick, get the lock!" Will screams.

It's too late. Nick is already rushing Matt. The force of the punch knocks Matt out of Paulo's arms. His gun skits across the dirt.

Will yells at them as they wrestle on the ground. Paulo pulls Matt off of Nick and holds him back.

Nick springs to his feet and wipes his mouth. It looks like Matt must have got a punch in. Nick's lip is bleeding. Nick picks up the gun and puts it in the waist of his pants.

"Nick, let's get out of here. You'll get your revenge on this little cock-blocker soon enough." Will looks around to make sure nobody heard the scuffle. There's nobody here, they're all at Arnie's funeral.

Once the gate is open, there is no stopping him. Nobody can save us. We can't leave the property. Will won't shoot us here. He can't. He needs Nick, he needs his money. Nick is still working the lock. I don't remember it taking this long when we pulled in. He's frazzled, so I try to make it even worse. "Nick, you're just going to let Will shoot me, shoot Matt?"

Will gives me a hard shake and I wince as the gun in his hand digs into my side. "Nick will do whatever I say. If I tell him to shoot you, then you're dead." Will presses his mouth to the side of my face. "But

I wouldn't do that to my nephew. Shit like that haunts you. I'll take you out myself. Maybe have a little fun with you first."

"Will!" Paulo screeches.

My eyes dart to Nick, he's holding a gun, Paulo's gun. It's pointed at me. At Will.

"What the fuck, kid?"

"Let her go." Tears roll down Nick's cheek. I don't know if he's crying because of me or the fact that he is holding a gun to Will, the man he's looked up to for most of his life.

Will grips me tighter and raises the gun from my waist to my head. "Nicky, come on, you're emotional."

"Shut up!" Nick looks at me, then to Matt. "I'm sorry."

"I forgive you," I cry. I don't what him to change his mind. I don't want Will to change his mind.

"Let them go and I'll leave with you." Nick is trying to negotiate with Will. "We can leave with the money I got for my birthday. We can set up someplace new."

"You know I can't do that." Will steps towards Nick. "Let's talk about this in the car. We can work it out on the way to the beach."

Nick shakes his head. "No, there's nothing to work out. This isn't happening. I'll give you the money. All of it. Then you leave."

"Nicky, no. We're family." Will sounds hurt.

"Family?" Nick scoffs. "This has nothing to do with family. It was always about the money. You used my father, and now you're using me."

Will pulls me to the side, holding the gun firmly to my right temple. "That's not true. You're my blood." He points at Nick with the gun then puts it back to my head. "I was setting you up to be the next Tony Montana, just like we talked about. Just like you wanted!"

Nick shakes his head. He runs his hand through his hair and smiles. At me. "I love you, Dani."

I almost tell him I love him back. The words catch in my throat.

"You fucking pussy. I knew you didn't have it in you," Will sneers.

"Let her go, and I'll leave with you," Nick says again.

"Fuck you. Drop the piece and maybe I'll let *you* live." Will grabs me by the throat.

I grab at his hands and he squeezes tighter. There's a ringing in my ears. It hurts.

Nick drops the gun and kicks it towards Paulo. Will throws me onto the ground. I taste dirt as I gasp for air. Nick is suddenly at my side.

"Are you ok?" He pulls me to him. "I'm sorry, Dani. I never meant for…"

Matt pushes Nick away from me. "You don't get to say sorry." He helps me stand. Nick looks devastated.

"Let's go," Will yells. We look up and see him standing next to the open gate with Paulo, their guns pointed at us.

Matt grips my hand and moves forward, but Nick holds us back. "Wait."

Matt pushes his hand away and pulls me closer. A helicopter flies over the house. A dozen men appear out of nowhere and rush towards Will and Paulo.

"What the fuck!" Will screams as he is surrounded.

Swirling lights come out of the tree line across the road and park in front of the gate. Cops come running up the path that leads to Nick's cottage. They've been here all along.

Nick walks up to Will, who is now in handcuffs. "I don't think I want to be the next Scarface." He smirks. "I was thinking more along the lines of Donnie Brasco." Nick lifts his shirt and exposes a wire taped to his chest.

Matt and I don't move, we don't speak. We're in shock. Just like Will.

48
Dani

The eight hours that followed were a blur. I learned that Nick contacted SFPD after the shooting at Will's bar. They had a plan to get Will to confess to shooting my parents, but Nick couldn't get him to talk. It was the detective's idea to have Nick pick me up and bring me to the cottage. Johnson and Lucy were not thrilled to hear they used me as bait, even though there were twenty members of law enforcement surrounding the property, ready to take Will out as soon as they had what they needed. Matt showing up almost blew the whole thing, but Nick stalled on the lock and gave them the time they needed to mobilize and take Will down without any casualties.

That isn't totally true. There was one casualty. Devon's attempt on Will's life came after Will made a deal with the Devil's Gold to partner up with a member from their San Francisco chapter. The guy turned out to be an old high school buddy of Will's. When Devon found out Will was keeping Humboldt, he decided to take him out. He failed and lost his life, taking Arnie with him.

The man who killed my parents, who ruined my life, is behind bars. If it wasn't for Will Walker, I would have never moved to Eureka. I wouldn't have met Matt or Nick. I would have never, ever, taken thizz. I can thank and blame Walker for all the good and bad that's happened in my life over the last six months.

The strangest change is my relationship with Heather. She practically lives in my room these days. Her parents adore Lucy. She helped nurse Heather's grandmother after triple bypass surgery two years ago. Once they found out she was my aunt, Heather was allowed to come over. Heather knows all my secrets now. She knows I miss Nick. She knows I loved Matt. And she knows some days I pull out the Big Red gum pack and hope to find a pill.

I don't think that craving will ever go away.

49

Dani

Five months later - San Francisco

I used to walk down Columbus Avenue thinking nothing existed past what I could see—dogs running in the park, a homeless man lying on a bench, kids playing in the school yard. As I walk along the crowded sidewalk on this fogless October morning, I know that the world extends far beyond my line of sight. I know that six hundred miles north of here, there is a happy family with a baby girl named Marguerite. Even though she was born two months early, she is perfect. I know there's a sick girl in Colorado wearing a turquoise necklace fighting for her life. I hope there is a God and he will heal her. I walk down this street, and I know there are people in this world that love me.

I round the corner onto Union Street and turn to the overweight bulldog behind me to offer words of encouragement. "Come on, Arnie! You can do it, boy!" He can only muster a slight gallop before running out of breathe. He wheezes and looks at me with his big brown eyes. "Ok buddy, take a break." He plops down on a shady patch of sidewalk and rests his head on his front paws. His tongue hangs from his mouth, and a pool of saliva forms on the cement in front of him. Walking up these steep San Francisco hills always wears him out.

I unlock the door to my flat, and Arnie pushes the door open with his large round head then scampers to his bed and falls straight to sleep. I look at the clock. I can't stop time, and I can't keep running from my past. Today is going to happen whether I want it to or not. With Arnie snoring in the corner, I settle into my favorite spot on the couch, pull out my history book, and begin to read. I have an hour before I have to meet them. I might as well make good use of it.

I'm only halfway through the first paragraph when my phone makes that tinkle sound. A sound I've grown to love, because I know it's him. *Cal-girl c u in 60*. I smile, but I can't ignore the anxiety I feel in the pit of my stomach.

I haven't taken a pill in months. I don't want one, but there are times I miss the rush. I don't think that will ever go away. I haven't had many moments like that since I left Eureka, but I can recall a few times I would've killed for a pill.

The day I told Nick I was going to CAL was one of them.

Things weren't the same after the incident with Will. Matt and Nick seemed to go back to normal, but there was no denying that something changed between me and Nick. Even after finding out he was working with the cops to bring Will down, I couldn't forget the look on his face the day he found out I was the one Will was looking for. Some part of him hated me for who I was. What I meant to his uncle. I hated him, too. He became tainted for loving the man who killed my parents.

The day after Matt left for Stanford, I asked Nick to meet me after work. He picked me up and took me to the beach. I remember thinking we'd come full circle. Our beginning and end at the beach. The sky was filled with fog when I told him I got into CAL. The same dank gray fog that filled the sky the night my parents were killed. Nick congratulated me and asked if I had a place to stay. He offered me one of his family's apartments in Nob Hill, and I told him I wanted to do this on my own. I knew Nick would happily follow me to the city, but I couldn't allow him to do that. Following me to school wasn't the best solution for him, for either of us. I would be using him just like I used the pills, to fill my void. Once Nick realized I wasn't including him in my plans, he started the car and drove me home.

I remember the song playing on the radio and the sweet metallic smell of jasmine and burnt oil, the smell of Nick when he stopped in front of Lucy's house and left the engine running.

"When are you leaving?" he finally asked.

"A week from tomorrow." From the corner of my eye, I saw him shake his head in disbelief at the short amount of time we had left together.

I felt his eyes on me, but I couldn't muster the strength to look at him. I didn't want to see the pain on his face that was so evident in his voice. I watched his hands gripping the steering wheel as if it would fly away if he let it go.

"You're just going to leave, that's it?" He paused and ran his hands through his hair. "We're over?" His strong, confident voice cracked, and he cleared his throat to hold back any sign of weakness.

Are we over? I didn't even know the answer myself. I never really considered what my choice meant for us. Going to Berkeley was my plan long before Nick Marino was part of my vocabulary. Nick and I never talked about the future, maybe it's because we were never destined to have one. As I fought to find the right words to say, Nick's phone buzzed in the ashtray. I glanced quickly at his face as he read the text. The hurt in his eyes was not caused by the words on the screen. He closed the phone without replying and placed it back in the ashtray. His face seemed less hard, less desperate. He looked almost relieved. I thought, maybe he realized that this truly was for the best. We both needed to move on, to grow. The whirlwind drug-induced romance that we shared was too much too soon. We needed to find ourselves before devoting our lives to each other.

The possibility that we could end up together someday soothed me. It made what I was about to say easier. I finally knew what I wanted to say and how to say it, but when I started to speak, Nick stopped me.

"I got into Stanford." He even allowed himself a small smile. He ran his hand through his hair twice and said, "Do you know what this means?"

I knew what it meant for Nick, an education, a chance at a real future.

"I'll be closer to you, nothing has to change." He leaned in close so our faces were just inches away. I thought he might kiss me, and for the first time ever, I hoped he wouldn't.

I don't know if it was the drugs that kept us together or just the fact that he loved the man that killed my parents that was pushing us apart. Nick was my first love. I just wasn't sure if I was ready for him to be my only love. I looked into his hopeful eyes, and I knew what I had to say.

"Nick, I love you." Tears brimmed at the corner of my eyes.

He whispered I love you then brushed his lips across mine. I felt my heart flutter as if this were our first kiss and not our last.

It took a lot to pull away from his mouth. He recovered quickly from my rejection and moved back to his side of the car. I touched my fingers to my lips to soothe the burning. I wouldn't let my heart or my desires cloud what I had to say. "I just don't know if being together is the best thing right now."

Nick looked at me, confused and embarrassed. "What are you trying to say?"

I didn't want to lose the moment to hostility, but I knew from the tone of his voice it was too late.

"It's going to be a huge change for both of us. The stress of trying to make this work will only make things harder." The weight of my words felt like a ton of bricks had been dropped on the car.

"You don't want to be with me?" His words cut through me. There was truth in what he was saying, no matter how I sugar coated it. Even as I formed the words and spoke them aloud, I lied to myself about their meaning. Watching Nick's reaction was forcing me to accept the fact that I was breaking up with him.

Nick pressed on the gas, and the roar of his engine echoed down the street. "I gotta go." He looked straight ahead, gripping the wheel, waiting for me to get out. I lifted the lock and pulled the handle until the heavy metal door clicked open. He pressed the gas again, and the smell of exhaust crept in the open door. I didn't hide the tear that escaped down my cheek.

"I love you, Dani." His words surprised me. He could have been cruel. I deserved it.

"I love you too," I told him, then forced myself out of the car.

I watched him fly down the street, barely stopping at the sign before disappearing around the corner with no promise to see him later, no assurance that he'd call.

I was addicted to Nick, addicted to his touch, his smell, his essence. I let his life become mine, and when he wasn't around, I turned to ecstasy. In the same way thizz is a drug, Nick was a drug to me. Just like thizz, I had to stop using Nick.

Another day I could have used a pill was the day I found out they were seizing my parents' assets. The confession Will Walker gave the police regarding my father being paid to lose Devon Brown's case launched a full investigation into my father's finances. Apparently tax evasion is looked upon more sternly than drug dealing and robbery. Some of my father's old clients are in trouble again and were offered leniency for their cooperation in proving a dead man was a crook. I don't care what they say about my father or what kind of person they want to paint him as. He will always be the patient man that taught me how to write my name. The person that soothed me when I was sick and made midnight runs to the store to get me orange juice. He was the only person on earth that could make my perfect hot dog.

Now that the IRS is involved, it's only a matter of time before they start to seize property, so today I'm going back to my old home to salvage whatever personal belongings I can. Lucy and I decided an estate sale would be a great way to earn some extra money for school. My parents did have a small life insurance policy that helped pay the rent on my apartment, but it won't last forever. I need to find another way to survive without taking money from Lucy and Johnson. They have their own family to support, and no matter how hard they insist on helping, I won't let them.

My childhood home is just a short walk from where I live now. I've managed to avoid going near the street ever since I've moved back. Just like I've avoided going anywhere near Will Walker's bar. He's in prison, but I don't think I can stand looking at the spot where Arnie was shot.

I decide to leave my Arnie at home; he's had enough exercise for the day. When I begin my ascent up Green Street, my calves start to burn. A feeling so familiar it's like the sound of my mother's laugh. It's been too long since I made this trek, and I'm winded when I reach the top. I pull out my key and insert it into the lock. I turn left and jiggle the handle until the lock clicks open. The smell of cinnamon and citrus potpourri fills the air. I knew Lucy was paying someone to maintain the house, but I didn't realize she told them to follow all the same protocols down to the air freshener. Just as I'm about to close the door, I hear Matt's car coming up the street.

He pulls in front of the house and parks. Matt jumps out, proudly sporting his Stanford colors. "Hey you," he says and scoops me into his arms. I don't realize how much I've missed him until this moment. I whisper I miss you in his ear and kiss his cheek.

He pulls back and smiles. "Me too."

Nick is standing behind him, waiting to greet me. Things were awkward when he first moved to Santa Clara. Especially because the day Nick arrived was also the same day I was going to spend the night with Matt.

Matt and I made a pact to hang out at least once a month. The first time he came to see me was right after Heather moved in. Her parents agreed to let her live with me after Lucy promised to get Heather an internship once she completed her first year in the nursing program at USF. She pays half the rent and utilities, and she doesn't mind doing the dishes.

The weekend Matt came to visit me, it was pouring rain. We spent the entire night watching MTV and eating pizza. After he made his nightly call to Ashely, well, our issues didn't really seem that important. Matt's parents found out Ashely was sick during spring break, but she didn't want to tell Matt, not until after he graduated. She didn't want to ruin his senior year with her problems. It was even her idea to buy Matt the Mustang. His parents moved to Colorado right after graduation. There is a specialist that's had some success with her type of leukemia. She's responding really well to treatment. Matt is going to see her for Christmas. If I can afford it, I might go with him.

When it was my turn to visit, I couldn't wait for the chance to be alone with him. I was hoping to finally see if my feelings were real.

I stepped off the train with my backpack over my shoulder and a little travel bag in my hand. Although I'd slept at his house before, this was without a doubt different. It was just me and Matt, no Nick and no thizz.

I could barely contain my enthusiasm and practically mowed down an old man as I ran down the platform towards the parking lot. The cloud I was riding on suddenly disappeared when I saw Nick standing beside Matt. It was a lot like the first time I'd met them in the parking lot at school. Except they were leaning against Matt's Mustang, and this time Matt stepped up. He greeted me with a hug and a soft kiss on the cheek. I didn't know if Nick understood why I was there or knew I was coming to spend the night with Matt. I was mortified. Matt quickly explained that Nick had driven down that afternoon and moved into the dorms. From the pained look on Nick's face, I was sure his presence wasn't his idea at all. It was Matt's. It was the first time we'd seen each other since he drive away from Lucy's. I hadn't spoken to him on the phone or even exchanged a text.

We left the train station and went straight to a college-friendly pub. After a few shots of Patron and a lot of beer, the reason for my visit was forgotten. The three of us were just old friends hanging out. We were on our fourth or fifth shot when Matt made a toast.

"May the best man win," he slurred and lifted his glass. The table fell silent, then I burst out laughing. I'm not sure why. Nick and Matt clinked their glasses and nodded to each other as if accepting the challenge. I told myself they weren't talking about me and took my shot, followed by two more.

Other than a few melancholy moments when Arnie's name was mentioned, it was a light-hearted reunion. Until we went back to Matt's room. We were falling up the stairs, clinging to each other for support as Matt fought to get his key in the door.

"Dude, come on," Nick yelled a little too loudly.

"Shh! I almost got it," Matt slurred and refocused on the lock.

"Let's just go to my room." Nick pointed to his door down the hall.

I didn't really understand why he was pointing it out to me until I felt his hand slide down my back. *Shit.*

When Matt finally opened the door, we didn't think about what came next. We fell into the room and stood uncomfortably in the cramped space, staring at the twin bed. I was horrified at the thought of Nick leaving me and Matt alone. When Matt made a bad joke about what side of the bed I preferred, I grabbed my bag and headed to the bathroom to brush my teeth and escape the awkwardness. My mind was foggy from the alcohol, and I was starting to feel a bit dizzy. I couldn't choose between them, not that I had a choice about who I would sleep with. I hoped they weren't flipping a coin to see who got me. I decided I would tell them I would take the bed and they could sleep on the floor. I opened the door, ready to state my proposition, only to find Matt and Nick passed out on the bed. Joining them wasn't an option. So I fished the keys from Nick's jacket and went to his room. It was dark and messy with boxes, but I found the bed under a pile of clothes and passed out.

A few hours later I woke to the sound of the lock clicking open. I felt a cold chill run through me. I knew Will Walker was in jail, but I have this fear that one of his crew will come after me. The thought made my already weak stomach turn. My entire body tensed until I recognized the tall, muscular figure moving in the darkness. I didn't know if I was strong enough to be alone with him. I closed my eyes and moved my head so the comforter shielded my face.

Nick made his way around the room. He was going through the boxes. Looking for something. The longer he stayed, the more I felt myself wanting to say something. The light from the hall was shining into the room. I peeked from under the covers and saw him pull his shirt off. I started to wonder if he was really looking for something to wear or was hoping I'd invite him to stay. He moved into the light and I stared at the muscles that rippled down his back. Just as I was starting to cave, he pulled a shirt over his head and left.

The next morning we had breakfast, and they drove me to the train. The weekend couldn't have turned out any better. I had my two best friends back.

"Hi Nick, thanks for coming." I leave Matt's arms and go to him.

"You know I'll always be here for you." His arms, the shape of his body, the curve of his neck are so familiar to me. Hugging him is like going home. When I feel his lips on my cheek, I break away.

"Let's go." I take a deep breath, and I lead them into my childhood home.

It is exactly as we left it. The pillows on the sofa are perfectly aligned, and the curtains are pulled back just enough to let the afternoon sun brighten the room. I round the corner and peek into the kitchen, almost certain I'd find my mother standing at the counter pouring a glass of wine. The sight of her apron hanging on the hook next to the refrigerator gives me chills.

"Is this you?" Nick asks from the hall. Seeing the silhouette of Matt and Nick in my hallway is very surreal. Something I never thought possible. It's like seeing a fish breathe out of water. I smile at the picture near Nick's head. It was taken when I had just learned to walk.

"Jeez you were fat," Matt teases. "Your mom must have put you on baby Weight Watchers."

"Shut up." I sock Matt in the arm and push them both out of the way. "It's right here." I point to the handle protruding from the ceiling. Nick barely has to tiptoe to reach it. He yanks on the handle and the hydraulic ladder unfolds in front of us.

They both marvel at the hidden door. Boys are so easy to impress.

The cobwebs and stale air of the attic overpower me. I pull my shirt over my mouth and swat at the webs until I reach the trunk.

"I can't believe you're leaving everything behind. I mean, you don't even want the flat screen?" Matt asks in disbelief.

"I'm not leaving it behind. I'm selling it. I need the money." The statement causes an awkward silence to fill the small, dusty space.

"Will you help me with this please?" I kick the trunk, and a lifetime of dust falls to the ground around our feet.

Matt and Nick pull the trunk to the middle of the attic and turn on the overhead light.

"What's in it?" Nick asks as I open the lock.

The combination is my birth month, my mother's day, and my father's year. I recall the day he dragged me up here to teach it to me. He had me open the lock at least a dozen times. "My whole life," I tell him as the lock clicks open. "All of my baby pictures and videos, old report cards and medical records. My mother called it my hope chest."

Nick places his hand on my back and kisses the top of my head. This is hard. But them being here helps. We get through the top layer of the chest, pulling out old Halloween costumes and Christmas dresses. There's a stack of photo albums and an old video marked "Best day of my life" in my father's writing.

"Hmmm, wonder what this could be?" Matt holds the video up.

"It's their wedding video, perv." I snatch it from him and drop it into the chest. It makes a hollow sound when it hits the bottom.

Nick looks into the chest, then runs his hand along the side. "This chest has to be at least twenty inches deep. This can't be the bottom."

Matt looks over the side. "You're right. This metal plate was screwed in." He points to some brackets. The boys look at each other with mysterious grins. Matt and Nick scour the attic until they find an old tool kit.

"What's the big deal?" I stand over the chest, protecting it. "What are you doing?"

Nick drops to his knees with a screw driver and starts removing the screws holding in the makeshift bottom.

"Wait." I grab Matt's hand when he reaches for the metal plate. "What if I'm not supposed to see what's in there?"

"You said your parents saved this trunk for you, right?" Nick kisses my hand.

"Yes." I shy away from his show of affection. Their little game of winning me over makes me uncomfortable at times. It's just a game they play to make me blush.

"Then they wouldn't put anything in here they didn't want you to see," Nick says.

"Yeah," Matt agrees. "I'm sure they didn't stash their honeymoon video in here or anything."

He's right. "Ok." I sit back and let them remove the bottom.

Matt lifts the large metal plate and a low whistle escapes Nick's lips. They look at each other with matching smiles.

"What is it?" I kneel over the chest and look inside.

My heart stops then kicks into action. Even though this confirms every horrible thing the police and the media are saying about my father, a slow smile spreads across my face.

My mother called it my hope chest because one day she hoped to fill it with things I would use when I had a family. Only it isn't filled with linens and china. It's filled with perfectly stacked hundred dollar bills.

Like I said before, I couldn't count on my father for much, but when he came through, he came through big.

acknowledgements

A big, fat, thank you to all the people that helped me research this book. To the laughs, the smiles, the good times that helped birth this story and inspired me to put down my drink and write! To long weekends in Tahoe and crazy all-nighters in Sac. To music festivals and Halloween parties. But most of all to anyone that ever hugged me at three in the morning. To my family for eating a lot of pizza for dinner and putting up with all my bullshit. Thank you.

about the author

Nicole Loufas is a San Francisco native. She loves books, music festivals, and bloody mary's. She prefers gin to wine, and hates the smell of fried fish. *Thizz, A Love Story* is her first novel. To find out more visit: nicoleloufas.com.